FUN REUNION!
MEET, GREET, MURDER

D.B. ELROGG

A MILO RATHKEY MYSTERY

Fun Reunion! Meet, Greet, Murder
A Milo Rathkey Mystery

ISBN 978-0-9998200-1-8 (Paperback)
ISBN 978-0-9998200-2-5 (e-book)
ISBN 979-8-9856252-2-6 (Hardcover)

If you wish to contact the authors, you may email them at: authors@dbelrogg.com

Cover Art by Drew Proffitt

Dedicated to Piper and Nick whose real life adventures somehow end up in the pages of these books.

SPECIAL THANKS TO

STAN JOHNSON
JODY EVANS
BRUCE CRAWFORD
DOUG OSELL
BILL HEAD
DREW PROFFITT

1

Milo Rathkey reached for the door of Ilene's bakery when two powerful arms crushed the barrel-chested detective in a vice lock. Shocked and angry, Milo stomped down trying to break his assailant's foot. He missed. Without warning, a hood came down over Milo's head, and he was dragged and shoved into the back seat of a waiting car.

"What the hell?" Milo shouted through the hood. *What is this?*

Tires squealing, the car lurched away from the curb. *Who would do this?* Milo struggled to comprehend the situation. Last week he and Duluth Police Lt. Ernie Gramm put one of the Kaminski brothers in jail. It could be the other two brothers, or any one of a number of thugs he crossed over the years.

Milo struggled to sit up but was forcibly pushed down by a strong, beefy hand, his head bouncing on the seat. *Think*

Milo, think. Where's the car is going? Traffic…stop and go… railroad track. Are we by the harbor? West Duluth? I'm not in the trunk, that's a good sign.

Trying to take calming deep breaths, Milo sucked in more cloth than air. He was beginning to feel light-headed. "If anybody cares, I can't breathe!" he yelled through the hood.

The same beefy hand jerked the hood up past his mouth and nose, but still covered his eyes. It wasn't great, but it was better.

Milo took in a deep breath as he heard the tires hit gravel. At the same time, cheap aftershave assaulted his nose. *Where had he smelled that before?* This wasn't the Kaminski brothers. They didn't use aftershave, or deodorant for that matter. If it's not personal, this was kidnapping for money, something that would have been laughable several months ago.

Who pays the ransom? Milo wondered. His estate co-owner Sutherland McKnight? His financial guy Creedence Durant?

The car skidded to a stop.

Crap! What now?

The beefy hand guy grabbed his upper arm and shoulder, roughly jerking him out of the car, slamming his head on the inside door frame. "Ow!" Milo yelled.

"Sorry," a voice said.

Sorry? Who the hell says sorry? Am I being kidnapped by the Boy Scouts?

Milo was hustled through a door and shoved into a hard wooden seat, a booth. The hood came off and Milo blinked, trying to focus. Milosh, also known as Mike, Morrie Wolf's chief body guard and Aqua Velva wearer, stood over him grinning. Milo slid into an upright position in the booth, blinked his eyes and ran his fingers through his dark curly hair. As his eyes adjusted to the early morning sun streaming through the transom of the Rasa Bar, he found himself looking at Wolf, the chief crime boss of Duluth. Morrie was head down, flipping through the day's gambling sheets, oblivious to the harsh way Milo had been deposited.

"Morrie?" Milo asked.

"Good to see you Milo," Morrie said, still studying the sheets.

"Good to see you too Morrie," Milo said with mild sarcasm, "Is this how you invite me over, pull a hood over my head and throw me into a car? I could do without the rough stuff."

"Rough stuff?" Morrie questioned, glancing at Mike.

"No rough stuff boss. We didn't hit him or nothin'."

Morrie smiled. "There you go Milo. They didn't hit you or nothin'. Don't be a whiner."

"Could I get some ice or a cold can here to hold against my head?" Milo asked. "It got slammed against the side of the car...when no rough stuff was going on."

"I said sorry," Mike defended himself.

Touching the knot on his forehead, Milo said, "I still need the ice."

"Get him a cold beer, and not the expensive stuff," Morrie ordered. Wolf, who always wore an outdated striped sport coat and skinny tie didn't realize he was now on the cutting edge of hipster fashion.

Bennie, the bartender, lumbered over with a can of Old Milwaukee. Milo pressed it to his head.

"What's with the hood?" Milo asked.

"Whaddaya mean?"

"I mean it's like out of an old movie."

"I didn't ask you to come here so we could talk hoods."

You didn't ask me to come here at all. You kidnapped me, Milo thought but kept silent. Getting too chippy with Morrie was unhealthy. He had a reputation for violence.

Morrie put his sheets aside, folded his hands, and focused on Milo for the first time. "I need a favor."

§

His long legs resting on the window sill, the sandy haired Sutherland McKnight watched an ore boat leave the Duluth harbor. Helen Munger, the head of McKnight Realty's HR department, strode into his office. "Boss, we have a problem employee."

"Really?" Sutherland was surprised. "Do you want to close the door?"

"No need. This will be quick. As you know, your father instituted a strict policy that all employees had to take at least two weeks of vacation every year. He considered it important for mental health."

Sutherland nodded.

"We have one employee who has refused to follow the company policy. At most, he's taken only one week in the last year, and that's a generous computation on my part."

"Well, send him on vacation!" Sutherland said with force.

"I thought you would see it that way. Thank you." She stood and moved to the door then turned. "Mr. McKnight. Go on vacation!"

"Me?"

"Yes, you."

"Can you do that?"

"By your order, I can." Helen stood unmoving, arms folded.

Sutherland swung his legs off the window sill, flipped through some files on his desk, and saw nothing pressing. Maybe he should take the rest of the day off. "Are you open to half days?"

Helen sighed. "No…full days…with one exception. If you leave now, this will be a half day."

Sutherland remembered her from when he was a boy, telling him to stop running in the office. She was the boss then, and it seems she's still the boss. "Yes ma'am," Sutherland said. "As soon as I put these files away, I'll give Bill and Marion a heads up this is going to happen."

Helen nodded and strode back to her desk.

Sutherland gazed out the window again; the ore boat was well on its way. *I could go sailing. Laura's Launch*, the thirty-two-foot sailboat named after his mother, had been overhauled this past winter and was waiting.

§

Jamal and Darian, younger brothers and wards of Lakesong's chef, Martha Gibbson, were racing their bikes on the roads of the estate. Sutherland caught their attention as they slid around the front driveway, gaining speed for the straight away which led to the work shed. He waved. They waved. Sutherland drove his Porsche into the massive garage.

"Home already?" Martha asked as he entered the kitchen.

"Playing hooky. Are your sibs doing the same?" Sutherland asked, using the nickname Martha had for her sister and two brothers who lived with her in the caretaker cottage on the estate.

Martha laughed. John, Sutherland's late father, always knew about school vacations. His son was oblivious.

"School's out for the summer Mr. McKnight and if you touch those cucumbers now, it will mean fewer cucumbers later."

"Live in the moment, I always say." He grabbed several cucumber slices.

"You never say that. Mr. Rathkey is rubbing off on you."

"That was dad's plan. He said I was dull and predictable. Now, I live on the edge. I'm a spur-of-the-moment cucumber thief!" Taking one more cucumber slice Sutherland asked, "I see Darian and Jamal out there doing the Tour de France. Where's Breanna?"

"At the cottage working on an essay. She's trying for the Patricia Lind Math Scholarship."

"Scholarship? Why? My dad left money in his will for their education."

"Shhhh," Martha said, glancing toward the hallway from the garage, making sure the sibs weren't within earshot. "I know, but I haven't told them. I want them to earn their way as much as possible." Martha set her knife down. "Don't get me wrong. I appreciate the money, but knowing Breanna and Jamal, that money will be needed for graduate school."

"What about Darian?"

"He's nine. Who knows?"

Sutherland wondered, if he were in Martha's place, how he would deal with having to become a parent to a younger sister and two younger brothers. He admired Martha's dedication. She put her life as an up-and-coming restaurant chef on hold after the death of her parents in a car accident five years ago.

"Speaking of my father's bequests, as trustees of their money, you and I need to have an official meeting twice a year to discuss the investments."

"Well…we're meeting now over cucumbers," Martha offered.

"True, but we need the financial reports, and maybe a few carrots with the cucumbers." Sutherland continued his vegetable theft.

"The rest of those are for Mr. Rathkey!" Martha admonished.

"You know he won't eat them. They're green. Milo doesn't eat green," Sutherland said.

"Except for iceberg lettuce."

"Right, iceberg lettuce smothered in the blue cheese dressing."

The *Gate Open* buzzer rang on the intercom indicating someone had activated the tall wrought iron estate gates.

Several minutes later Agnes Larson, the Lakesong house manager, yelled from the foyer, "Hey Martha! I'm here! I'm meeting the elevator guy."

"In the kitchen," Martha called, "Come in, let's see the new haircut."

"Oh!" Agnes said startled upon seeing Sutherland. "I didn't know it was a full house."

"I like it!" he blurted, as the pretty twenty-eight-year-old fluffed her new shorter summer hairdo in a flirty manner.

"Thanks," she said as she flipped it a couple more times. "It's shorter than I wanted, but I'll get used to it."

"It's nice," Martha said. "Sophisticated…will send the right message."

"The right message?" Sutherland questioned.

Agnes smiled. She had shared with Martha her anxiety about attending her upcoming high school reunion. Both agreed the shorter, sassier do' would give her the desired pizazz.

Agnes, who enjoyed teasing Sutherland, quipped, "I got it cut for the elevator guy."

Sutherland felt a slight pang of jealousy. "You want to be sophisticated for the elevator guy? Besides, I thought he was coming tomorrow."

"He was, but I moved it up. My reunion's tomorrow, and I have the day off, remember?"

"Ah yes, the Thrana Hall all school reunion." Sutherland reached for another cucumber only to have Martha remove the plate and place it on the back counter. "I'm confused. When you asked for the day off, you said you weren't looking forward to going. Why get your hair cut?"

"Just because I don't want to go, doesn't mean I don't want to look good when I do," Agnes explained.

Confused by the contradictory statement, Sutherland offered as to how he enjoyed his last reunion.

"Did you also get a new 'do?" Martha joked.

"I did." He grinned while mimicking Agnes. "It was too short, but I got used to it."

Agnes smirked at his sarcasm.

"Why don't you want to go?" Sutherland asked.

"There was an incident my sophomore year. It's complicated."

"What happened?" he pressed.

Agnes thought she made it clear she didn't want to talk about it, but Sutherland wasn't going to drop it. "Well, if you must know," she said with uncharacteristic sharpness, "a girl died." This was something she hadn't even shared with Martha. "Another girl was involved and people blame her for Molly's death. I don't like to think or talk about it."

The intercom buzzed; the elevator man was at the front gate. Agnes, glad for the interruption, hurried to the intercom. "I buzzed you in Mr. Otis."

Sutherland turned to Martha. "Otis?"

§

Morrie's 'boys' dropped Milo back at Ilene's Bakery. They said goodbye as if they were friends giving him a lift. Milo had hoped the violence-to-person part of his life was over. It wasn't.

As Milosh and Benny squealed out, Milo looked at the door next to Ilene's. It used to be a red, battered, wooden door with RAT KEY INVESTIGATIONS painted in the middle. The *H* had faded years before. Now the door was metal with a shiny brass toe plate and a professional sign that advertised accounting services. He thought he should feel sad, but he didn't. This situation looked better. The door was classy, and Milo bet Ilene was getting more rent and on time.

Even though he and Ilene no longer had a business relationship, she let him visit his beloved cream puffs any time he wanted. She looked up and smiled as he entered. "Milo where did you go? I saw your vintage vehicle pull up about an hour ago."

Ilene's ever-changing hair streaks on her white blond spikes had gone green for spring and were fading. Her nose had a small bit of bling, and Milo thought she had added another tat to the growing art work on her left arm. "I had an appointment I didn't know about," Milo said cryptically.

"The usual Milo?"

He nodded as he sat down at the employees table. "Do you have any Excedrin?"

"Now what happened?" she asked, placing a cream puff on a plate.

"I bumped my head, nothing serious, a little headache."

"And a growing welt. I thought you stopped the rough stuff."

"It finds me."

With water, two Excedrin, and a cream puff in hand Ilene poured them each a cup of coffee and sat down across from him. "So, what's new?"

Milo had a mouth full of cream puff, and Ilene waited until he could speak. "My old door is gone."

Ilene bolted up. "I almost forgot!" She grabbed the coffee pot, returned it to the heater and rushed into her back room.

"Was it something I said?" Milo yelled after her.

Ilene returned with a large square wrapped in white bakery paper and presented it to Milo. "Here. For old time's sake."

Unwrapping it, he recognized the center piece of his old door, *RAT KEY INVESTIGATIONS*. "This is great!"

"I figure you can hang it in that fancy estate you live in. You know next to the Rembrandt."

"The Picasso would be pissed, but it'll be great in my office to remind me what could have been if I only applied myself."

"Yeah, your life's crap now." The bells on the door rang announcing a new customer. Ilene got up. "Get your credit card ready."

Milo sighed. There was a time when the cream puffs were free. Six months had passed since Milo's life had been turned upside down moving from struggling private eye to wealthy estate owner. Rubbing the welt on his head he realized some things remained the same.

2

David Bonner, older brother of the recently murdered real estate mogul James Bonner, picked up the phone and sat down. Opposite him, a thin, wiry, man in a three-piece suit cleaned his horn-rimmed glasses with a white monogrammed handkerchief. Bonner, facing charges for extortion in connection with his brother's scam, didn't remember hiring a high-priced lawyer.

The man scoped out the surroundings as he tended to his glasses before readjusting them back on his hawkish face. They were almost alone in the visitor's area except for a crying woman yelling at her husband several seats down. The ever-present guard was at the other end of the room reading the paper.

Satisfied they would not be overheard, the man began, "My name is Kozlov...Koz."

Bonner had heard the name. He knew enough to be polite. Koz was no lawyer. He nodded.

Almost in a whisper, Koz began, "I have clients who believe you might be of help to them because of your association with your brother's real estate ventures."

David remained silent.

Koz removed a picture from inside his left suit jacket pocket and held it up for David to see through the glass. "This woman sold condos kinda like what your brother did only in Atlanta."

Bonner studied the dark-haired attractive woman in the black suit. He glanced again at Koz and shook his head. "Don't know her. James might have, but I was just the muscle."

Koz replaced the picture in his pocket. "Can you check with your brother's associates?"

Bonner thought there wasn't a chance in hell he could be of help, but he knew better than to say that out loud. He nodded.

"I'll check back." Koz stood up, buttoned his coat, and walked away leaving David Bonner looking at an empty chair.

Bonner returned to his routine, a morning card game for Honeybuns and gum in the general population area. He wondered who he could ask about an unknown woman doing things he knew nothing about.

§

This overcast June day was a Feinberg pro bono day. Rather than remain idle, Milo still worked for lawyer Saul Feinberg as well as being a consultant to the Duluth Police Department.

Milo's morning kidnapping caused him to miss scumbag Dean Ford teeing off from the first hole. Pretending to use the ball washer, Milo waited on the tenth tee. He waved Ford's foursome through saying he was waiting for his guys to get out of the club house. As Ford set the ball on the tee, Milo sat down on a nearby bench and adjusted a camera hidden in his golf bag.

Ford teed up and after the thwack of a solid connection, roared to his companions about the stroke. Milo smirked at the roundhouse slice that left the ball in a sand trap. His job was done. No arm injury there. Saul Feinberg's client was without liability.

As he slid into the golf cart Milo marveled at his day, kidnapped by a mobster followed by successful undercover camera work all before lunch. This was like old times.

§

Since John McKnight had willed the Lakesong estate and his considerable fortune to both his son, Sutherland, and to Milo, who had grown up on the estate, Morrie's request this morning created a problem. On the way home Milo thought about how to sell Sutherland on granting Morrie's favor.

As Milo arrived at Lakesong, a panel truck advertising elevator maintenance was driving out of the gate. Lakesong had an army of guys who kept the estate functioning, and now *Up N Down Elevator Repair* had been added to the list.

"I see we have an elevator guy," Milo called from the hallway leading to the kitchen. Having seen the Porsche in the garage Rathkey knew Sutherland was home

"Have a cucumber," Martha offered. "It's not green."

"The outside is green. I don't do green," Milo complained.

"I told you so," Sutherland said taking three or four more slices.

Martha, who didn't fix lunch, pointed to the refrigerator. "Mr. Rathkey, choose your own color palette."

Grabbing a slice of ham, Milo asked Sutherland, "Don't you go to work anymore? Did you fire yourself?"

"If you must know, I've been ordered to take vacation time."

Agnes was confused. "You're the boss. Who orders the boss?"

"Helen Munger, the head of HR. She says I'm violating company policy by not taking vacation, so I'm taking vacation...thinking of weighing anchor and hoisting the mainsail and..."

"Hold that thought Captain Ahab, I also have news," Milo said. "We are going to have a wedding."

"You're getting married?" Agnes asked, eyes wide.

"Not me. I bumped into a...friend today. This guy has a granddaughter." Milo began uncharacteristically describing this friend's large, loving family.

The trio stared at him waiting for the story to get around to a wedding. Agnes weighed-in. "The wedding?"

Having downed the ham, Milo grabbed a piece of cheese. "I'm getting to that." He said between chews. "The wedding is about the granddaughter—delightful girl, about to start medical school, smart lady, lives in Minneapolis. She was supposed to be married at Bullard Hall, but they had that fire. The bride was devastated. It was terrible. Broke her heart.

She and her fiancée didn't know what to do. She cried for days." Milo was wondering if he was overselling. After all he was making most of it up on the fly. "Anyway, I thought they could have it here, out on the lawn. It's not like we don't have the room."

Agnes was embracing the possibility. "When's the wedding?"

"Two weeks," Milo said.

"Oh wow. You're right. They could never find a venue in two weeks," Agnes agreed.

Martha was also warming to the idea. "Were they using Bullard's in-house caterer?"

"That's food, right?"

"Yes, Mr. Rathkey, it's food and drink."

"I remember he said they need food, but they have flowers."

Sutherland was munching on a carrot he found in the refrigerator.

"Well, I can bring in temp help and use that kitchen in the basement," Martha said, thinking out loud.

"How many guests?" Agnes asked.

"Don't have a clue. He didn't say."

"Give me a contact number, I'll get the specifics," Agnes said shifting into party planner mode.

Sutherland finally spoke up. "Look, I don't want this poor young lady, her beau, and their 'huge close knit' families married on the street, but I'm missing key facts. I don't have a name. You haven't given us a name."

"The bride's name is Brittany Walker."

"The groom?"

"Joe."

"Joe?"

"Joe, that's all I remember."

"We never hosted a wedding at Lakesong," Sutherland mused. His brief engagement several years ago flew through his thoughts. "We could do it down by the lake."

"That's what I thought," Milo said, agreeing with Sutherland. "Might be fun."

Sutherland crossed the kitchen heading up stairs to change into his sailing clothes. Milo was self-congratulating. He had pulled this off and never once mentioned Morrie.

"Wait!" Sutherland came back into the room. "What's your friend's name?"

Damn! So close, Milo thought. "Oh, I think you'll like him. In fact, you once suggested we invite him over for brunch."

"That's nice. I still want a name."

"Wolf, Morris," Milo mumbled as he took another bite of sandwich.

It took a second for Sutherland to turn Morris into Morrie. "Oh, hell no!" Sutherland erupted.

Agnes jumped a little.

"You want to throw a wedding for the granddaughter of Morrie Wolf! The 'I put dead guys in the trunk of cars' Morrie Wolf?"

Agnes and Martha looked first at Sutherland then at Rathkey.

Milo began carefully, "Morrie does have his faults, but his granddaughter is in a pickle. Besides, when Morrie asks for a personal favor, you do him a personal favor. Nothing about this is illegal. It's a wedding."

"Does he really kill people?" Agnes asked.

Milo scoffed. "It's a legend."

"Could this wedding put us in danger?" Martha asked, thinking about her siblings.

"Absolutely not," Milo said emphatically. "Morrie insisted that no one knows the bride's relation to him. The bride is just a girl who was lucky enough to find an alternative place for her wedding, Lakesong."

"So, our client is the bride and groom and their families… not this Morrie Wolf?" Martha questioned.

"Yes."

"I'm still in," Agnes offered. "The girl is trying to get married. If she didn't set the fire, I don't have a problem helping her out."

Milo, sensing he had the backing of the crowd, turned to Sutherland.

Feeling outnumbered Sutherland argued, "Look, I feel sorry for this girl. I do. But I have a business to run, and I can't have gangsters roaming around Lakesong. Something like that is bound to get out."

"Morrie doesn't roam, and there will not be gangsters. No one knows Morrie has a daughter, let alone a grand-daughter. He will be here for the wedding and leave. None of the guests—none of them—know Morrie or what he does for a living. To them he's an old guy who was invited to the wedding. He assured me he will disappear as quickly as he appears."

Sutherland wondered if he could really trust Milo Rathkey, who until six months ago was a name on an occasional greeting card sent to his father. In his will, Sutherland's father had described Sutherland's life as uneventful and predictable. Within days of Milo's moving to Lakesong, Sutherland had been involved in a murder and now six months later, a gangster's wedding. Neither could be described as uneventful nor predictable.

Sutherland surveyed the small group of co-conspirators. "Okay. We'll hold this wedding, but no criminals other than Morrie…"

"And his body guard," Milo interrupted.

Sutherland rolled his eyes and sighed. "And his body guard. Of course. But Milo, I'm holding you responsible for the safety of everyone and everything here at Lakesong." He would have continued but his phone began to vibrate. Sutherland excused himself and stepped into the hearth room to take the call.

"Oh yeah. That was something else I forgot," Milo said. "Do not mention Morrie's name to anyone."

Sutherland came back in the room smiling.

Milo was wary. "I don't like the look of that smile."

The smile grew into a grin. "Here's the deal. I'll agree to this wedding which you offered to do as a favor, but now, I want a favor."

Doing a favor for Morrie Wolf was frightening. A Sutherland favor couldn't possibly be in the same league. "Who's the gangster now?" Milo kidded. "Right out of *The Godfather*. What's your favor?"

"I want you to join my cycling group."

Milo's eyes widened. This was unexpected.

"Wait," Sutherland challenged. "Before you crack wise, let me explain. I have been a promoter and supporter of the biking trail system in Duluth for years. A national newspaper is in town to write an extensive article on our mountain bike trails for their Sunday magazine. The article will include a picture of my group, the Zenith City Cyclers. That phone call was a couple, big bike enthusiasts, saying they couldn't attend. We need more people for the picture, and you will now be one of them."

"How am I going to look like a guy on a bike? I don't even own a bike."

"You can buy everything you need. We'll go this afternoon and get you outfitted."

Milo got the message. "Okay. I'll buy a bike. I'll pose for a picture. That's it…right?"

"Nope. You actually have to ride. I don't want to use ringers. You have to be a legitimate member of the group even if you only ride a couple of times. I will get you up to speed."

"I know how to ride a bike."

"Not these bikes you don't. Your first lesson is tomorrow." In true positive Sutherland style, he assured Milo it would be painless. Then he hit him with part two of the favor. "Oh, by the way, the newspaper people will be over tonight for dinner, and your attendance is mandatory."

Milo sighed. He was being held hostage by both Morrie and Sutherland. He had already agreed to do the Morrie favor. There was no backing out now. If he had to ride a bike, he had to ride a bike.

Martha, sensing an agreement, brought the conversation back to the bride. "So, it's set? We're hosting a wedding?"

Milo and Sutherland eyed each other in wariness but shook their heads in agreement.

"I can ride, and I have a trail bike if anyone's interested," Agnes said coyly.

Sutherland's eyes lit up. "Absolutely! Welcome to the Zenith City Cyclers! Great! This is going to work out. Come on Milo, let's get you outfitted."

"As much as I can't wait to buy a bike, I have a prior commitment."

"No, no, no. This is your commitment to me," Sutherland charged.

Noticing Sutherland was about to go off on fair play and favor for favor, Milo put up his hands to stop the lecture. "Hold up! You know I'm a police consultant."

Sutherland was wary.

"Today, along with you and Morrie, I've got Gramm on my butt," he said referring to his friend Lt. Ernie Gramm. "Before I can carry my gun, I've got to qualify, so I reserved time to practice on the gun range. It'll only take a couple of hours, and then I'll meet you in the parking lot of the... where the hell do you buy a bike?"

"Ski Chalet."

"Of course. You know that makes no sense," Milo pointed out.

"You have a gun?" Sutherland asked.

"Of course, I have a gun. I've always had a gun. I was a PI and before that a cop and before that I was shore patrol in the Navy. How would I not have a gun?"

"My first day of vacation I learn we'll have a mobster wedding, and Milo has a gun. Can't wait for day two." Sutherland jumped up. "I'm going sailing. I won't be back until the cool lake air cleanses me of this nightmare and helps me cope with this clown show that has become my life."

Watching him leave, Milo called after him, "Kinda dramatic doncha think?"

Martha and Agnes exchanged glances but said nothing. Milo went to his bedroom to retrieve his gun bag from the bedroom safe. The room's massive walk in closet created for a gentleman of another century was still almost empty. N&J clothiers had managed to fill in a few items of high-end winter wear, including the suit he wore to Mary Alice Bonner's New Year's Eve party.

Milo changed out of his golf clothes, putting them at the end of the closet, behind the ladder which led to unused shoe cubicles. In his mind he categorized that area of closet for disguises. Currently, it held only the golf clothes. His summer casual wear remained unchanged, khaki Dockers, t-shirts, and a wind breaker a must for Duluth even in the summer.

Milo picked up the jacket, his gun bag, and headed to the range.

Agnes, still in the kitchen, sipped her coffee.

"I would give a month's salary to see Milo in spandex bike shorts," Martha said almost to herself.

Agnes erupted in an explosive laugh. "Keep your money. I'll be there. I'll capture it for us on my phone."

§

Jessica Vogel flipped her fingers through her ombre hair pushing it up out of her face. Her colorist had done a great job. Expensive, certainly, but her outside revenue stream was about to explode. She smiled at the pricy drop-dead red dress on her closet door. Another extravagance that would be her new normal.

Pairing her phone to Alexa, she called up her favorite Zumba workout, "Uptown Funk" by Bruno Mars, and cranked it. Putting her hair up in a rubber band, she began to dance. Hands in the air, point to the right, point to the left. Roll right. Roll left. Spin in! Spin out.

She was hot, fit, and charged to confront perv Paul and Matron Maureen, two potential contributors to her lifestyle. Naughty Paul had stopped his payments. Maureen's contribution, idle since high school, would double, no, triple, in light of her husband's family value run for the state senate. Jessica had the power. She had the goods.

Taking her hair down, she fluffed it out. The auburn tones complemented her brown eyes. As a realtor she couldn't be too outrageous, but the highlights were subtle and brightened her face. Turning thirty was depressing; she refused to look it.

Jessica grabbed the red dress, rolled it and put it in the suitcase along with matching red lingerie and shoes. *Friday Night. Check. Next, prissy, sissy Saturday luncheon with the girls. Barf. Dog meat canapés.*

Checking the closet, she chose the fit and flare floral dress and a red power blazer. She debated between her new Kate Spade satchel, and the more expensive Prada tote, another new extravagance. She tossed in the Prada and matching shoes.

Jessica locked up her house and made sure her bike was secure in its rack on the new red Audi Q5 SUV. She threw the suitcase and biking gear in the backseat and headed for Duluth. Some of those dreary mopes were bound to bring up that clumsy Molly girl. Jessica was ready. She had money to collect. She was confident as she cranked up more Bruno.

3

As Milo turned right into the gun range parking lot, a bright red Mercedes convertible swerved from the left lane cutting him off.

"What the hell? Are you blind?" he yelled slamming on his brakes.

The Mercedes drove to the nearest empty space in the back of the almost filled parking lot. Milo parked close by with the intention of having words with the driver. He could see a blond ponytail being adjusted and makeup being checked in the rear-view mirror. The scene looked somehow familiar.

Milo's déjà vu moment was interrupted by a reminder call from Gramm. "Are you going to the gun range?" he demanded in his gruff manner.

"Ernie get lunch. I'm here…"

The blond driver got out of her car, turned to Milo, mouthed the word 'sorry' and wove her way toward the building. Milo's anger dissipated in a flash. He recognized her at once, deep blue eyes, pretty smile, Mary Alice Bonner.

"Gotta go Ernie...just saw an old friend."

"You're qualifying tomorrow at..."

Milo hung up.

Gramm called back. Milo ignored the call, catching up with Mary Alice as she reached the steps.

"Hi there," Milo said, at once regretting his mundane, school boy greeting.

She turned, looked at him, and smiled the Mary Alice all-accepting smile. "I know you...Milo...Rathkey. I remember. Was that you I cut off? Again, sorry. What are you doing here?"

Milo tried not to stare at those beautiful blue eyes, failing miserably. "I...have to...shoot...qualify, you know, for the cops. I'm still a consultant."

"We never did have our conversation," she said as she walked up the steps, slowing down, allowing Milo to escort her.

"Conversation?"

"You've forgotten!" She feigned hurt feelings. "At my New Year's Eve party, I said I wanted to know every little detail of how you came to be the co-owner of Lakesong. As I remember, we joked about uncovering skeletons in the McKnight's closet."

"Oh, I didn't forget...events got in the way," Milo said as he opened the door, allowing her to enter.

She turned and said, "We shouldn't let anymore... events...get in the way of our chat. I am still intensely curious as to how Milo Rathkey became my neighbor."

Milo could not remember any other neighbor being intensely curious about him. The flirtatious tongue-in-cheek banter with Mary Alice was fun. Six months had passed since her husband's murder, and if she had been in mourning, her bright yellow outfit signaled it was over.

"Do you have time for coffee after we shoot?" she asked.

We shoot? Milo thought. *She's done it again. It's not just a pronoun change from I to we, it's her manner. At least for now, we're a couple.* "Coffee's good."

Mary Alice smiled and turned to the attendant to get her lane only to be told they were all taken. She would have to wait.

Milo came to the rescue. Showing his police identification, he asked if Mary Alice could join him in the three-lane range reserved for law enforcement. The attendant agreed as the police range wasn't being used. They bought their targets, and Milo led the way.

Mary Alice stopped to put on her earmuffs which were usually required before entering the lane area.

Milo stopped her. "It's quiet in there; we don't have to do that until we shoot."

Inside the range, they clipped their targets to the hanger and sent them out twenty-five feet. Milo's qualifying distance. Mary Alice removed a Glock 19 from her shooting bag.

She noticed Milo's silent stare. "Yes, in answer to your unasked question. It's one and the same. The object of my husband's demise and my new favorite pistol. The police returned it to me."

Remembering that the gun had a hair trigger, Milo stepped back even though she was pointing it down range.

Laughing at Milo's defensive move, she assured him it was safe. "The trigger's fixed. I did it myself. Remember, I told you my father taught me about guns."

They put on their protective eye and ear gear and shot fifteen rounds before pulling the targets back. Milo had his usual problem. Most of his shots were to the left and down, only one close to the bullseye. Not good enough to qualify. Mary Alice's shots, however, were so closely grouped in the bullseye, one shot could not be distinguished from another.

She looked at his target. "Low and to the left. Your finger is too deep into the trigger. Bring it out."

"It's a personality flaw of my trigger finger."

Mary Alice laughed. "Really?"

"Yes. No lie."

As they sent the targets out again, Milo held up his trigger finger and instructed it to behave. Blue eyes glanced and smiled at Milo's silliness. This time Milo did much better, not Mary Alice better, but good enough to qualify.

After five more rounds, Milo was beginning to be bored by continued conversations with his trigger finger, and his own success. He suggested he and Mary Alice go for that coffee.

"Coffee's good," Mary Alice said parroting Milo earlier response as if it wasn't her initial idea. "There's a new coffee place I've been meaning to try. It's a few doors down. We can walk there."

They stowed the guns in their respective cars and walked to La French Press. Having had an active morning, fueled only by a cream puff, and a small snack, Milo's stomach wanted something substantial with his coffee.

Looking at the menu board, he didn't see anything he recognized, only a series of French sandwich names. "I was hoping for a ham and cheese sandwich."

"Try the Croque Monsieur," Mary Alice suggested.

"What's that?"

"Ham and cheese, on brioche."

"I can work with that."

Mary Alice ordered a small plate of brie with almonds, fig jam, and apples.

They took their food and coffee to a small table in the corner where Mary Alice began her interrogation of Rathkey. "So, I want your version of how you came to be co-owner of Lakesong and my neighbor. I never did get the story...from you."

"My version? That indicates you have other versions."

"Rumors...only rumors. However, some were quite exciting."

"Really? What?"

"The two I most enjoyed were you're a spy or John McKnight's long-lost love child."

"I can't be both?"

Mary Alice rested her chin on her hand. "I suppose you could, but that would be a little piggish. Leave some drama for the rest of us."

"You haven't had enough drama?"

"Hmm, good point."

"Okay, here's the quick version. After my dad died, my mom became John's cook. I was eight. We moved into Lakesong, and I grew up there. I knew John longer than I knew my dad. I left Lakesong for the Navy when I eighteen, and Sutherland was about to be born."

"Interesting. Did you expect the bequest?"

"No. John and I shared a love of mysteries, so when I heard about the will reading, I expected a book, or two. I was shocked, and quite frankly I still am."

"Your mother must have been a great cook for John to leave you half the estate," Mary Alice joked.

"She was."

"Why did Sutherland go along with it? Everyone was waiting for him to challenge the will."

"Me too, but Sutherland said he and his dad talked about it for a long time and agreed." Milo tasted his sandwich, admitting to himself it was delicious despite its peculiar name. "I told you my story. What have you been doing since the last time I...interrogated you?"

"You did, didn't you?" Mary Alice tilted her head allowing a brief frown to flit across her face and then disappear. "I'm a socialite turned career woman these days. I took over James' business."

"Sounds like work. How's that going?"

"Well, don't get me wrong. I don't go into the office every day. I hired a new vice president, a woman from the cities to do the heavy lifting. She's moving our reputation from shady to trusted. It's an uphill struggle, and my new public relations guy has his work cut out for him."

"You know business?" Milo asked.

"Oh yes, I always liked business. I completed my MBA years ago." Mary Alice took a thick slice of brie, balanced it on an apple wedge, dolloped it with fig jam, and topped it with an almond. She expertly brought it to her mouth and consumed it as if it were a piece of toast, not a Leaning Tower of Pisa. After she was finished, she began building again.

"How do you do that?" Milo asked.

"Do what?"

"Pile it like that and not wear it. Everything would be on my shirt."

Other than her father, the men in her life never asked her how she did anything. She didn't think they even noticed. Keeping it light, she replied. "It's all in the trigger finger. You can't go deep."

Milo took another bite of his sandwich to give his brain time to digest her comment. *Does that have a double meaning? I don't have a clue.*

Mary Alice took a bite of her latest creation before saying, "Besides trying to transform the company, I'm also looking for a new tennis partner."

"What about…ahh what's his name…Brad…"

"Nelson. Not in the picture," Mary Alice said referring to her husband's business rival, and her old tennis partner.

Milo suspected that tennis was not all she and Brad Nelson shared. Either way Brad not in the picture was good. "I play tennis."

The blue eyes opened wide. "Are you any good? I take my tennis seriously."

"I played in high school, in the Navy, and I still play pickup games from time to time. A couple of practice sessions should bring me up to speed."

Mary Alice crossed her arms and gave him an unbelieving head tilt. "You got one shot with me. One and done." She was smiling, but she meant every word.

"Bring it on. Your court or mine?" Milo shook his head. "I don't believe I said that."

Mary Alice laughed. "Yours. Mine is being restriped. They're almost finished." She tossed back a couple of almonds she had dipped in the fig jam, sat back and stared at Milo. "This could be interesting."

"How so?" Milo asked, feeling a bit like a bug under a microscope.

"My therapist says I have a type, whether it's husbands or tennis partners. You may break that type."

"Is that good or bad?"

"Let's see how you play tennis."

§

Leroy Thompson had his head down on a back table in the general population area where prisoners played cards and passed the time. He hated jail as much as he hated juvie as a kid. His partner and protector, Stan Shultz, was dead leaving Leroy on his own once again. He had two things to do, survive jail and pay back Morrie Wolf. Cheating Morrie sounded good at the time, but Leroy knew he was lucky to be alive. He hadn't cut Morrie in the now infamous Bonner real estate scam.

Leroy usually wore a pencil-thin mustache and goatee, but a few goons poked fun at him, so Leroy shaved it off. Go along, get along.

Leroy longed for his 'Miami in Duluth' look, a white tropical suit and purple shirt. Prison orange was not his color.

I gotta get out of here. I'll figure it out. I'm Leroy Thompson goddamn it!

David Bonner, who ignored Leroy most of the time, sat down next to him. "You can drop the sleeping act, Leroy. Everyone knows you're faking."

Leroy looked up, his eyes darting, assessing the degree of danger. "Whaddaya want?"

"You and my brother…"

Leroy leaned in whispering. "I told you. Stan Shultz killed your brother. I had nothin' to do with it!"

"I don't care. I'm lookin' for somebody that builds stuff… you know condos. I figured you hustled for my brother so you'd know."

Leroy was confused. "Builds stuff? I'm a con man. I don't know anybody. I do what I'm told."

Bonner sneered. "Who would know?"

"Know what? I'm not getting what you're lookin' for."

"A broad with long dark hair, kinda pretty…sold condos in Atlanta…and now sells 'em here. People want to *talk* to her. I'm helping them."

Leroy thought his question was stupid but pondered how helping Bonner could benefit him. "Ask the kid."

"Kid?"

"You know, Dickie boy…"

It was Bonner's turn to look puzzled.

"Richard, your brother's kid. I hear he now does crap like that. Or you can ask your brother's wife."

David nodded.

Leroy, always working an angle, thought he would push his luck. "So, why do these people want to talk to her?"

"Their business. Not yours."

It was time to shut up.

§

The Honda slid into a waiting parking space behind the Ski Chalet next to Sutherland's Porsche. He knew the familiar Tyrolean themed building, it was a Duluth landmark, but he never had a reason to shop.

"Are you sure the Ski Chalet sells bikes?" Milo asked.

"Of course. It gives them something to sell in the summer. My friend Larry, who's a part owner, says they sell more bikes than skis."

Milo looked doubtful.

"You can ask him yourself, he's outfitting you as a personal favor to me. We're riding buddies," Sutherland said as he yanked open one of the beat-up double metal back doors revealing lines of hanging bikes waiting to be repaired or adjusted. Sutherland called out to one of the guys who was working on a blue mountain bike.

"They sure have enough of these mechanics," Milo said counting five people working on bikes.

"Wrenches," Sutherland corrected.

"What?"

"The mechanics. They call themselves wrenches."

"So, if a wrench is using a wrench…"

"Don't worry about it," Sutherland cut him off, shaking his head while directing Milo up the stairs to the sales area.

"Sutherland! Good to see you!" A friendly looking man with tousled dark hair and a close-cropped summer beard shook Sutherland's hand with enthusiasm. He was wearing full spandex, shorts and shirt. Milo was not a member of the spandex fan club.

"Larry, this is my friend Milo Rathkey. Milo, Larry Ashbach. He knows bikes."

"I try. What are you looking for today Sutherland?"

"I'm good, but Milo needs a bike, clothes, shoes, a helmet—the works. He's a beginner," Sutherland said, emphasizing the word beginner.

"Whoa! I don't need training wheels," Milo objected. "I have ridden a bike before. But nothing like what I'm seeing here."

"These are not your father's three speeds," Larry joked. "Where are you going to ride?"

"I have no clue. I am here against my will," Milo mumbled as he began to look at the multitude of bikes.

Sutherland filled in the blanks. "Street riding primarily, maybe a couple of easy trails with the emphasis on easy."

Milo stopped at a row of wide-tired bikes. "I like these. Big fat tires…like when I was a kid."

Larry laughed. "Those are snow trail bikes Milo. We have a few left over on sale."

"Snow trail bikes. There are snow trails?"

"Yeah," Sutherland chimed in. "Although I've never used them. During the winter I stick to my stationary bike."

"Let's start with a road bike," Larry suggested.

Milo shrugged and followed Larry to a long rack of bikes with narrow tires, down curving handlebars, and small seats. It took Milo only seconds to declare the road bikes uncomfortable. "The seat hurts, and I don't like bending over the handlebars like that. All I can see is the pavement."

"Seats and handlebars can be changed," Larry offered, "but I think you might like a hybrid."

They moved over to another row of bikes. "These have front suspension, straight handlebars, and look, a padded seat," Larry explained. "The tires are wider but not as wide as mountain bikes and nowhere close to snow bikes."

Milo got up on a hybrid, and had to admit, it felt fairly comfortable. Larry spent the next fifteen minutes asking him questions and making minor adjustments. "I'll send all these adjustments downstairs after you get your riding clothes."

"I can tell you right now, Larry, this body doesn't do spandex," Milo warned.

Sutherland rolled his eyes. "Let's try the quick dry poly shorts, a jersey, and a bike helmet."

"What kind of shoe?" Larry asked.

"A regular biking shoe, and platform pedals. That way if he falls off, he can stop himself."

Milo waved his hands. "I'm right here in the room guys. I'm not three."

"If you start to fall, you can get your feet off the pedals to steady yourself," Sutherland explained as his phone rang. He glanced at the name of the caller and smiled. "Hello? Mary Alice?"

Milo looked up with interest.

"I can, but he's right here. Do you want to talk to him?" Sutherland handed Rathkey his phone with a giant question mark on his face.

Milo answered Sutherland's expression with a shrug and said, "Hello Mary Alice. What can I do for you?"

"After we had coffee, I forgot to get your number. Could you text it to me?"

"Sure, no problem," Milo answered, hiding his amusement at Sutherland's heightened curiosity.

"Also, the reason I'm calling, I need to do tennis at noon instead of eleven," Mary Alice said.

"Works for me. See you then." *Every sport has its outfit… Mary Alice in a tennis dress or shorts has to be spectacular.*

Milo texted his number to her on Sutherland's phone and handed it back to him.

"What was that?" Sutherland demanded.

"Mary Alice," Milo said. "Yeah, let's go with the quick dry shorts, and I don't want to know why they have to be quick dry."

While Milo left the store with unwanted biking clothes, shoes, helmet, and hybrid bike, Sutherland left the store still wondering why Mary Alice Bonner called Milo.

§

"Martha, I talked to the bride," Agnes said. "She and her mother asked to meet with us tomorrow…early afternoon. I tentatively said yes. Does that work for you?"

"Tomorrow's fine. What's her mood?"

Agnes pursed her lips and searched for the right descriptor. "I think hysterical covers it. At this point, if we served hot dogs and potato chips, she'd be okay with it."

Martha laughed. "Oh, I know I can do better than that. Would you like some iced tea?"

"That'd be great!"

They both sat down on the back terrace overlooking the dappled expansive lawn leading down to the big lake. Superior's mood today was calm and glassy, stirring from time to time by a deep undulating wave which never broke the surface. It was soothing.

Martha interrupted the silence, continuing an earlier conversation about Agnes' high school reunion. "I went to East High."

"I would have liked that, but my foster mom had both me and my sister go to Thrana Hall. She thought it would be more disciplined, and she had connections there. We were scholarship kids."

Martha could hear the resentment in Agnes' voice but was not sure if it was toward her foster parents or the school. Silence fell again as both women stretched out, and closed their eyes, absorbing the sun's warmth.

"Can I stay here forever?" Agnes said, half seriously.

"Sure, but it might get chilly at night."

"Oh, but not now. I so need this, and I want to thank you for recommending Dr. Taylor. She has helped me deal with the trauma and loss over the last six months."

"She is helpful. I couldn't have gotten past my parents' death and taking on my new role without her. I'm glad she's helping you with the loss of your sister."

Agnes didn't share the other issue besides the death of her sister, a horrific scene which kept haunting her and causing nightmares.

Martha turned to look at her. "Are you also stressed about the wedding?"

"Not yet. I'm stressed about the reunion. I tell myself daily I don't have to go, but part of me says it would be good. I hear this argument in my head every single day."

Martha sipped her iced tea and said nothing. Agnes seemed to need a sounding board today.

"I can deal with the sadness of my sister not being there. I mean she died, and everyone will say how sorry they are. What I dread is the rehashing of Molly's death—so many questions."

"That's the girl that died when you were a sophomore?"

"Molly Edwards. She was my friend. She came from a big family, lots of sisters—loved music and was tech savvy. Remember Limewire?"

"Oh yeah, that takes me back—great music and free."

"Well, Molly was the queen of Limewire. She would download a ton of music and make mixed CDs for everyone. I loved it, and a lot of the cool girls did too."

"Ah yes, the 'cool' girls. You had them too? How lovely life would be without them."

"Molly's life might have continued without them," Agnes said bitterly as she stared off into the distance.

Martha hesitated. "Can I ask what happened?"

Agnes hadn't discussed Molly's death in years. She sat up, staring at the water. She was hoping the hugeness of the lake would somehow make her problems smaller. It had worked in the past. It didn't today. Maybe talking to Martha would help. "It was a Friday night in October. The older girls took us along on their drinking escapade up at Enger Tower. For most of us this was our first time going."

"Getting to tag along with the older kids at that age is a rite of passage," Martha said.

"It should have been," Agnes agreed taking a sip of her tea. "You know how spooky that place is, especially in the fall and that night it was even more frightening—cold, dark, and windy. We kept hearing moaning sounds, which I'm sure was the wind moving through the tower, but back then it was scary. The older girls were retelling a spooky story of a man being frightened to death by the tower spirits. They had us believing that he and the other spirits walk the top of the tower each day around Halloween looking for the next person to scare to death and join them."

"That's silly," Martha said.

"Easy to say now, but we were young and stupid. On a dare, we paired off. One at a time, an older girl took a younger girl up to the top to confront the ghost. It was scary but meant to be fun. There were no lights. We had to feel our way up, using the walls as a guide. That was good because I remember the beer was making me a little tipsy. Going up wasn't bad, but coming down was too hard and scary. I inched down on my butt. Molly refused to go at first, but Jessica Raymond, nastier than the girl that took me up, bullied her into it. We don't know what happened, but on the way down, Molly fell. She died."

"I remember hearing about that. Nobody went to Enger Tower for a long time after that," Martha said.

"We all thought Jessica pushed her, including Molly's closest sister, Liz. If Jessica shows up, and Liz is there, I don't know what will happen."

§

"I've heard the mosquitoes in Minnesota are as big as birds," Megan Davis said to Sutherland after he suggested dinner out on the terrace.

"The local joke is the mosquito is the state bird," Sutherland joked, leading the group outside. "We fog."

"Do we have a fog guy?" Milo asked.

"We have a fog couple."

Milo had hoped for a quiet night, forgetting about the Sutherland-manipulated dinner with a newspaper reporter and photographer.

Megan looked around as she sat at the terrace table. "You have a lovely home. What do estates like this sell for in Duluth?"

"Just a little nosey, Megan," Photographer Reggie Cuff admonished. The two made an interesting pair—the short and blond Megan, the tall and dark Reggie with shoulder length dreads.

Megan curled her hair behind her right ear. "Reggie, I'm a reporter. I ask questions. Besides in my previous life, I worked in a real estate office."

This was news to Reggie. "When was that?"

"In college when I was at Emory—part time."

"Duluth was once filled with lumber, ore, and fur millionaires," Sutherland explained, "but that was the turn of the last century. Today, no matter what this estate is worth, finding a buyer would be difficult." He detailed his father's worry that the house would not sell as a home and at best would become a museum.

"Where do you live Mr. Rathkey?" Reggie asked.

"It's complicated, but I own half of this."

Seeing the confusion on his guest's faces, Sutherland elaborated, "My father thought if he willed it to two of us, there was a greater chance of the estate remaining as a private home for at least one more generation."

"Interesting," Reggie said. "What do you do Milo?"

"I'm a private detective," Milo answered.

"Even more interesting."

"Do you cycle?" Megan asked Milo.

"Sure, I was pretty good at it as a kid."

Sutherland cleared his throat. "Several of our mountain bikers went up to the Boundary Waters on a camping trip, and a couple canceled…don't know why. So, we've added a few newbies. Milo is a newbie."

"Help. I am being held against my will," Milo whispered to Megan.

"Ignore him. He's looking forward to the experience," Sutherland lied, and asked the pair what other events they would be covering.

"The story is about extreme sports in the area," Megan explained. "Tomorrow we're going kayaking on the Lester River."

Looking at Reggie's tall frame, Milo asked if he could fit into a kayak. Reggie assured him, he could.

Megan continued, "And on Sunday we'll be hang gliding out over the lake."

"I'm afraid our mountain trails may seem tame after that," Sutherland said.

"I've heard your diamond trails are far from it. I'm riding one tomorrow with another local group."

Sutherland was a bit put out that Megan would be riding with a group other than the Zenith City Cyclers.

Megan noticed Sutherland's frown and offered a further explanation. "It's a group of business women who ride during the week before work. I find it an interesting phenomenon, and that's my job."

"I've arranged for my friend Larry, a bike shop owner, to provide you with bikes and whatever other equipment you need—gloves, shoes, helmets."

"I brought my own helmet," Megan said. "It works for various sports so I always have it with me."

"Yeah," Reggie laughed. "I like that helmet. I can always spot her; it's bright red."

Martha began to serve dinner, lake trout in lemon butter garlic sauce with sides of asparagus and julienne carrots.

"I'm hoping to run in the Grandma's Marathon," Reggie said. "Who was grandma?"

"It's a restaurant," Sutherland explained. "Are you running too?" he asked Megan.

"These short legs pedal, they don't run. I'm dropping him off at the starting point. Speaking of pedaling when are we going to ride the trails with your group?"

"Between kayaking, parasailing, and Grandma's, sounds like you're busy this week. Why don't we set it for next week?" Sutherland said.

Reggie checked the schedule on his phone. "How about next Thursday?"

"Sounds good to me," Sutherland said. "Milo?"

"Sure…can't wait."

4

Jessica did her pre-ride stretching in the gravel Twin Ponds parking area off of Skyline Drive. Despite the early hour, a number of other bikers were doing the same, with more already on the trail.

"Great day for it," a woman coming off the trail told her. "I love getting my ride in before work. You from around here?"

"Used to be," Jessica said. "Visiting now."

"Well, enjoy."

Jessica nodded, wondering if she could endure all this Northern Minnesota friendliness for the entire weekend. The early morning chill was already beginning to warm as she strapped on her helmet, mounted the bike, and headed up the trail. Her muscles strained as she climbed the rocky path that followed the ridgeline. Most of the riders took it slow, so they could enjoy the view of Lake Superior and the Duluth Harbor in the far distance. Jessica took it fast, scaling the switchback curves easily in anticipation of pumping and jumping over the berms and boulders on the trip back down. One misplaced rock could spell disaster. For Jessica it was about the rush.

After full out climbing for fifteen minutes, she stopped to hydrate. Other bikers came up and paused in the same general area. They all had red helmets, apparently part of a group identity. Jessica laughed. As they took off their helmets, she vaguely recognized one of them. They locked eyes. There was mutual recognition, but nothing said. Not even a nod.

How do I know you? Duluth? Minneapolis? Atlanta? Jessica continued to stare at the group trying to remember. *Oh my God! Could it be?*

Her thoughts were interrupted by the abrupt turn and rush downhill of the recognized biker.

Where are you going? Are you running from me?

Jessica pursued. A surge of adrenaline enveloped her. Her quarry handled the trail like an expert, but Jessica, who knew no fear, flew down after her, jumping rollers with abandon. This was a no brakes trip. Bikers coming up the single-track squeezed to get out of her way, several shouted at them to slow down. Ignoring the shouts, the two continued at breakneck speed, a tandem menace on the morning trail. Seconds before the parking lot, a family of four blocked the way leaving little room to maneuver. The mystery cycler skidded off the trail but managed to keep upright. Jessica hit her brakes. Too much! Her front wheel lost its traction and slipped out from under, throwing her to the ground, skinning her leg and bruising her shoulder

Damn it!

Wincing, she remounted her bike, pushing beyond the family before they could slow her down again. She careened back down the trail.

As she skidded to a stop in the parking lot, a Land Rover was swerving through a quick left turn onto Skyline Drive. Standing there, catching her breath, numb to her aching shoulder and bruised leg, she knew.

No wonder! I'd run too.

§

Milo finished his early morning swim in Lakesong's indoor pool when Saul Feinberg called wanting the golf video.

"I'll be over after I qualify on the gun range…right around noon," Milo said without a hello.

"Why don't you email it to me?" Saul asked.

"Because I love the ripping sound of my fee coming out of your checkbook."

"Bull…you just want a free pastry, besides, the checks don't even go to you anymore," Saul said, referring to their new arrangement where Milo's fee went to the Boys and Girls Club.

"But you still write the checks, and I still love the sound."

Feinberg sighed. "I'll save you a bear claw."

As Milo toweled off, he caught his reflection in the surrounding pool windows. Five months of steady swimming had shrunk the tire around his middle. He was feeling good, not his old Navy days good, but good for mid-forties.

He dressed and headed for breakfast in the morning room. Per usual, Annie joined him, anticipating a share of his breakfast.

"Welcome Annie," Sutherland said. "I see you brought your pet human with you."

Annie gave him a silent meow. Sutherland often interpreted this as a negative assessment of him, but today he thought Annie was laughing with him.

Milo poured himself a cup of coffee and sat down, waiting for Martha to deliver his eggs and bacon. No full lumberjack breakfast with hash browns and pancakes, but still a counter point to Sutherland's green protein smoothies.

Sutherland was engrossed in his Wall Street Journal prompting Milo to interrupt his concentration just for fun. "So, who won?"

Sutherland peeked around the paper. "Won what?"

"I don't know. Your paper has no sports page; I figured they keep track of real estate scores."

Sutherland huffed good naturedly at Milo's usual chiding. "If you must know, I'm reading about crime—money laundering in major cities involving real estate developers and drug gangs. The article says it's been going on for ten or fifteen years."

"Wow, so exciting. Can I read it after you? No wait, I have to pound a nail through my foot first."

"Okay, it's not murder, but it's crime and it's in my business. This is the third story I've read about it. It keeps getting bigger...more widespread, Miami first but now Atlanta and Dallas."

Milo broke off small pieces of bacon, dropping them on the floor for Annie. Sutherland followed the action, folded his paper, and cleared his throat. "Well?"

"Well what?" Milo asked still, dealing with the cat.

"I haven't crowded you, but I want an explanation."

Milo looked up. "I always feed the cat."

"Not the cat, the widow. Why did Mary Alice call me looking for you?"

"Let me check to see if you're on the list of people who are authorized to know." Milo followed down an imaginary list with his index finger. "Nope, don't see your name anywhere."

"You're kidding me. You're not going to tell me?"

"She's planning a surprise birthday party for you."

"My birthday is in January. This is June."

"She wants to get a jump on it," Milo said dragging his scrambled eggs through a pool of ketchup.

"I could employ the techniques I learned from you and Lt. Gramm …you know on the Bonner murder."

"I refuse to talk."

"We could do this downtown," Sutherland mocked Gramm's favorite line.

"To a real estate office?" Milo questioned.

Sutherland sighed. "My technique needs work." Sutherland finished his green smoothie. "The more evasive you are, the more curious I become —just saying."

"You'll know soon enough." Milo gave Annie one last piece of bacon.

§

Agnes had taken over the bright and airy reception room next to Milo's office. It was a perfect location as it faced the front of the house and had a door to a small courtyard allowing tradesmen and others to reach her without having to go through the main entrance to the house. Her new bosses gave her a budget to add her own personal touches to the workspace: a few favorite art prints, modern furniture, and flowers, real ones, something James Bonner her old boss would have never allowed. It was comfortable but professional. Something she thought reflected her style.

The calendar on her phone chimed, reminding Agnes that the bride and her mother were due in thirty minutes. The gate intercom buzzer surprised her.

"Yes?" she asked.

"This is Linda Baer," the gravelly voice on the other end proclaimed.

The name didn't register with Agnes. She checked the closed-circuit feed and saw a white pickup truck with a tarp hiding something in the bed. "I'm sorry. Do we have an appointment?"

"In a way. I'm Brittany's grandmother."

"Oh, yes. Of course," Agnes said, being polite. A grandmother had not been mentioned. This woman looked a little rough. *I wonder what's under the tarp.*

Agnes headed out of her office to the courtyard to meet Mrs. Baer.

Linda Wolf Baer was a petite, gray-haired, energetic seventy-year-old who looked and acted twenty years younger.

"Sorry about the pickup truck," Baer said. "My husband and I run a trucking company, and it comes with the terri-tory." That explained the work jeans, t-shirt, and scuffed up steel-toed boots.

"That's fine," Agnes said, introducing herself. After a brief handshake, Agnes invited Linda inside and texted Martha to join them in the gallery.

Looking around the glass-domed, park-like setting of trees and foliage, Baer asked abruptly, "Are we inside or outside?"

Agnes assured her that they were inside as they wound their way to one of the small sitting areas overlooking the back lawn, gardens, and Lake Superior. Martha introduced herself and offered coffee and cookies.

Linda Wolf Baer sat on the edge of a chair and looked from Agnes to Martha with little friendliness on her face. Her husky voice, a product of a tough life and too many cigarettes, began with a serious tone. "I came early because I need to get something straight with you people before any of this goes forward."

Agnes was uncomfortable but said nothing.

Baer again looked hard from Agnes to Martha. "In case you haven't figured it out, I am Morrie's ex-wife. My granddaughter doesn't know anything about Morrie, and I don't want her to. Do you understand?"

Remembering Milo's warning about mentioning Morrie to anyone, Agnes decided to play dumb. "Morrie?"

Linda's eyes narrowed. "Yeah, Morrie—Morrie Wolf." She watched Agnes consult the papers in her lap as if looking for the name. "Okay who are you people?"

Martha, used to being bullied by executive chefs, was having none of it. "Our clients are Brittany Walker and Joe Nowicki. One of our employers, Milo Rathkey, agreed to host their wedding as a favor to them, and our other boss, Sutherland McKnight is on board."

Agnes, wishing she had been as assertive as Martha, said, "That's right."

Linda sat back and ran her hands through her pixie salt and pepper hair. "A favor, huh? So, what's this Milton into Morrie for?"

Agnes once again was lost. "Milton? Into? Do you mean Milo? I don't know what you mean?"

Linda became more aggressive. "Look, whatever his name is, he owes Morrie. That's obvious. Is it gambling or did Morrie lend him money?"

Agnes laughed. "Neither."

Martha chimed in, "They both have plenty of money."

Agnes wondered how she knew that with such a certainty or was that a bluff.

Linda topped off her coffee and munched on a cookie. "If Morrie's not extorting a favor, do you do weddings? Are you a venue?"

"We're not in the wedding business. This will be our first, but we are glad to help," Agnes said smiling, hoping to defuse the aggressive back-and-forth.

Martha wasn't interested in defusing anything. "As long as we are being forthright, I have a few questions myself. Who are you? You say you're the bride's grandmother. How do we know that? A grandmother hasn't been mentioned."

Linda laughed. "I like you. My daughter and Brittany will be here in a few minutes and vouch for me. If I wasn't the grandmother, I'd be making an exit right about now."

That made sense to Martha, who decided to break Milo's rule and mention Morrie Wolf by name. "Let me add, I'm not any more comfortable with Mr. Wolf's proximity than you are."

Worried she may be causing a problem, Linda backed off. "If you don't owe him, but you're doing him a favor there's no problem. Does that make everybody feel better?"

"I guess," Martha said.

Finishing her coffee, Linda sat further back in the chair and crossed her arms. "The fact he's showing his face here at all was a deal he struck with my daughter. Morrie finds a venue, he's welcome at the wedding. I was not consulted."

This wedding is coming with angry undertones, Agnes thought. *Maybe this is what families do.*

Linda continued, "I believe you two, but at some point, I have to meet this Rathman and McDougal to check them out for myself."

"Rathkey and McKnight," Agnes corrected. "I'm sure they would be glad to meet with you."

"Good. I guess I better get the names straight. Let's set that meeting up as soon as possible," Linda said, reaching for another cookie and giving Agnes her cell phone number. "Good cookies by the way."

The intercom buzzer went off again. Agnes walked over and said, "Can I help you?" but thought, *what now?*

The voice on the other end was young. "Ah, I don't know if we're at the right place. I'm Brittany Walker."

"You're in the right place," Agnes said, pushing the *Gate Open* button. She headed to the front door while Martha went to the kitchen to replenish the cookie plate and grab the menu options for the wedding.

Brittany had a young bride-to-be spring in her step which increased the bounce of her long brown hair. Like her grandmother, she too wore jeans and a t-shirt, except hers were pink and did not have a lived-in look. Agnes led her and her mother, Stephanie, into the gallery. Stephanie had recognized her mother's pickup in the driveway and was sure Linda was fear mongering, blowing this venue for her Brittany.

"Mother," Stephanie said coldly, "why are you here?" Except for the same nose, it would be difficult to discern a relationship between the two. Linda, like her personality, styled her salt and pepper hair 'wash and go' spikey. Stephanie's blond hair was smooth and controlled. She wore large hooped earrings, and a white linen blouse, the last vestiges of a hippy past.

"Grandmother!" Brittany shouted, hugging Linda who stood taking Brittany's young face in her worn hands. "You're wonderful, and you will be a beautiful bride!"

"Mother, again," Stephanie interjected, "why are you here?"

Still gazing at Brittany, she answered, "I had a few minutes before I had to drop the transmission at the shop and thought I would stop by and see the place for myself. It's beautiful!" She dropped her hands and stepped away as if to leave. "I know it will break your heart, Steph, but I can't stay. I'll leave you to it." Stephanie accompanied her mother to the front door.

"Okay, what gives here? What did you say about Morrie?" Stephanie demanded.

"Relax. I didn't say anything. I need to know who these people are, for Brittany's protection."

"Oh Mother! You make it sound like Morrie is…"

"Stephanie, he's a gangster. Go! Plan the wedding." With that, Linda left.

Martha had been talking with Brittany and got the idea that the bride wanted a cocktail and hors d'oeuvre time, followed by informal food stations and festival seating.

"We've already ordered the cake from Ilene's." Stephanie re-entered the room and the conversation. "I told her about the change in venue and she insisted on delivering it herself."

"We have a strong relationship with Ilene," Martha said, smiling.

Agnes pulled out her computer tablet and asked how many people were expected at the wedding. Brittany said a hundred and fifty were expected. They walked around the gallery and the rear terrace before going down to the lawn and garden.

"This is incredible!" Brittany exclaimed, looking around the garden.

They sat on the terrace and talked about tents, chairs, and sound systems. Brittany had hoped to have twinkle lights on one wall, but as there were no walls, she gave up the idea. Martha gave them several options about the menu and how it could be served.

Then Brittany asked a question that made it clear to Martha and Agnes that this family didn't communicate well. "This is so much more beautiful than the Bullard House, how is this venue available on such short notice?"

Agnes looked at Martha. Then both turned to Stephanie.

"This isn't a wedding venue honey, it's a private house. They are doing this as a favor."

"A favor? They don't know us?" Brittany questioned. "Do you know us?"

Once again Stephanie jumped in. "It's a favor for your grandfather. He asked these nice people to help."

"Oh," Brittany said, "the grandfather whose name we don't mention?"

"Just not around your grandmother," Stephanie added. Brittany laughed. "He's a gangster, Mother. I know he's a gangster."

No one said a word. Lakesong for a brief time was left to the crickets. Surprised, Stephanie asked, "How long have you known?"

"Since I could Google," Brittany said. "I know it's supposed to be a huge secret but come on—I'm an adult. All I know is he's doing me a favor which I appreciate."

"For god's sake don't tell your grandmother you know about Morrie!" Stephanie admonished.

"That's between you and grandma. I'm looking forward to meeting him. It's time for these old secrets to end."

5

Milo parked at the rear of the courthouse next to Saul Feinberg's office, a customized Mercedes Van. The van was more convenient and less intimidating for most of Feinberg's clients. Despite Milo's recent inheritance, he still hated to pay for parking, making Saul's situation perfect. The parking was free.

Milo noticed that Saul now had a sign marking his parking spot. *Reserved for Saul Feinberg. All others towed at owner's expense.* Rathkey wondered how much of his grandparents' pastrami fortune that cost him.

The routine was the same. Milo knocked. Sometimes Milo had to wait until Saul finished with a client, but not today. The dark-haired, thirtyish, thin lawyer with a well-trimmed beard was sitting behind his desk, checking his computer and jotting something down on a yellow legal pad.

"Pull up a seat, Milo, the bear claw is waiting for you," Saul said.

"What's with the sign?" Milo asked.

"Sign?"

"The reserved for Feinberg sign."

"Oh yeah. Our beloved district attorney tried to get me bounced out of here, so I went to the county administrator and offered to rent the space. Grandpa's deli money put to good use."

"I bet our beloved district attorney was not happy."

"He's never happy. By the way, did you qualify on the gun range, so you can continue oppressing the masses?"

"Yeah, barely. My trigger finger had a problem. A friend fixed it."

"Sounds medical. Let's move on."

Milo tossed the lime green thumb drive on Saul's desk as he grabbed the bear claw and settled himself in one of two client chairs. As Saul fiddled with the thumb drive, Milo chewed and talked at the same time. "I have Dean Ford kinda bringing his body through a little late and slicing badly."

"He swore in his deposition he couldn't use his right arm. All he could do was rest and go to physical therapy," Feinberg explained.

"You know, that injury could have accounted for the slice. Maybe I was too quick to judge."

"I gotta admire his commitment to golf." Feinberg finally plugged the drive into his computer and watched Ford tee the ball up and hit away with no concern for the injured arm. "Yes! Once again you've come to the aid of all of mankind!" Feinberg bellowed, slapping his hands together.

"Really? All of mankind? I thought your client was just a taxi driver."

"Maybe not all of mankind but the common man, in this case a taxi driver with four kids. You're right, Ford's slice is terrible. The man should invest in lessons. But first he'll have to deal with my counter suit. I want a week at Disney World for the family, and my fee."

"You never charge a fee. You do all this for free."

"I'm charging this time, and Dean Ford is going to pay it."

"Haven't you forgotten something?"

"What?" Saul asked.

"My check."

Saul sighed. "You're set on me writing this check in front of you?"

"I am. I've come to love the ripping sound of the check."

"I could give you the checkbook, and you could rip all the checks."

"It wouldn't be the same," Milo said.

Saul wrote a check to the Boys and Girls Club and eased it out.

"Ahhh, that sounds so good," Milo feigned. "I think as additional payback, you should let me win at poker this Sunday."

"Yeah, ain't gonna happen."

"Just a thought."

"Where's the game this week?" Feinberg asked.

"Gramm's."

"Good…Amy's cornbread."

"Do you have anything else for me in the next few days?

I'm kinda busy," Milo said, not wanting to mention the biking.

"No, I'm in court all this week. Next week I'm out of clients. Maybe I should take a vacation, which leaves you free unless Gramm has something."

"Maybe I have other clients," Milo countered, while finishing the bear claw.

"I thought you gave up your rowdy life as a PI. So, do you have other clients?"

"No, but I could."

Feinberg laughed. "Maybe you need a vacation. Do you even know how to vacation?"

"Vacation? Why? I live in a house that outranks any resort...with...what do you call 'em—Amenities—indoor pool, tennis court, personal chef, sail boat and yacht. Oh crap, tennis court reminds me, I gotta go." Milo inched to the edge of his chair, brushing off bear claw crumbs.

"Are you taking up tennis again?"

"I'm...auditioning to be a tennis partner."

"With whom?"

"Mary Alice Bonner."

Feinberg stared at Milo, took a long drink of his coffee, and said, "People were betting on her next tennis partner. Gotta say, nobody picked you."

"I'm a dark horse."

"Only because the country club set has never seen you play, but I have—up close and personal. I never need that humiliation again."

"Oh, come on, it was a close match."

"Yeah? One-six, two-six and I'm ten years younger, in great shape, and you're...you."

Milo ignored the jab. "Is Mary Alice good?"

Saul sat back and smiled. "Deadly."

§

After the bride and her mother left, Martha went to finalize the wedding menu, while Agnes, clipboard in hand, walked the terrace and grounds taking approximate measurements. Reaching a stone wall, she stopped and watched the waves bump up against the black boulders lining the shore. In the distance, the gray-white gulls were soaring taking turns diving for lunch.

This will be a beautiful place for a wedding. Agnes thought as she continued her walk to the shore. Turning back to the house she envisioned the ceremony, the tent, the tables, the flowers, and the flow of guests celebrating the day. Satisfied with her design, she began her walk back to the house.

Thwack! Agnes turned toward the sound. Thwack! Ponk! Someone was playing tennis. Agnes was used to that sound when she worked for James Bonner. Bonner's wife, Mary Alice, played all the time, but this was a first for Lakesong. The court was on the side of the house out of clear sight. She headed that way to see if it was Sutherland. It wasn't. It was Milo and to her surprise, Mrs. Bonner.

Agnes had played Mrs. Bonner from time to time, like a sparring partner, getting her ready for a match. Mary Alice was skilled, but she said she liked to play Agnes' younger legs, to keep her game sharp. Agnes only beat her a couple of times, but beating Mary Alice at all was significant.

Watching from the distance, she saw Milo making Mary Alice work. His ball placement was superb, forcing her to use every shot in her arsenal. It was a good match.

Agnes continued to watch as the serve moved to Milo. Mary Alice set up behind the baseline. Agnes had never seen her back so far. Milo threw the ball up and came through it with blinding speed. The ball hit the corner of the service line, chirped, and raced for the fence. Mary Alice caught up to it, not an easy feat, but popped it up because of the speed and the spin, giving Milo an easy put away.

Milo Rathkey? Tennis player? Agnes marveled, as she headed back inside to her office to contact vendors.

§

"How am I doin'?" Milo asked, as they took a break.

Mary Alice picked up her tennis towel and wiped sweat from her forehead and the back of her neck. "You've played before."

"I think I mentioned that, but I need to get rid of the rust."

"Yeah rust," She said as she took a long drink of water. "I can see you need to deal with the rust." Sitting down to towel off again, she added, "I'm glad you're on my side, and by the way, you're my new partner."

"Glad to have made the cut," Milo joked. "I've been told people were betting on your next tennis partner. None of the money was on me."

Mary Alice smiled as Milo joined her on the bench. Taking a couple of bites from her protein bar, she looked at Milo and asked, "Are you doing anything Sunday morning?"

"Nope," he said, knowing even if he was, he would cancel.

"Good," She said, pulling out her phone.

"Who are you calling?"

"I'm setting up a doubles match with Sutherland. You and I need to see how we play together."

Milo wondered if that was another double meaning, but let it go. "I don't know if he has a partner."

"Of course, he does. Agnes Larson. She's an ace," Mary Alice said, walking back to the court.

§

Agnes was texting while crossing the gallery heading to her office when she almost ran into Sutherland. "Oops! Sorry," she said.

"Maybe we need a traffic light," Sutherland kidded.

"You're not usually home this time of day. I'm not used to running into anyone besides Martha. Not literally of course," She laughed.

"I'm on ordered vacation, remember?" Sutherland's eyes lit up as he asked, "Are you doing anything Sunday morning?"

"No"

"Good! We're playing tennis, mixed doubles. I can't wait!"

Puzzled at his exuberance she asked, "Who are we playing and why are you so excited?"

"Okay, are you ready? Mary Alice has asked Milo to be her tennis partner." He hustled over to a seating area. "What can she be thinking of?" Leaning against one of the chairs, he continued his monologue. "I'd be a much better tennis partner, and my game is nowhere near Mary Alice's skill set."

"I don't know about that…I just saw…" Agnes said trying to join the conversation.

Sutherland wheeled around. "How well do you play?"

"I'm…

"Don't worry about it. Even though Mary Alice is an ace, Milo will mess up her game. I could handle this by

myself. Anything you add to my game will be gravy. I am...
well...I have to be so much better than Milo," Sutherland
said almost giddy.

In Sutherland's excitement, he didn't realize he had not
included Agnes in the conversation. It ticked her off.

"Yeah, I'll be the gravy," Agnes mumbled under her
breath, wondering if Sutherland could be any more insulting.

Sutherland noticed her cold expression and said, "I'm
sorry. I got carried away. You were saying you saw something."

"I was? I don't remember." Agnes could not wait for
Sunday morning.

"It's gonna be a hoot," Sutherland chortled.

"A hoot. Yeah, it's gonna be that all right," Agnes said, as
she headed for the kitchen leaving Sutherland still plotting
his strategy.

Agnes parked herself down on one of the kitchen stools.
"I need a drink!"

Martha looked at her with concern. "I have iced tea or
lemonade...or are we talking about something stronger."

Agnes sighed. "I still have work to do; make it lemonade."

"So, what gives?"

"Our boss, Mr. Sutherland McKnight, invited me to
play tennis on Sunday against Mary Alice Bonner and her
partner. Now, that's nice. Right?"

Martha, not knowing where this was going, said nothing.
She found herself doing that often these days.

"I like Sutherland. He's been a good friend. This could
have been fun, but do you know what he did?"

Recognizing a woman having been wronged, Martha
shook her head.

Agnes continued her rant. "Having never seen me play, he assumed I had no game. He called me gravy!"

"Gravy?"

"Yeah, gravy, but in a bad way, like I'm not necessary. Oh, but there's more. He said his brilliant play would make up for my poor play."

"Ouch," Martha said, taking a drink of lemonade. "Do you play?"

"Thank you for asking. Yes, I do, and I'm pretty damn good. I've played Mary Alice Bonner and held my own. I tried to tell him about Mr. Rathkey, but he prattled on with his fantasy of one-upmanship."

Martha was confused. "Mr. Rathkey? How does he fit in?"

Agnes smiled, took Martha's arm, and escorted her into the morning room. "Look at the tennis court. Mr. Rathkey is Mary Alice's new tennis partner."

Martha watched Milo and Mary Alice for a few minutes before responding. "I take it we are not going to tell our boss, Mr. Sutherland McKnight."

"No, we are not. He had his chance. He needs this bit of humiliation. It's good for the soul," Agnes offered.

"Love it," Martha laughed. "I saw nothing. I know nothing.

§

Since the evening was still warm, Sutherland suggested they eat out on the terrace. Milo protested he wasn't a picnic kind of guy, but Sutherland said he had a mystery that needed solving, and it began at the wall between the terrace and the lake. Milo was without work and intrigued, so dinner was served on the outdoor glass-covered wrought-iron table. Thankfully, the chairs were padded for comfort.

Milo had explored the extensive wine cellar when he first moved to Lakesong and was no longer surprised to find a bottle of wine waiting with every dinner. Tonight, it was the oak-aged chardonnay which complemented their trout with quinoa and asparagus tips.

After dinner, and a second glass of wine, Sutherland blurted, "I hear I'm playing tennis on Sunday."

"Yup."

"You want to tell me how you and Mary Alice came to be tennis partners?"

"Nope."

Sutherland tried to stifle a smirk that was bubbling up inside of him.

If Milo noticed, he didn't show it and changed the conversation. "What's the mystery you mentioned tonight?"

Sutherland handed Milo the picture they had found several months ago in Lakesong's massive basement vault. "Remember this?"

Milo glanced at the picture of four young children sitting on a wall, the same wall that was beyond the terrace. "Yes, it was in that black and gold jazzy frame. What about it?"

"On the back are the names of the kids. Second from the right is Dad, around age eight. The girl next to him is Annie."

Milo examined the picture with new interest. "Annie? Our Annie? All the cat's namesake Annie?"

"Yeah. Now look at the back…the question."

"Where is Annie?" Milo read. "A kid's printing—your dad?"

"I think so. Remember that unusual first day we met?"

"Yeah, the will reading. What was unusual about it?"

"I wore blue, and you wore band aids."

"I was bleeding! What's your point?"

"When you were downing two burgers and a side of Excedrin washed down with Diet Coke, you told me about a recent meeting between you and Dad. You said he wanted to keep in contact with you. He wasn't just being nice. I think he needed your skills. Today I had time, so I went through some of his personal papers and found this." Sutherland handed Milo a piece of paper. "It looks like a list of talking points or notes for a more concise letter."

- *Annie, age eight, disappeared from Lakesong.*
- *Lakesong was owned by the Pattersons*
- *Played with her until she disappeared.*
- *Played the spy game all summer.*
- *Different—kids made fun of her.*
- *It may be innocent, but my parents wouldn't tell me what happened to her. Maybe they didn't know.*
- *I liked her.*
- *Annie wanted to be a cat.*
- *Cats and codes to remind me.*
- *Clues—dead ends. Never solved.*
- *Milo Rathkey.*

"That explains the mystery of all the cats named Annie," Milo said.

"And the codes to the front gate and the vault. He didn't want to forget," Sutherland added. "So, that's the mystery. Down there on the wall is where it began."

"So, Annie is Annie Patterson. Does that name mean anything to you? Have you ever heard it before?" Milo asked.

"My dad bought this house from the Patterson estate. Most of that stuff in the back of the vault belonged to the Patterson's. We should look through it."

"Good start, but what about your week long sailing vacation?"

"I postponed it when I agreed to the wedding. Day sails will allow me to protect my home from gangsters," Sutherland said, pointedly.

Milo shrugged.

"I also have the newspaper people in town. After I discovered Dad's note, I added a bit of sleuthing to my week."

"Sleuthing? Really? Sleuthing?" Milo mocked. He figured the search for Annie would be more slogging than sleuthing. "The other two kids, according to the back of the picture, are Bennie Parsons and Susan Reading. We need to see if they are still alive. I can use my software to trace them. Annie Patterson, your father's friend disappeared when he was eight...what? 1952?"

"That's about right."

"After we check the vault for clues, let's hook Gramm in to see if she was ever reported missing. I got a guy who can go through the Trib archives to see if her disappearance made the paper."

Sutherland held up his wine glass. Rathkey did the same.

They drank and both looked at the empty wall, wondering what happened to the little girl who sat there so many years ago.

6

"Is there an initiation? Do I have to fly over a cliff blindfolded?" Milo asked as he lifted his new bike off the rack of the SUV. He didn't let on that the try-out tennis match with Mary Alice had left his muscles tight and sore.

"Never thought of that cliff thing. This could be a good time to start," Sutherland said, beginning his stretching exercises.

Milo waved at his toes once. His warm up was over. The Excedrin had not yet kicked in.

"Is that all the stretching you plan to do?"

"I'm not a stretching kind of guy."

"By the way you cut a mean figure in those bike shorts," Sutherland laughed.

"Water proof quick-dry shorts," Milo corrected.

Milo was concentrating on how this bike differed from a simple three speed. Several other members of the Zenith

City Cyclers arrived and were introduced to him. The only one he recognized was Larry from the bike shop. Apparently, the attractive angular looking woman with him was his wife, Danielle. Milo saw her as a study in brown: brown hair, brown eyes, brown outfit, and brown gloves. Only her red helmet broke the ode to brown.

Sutherland explained the gears to Milo along with the function of the two levers on either side of the handlebars. He also pointed out the two brake handles. "Squeeze the back brakes first, and if you have to use the front brakes, lean back on the bike. We're going to stay on the pavement today and most of it is level. When you see a hill get in the low range gears or you won't make it up."

"Don't worry," Larry said to Milo. "Almost no one dies on their first ride."

"Good to know," Milo said, wondering if all of this was worth it only to do a favor for Morrie.

"When was the last time you rode?" Danielle asked.

"I got my driver's license when I was sixteen so…sixteen minus…I have to do the math."

"You're scaring him Danielle, reminding him how rusty he is," Larry chided.

She shot him a look of disdain. "And *nobody hardly dies on their first ride* gives him confidence? You're an idiot!"

For Milo it was an awkward moment, but nobody else seemed to care. The group began to roll, following Sutherland out onto Skyline Drive. Milo's muscle soreness dissipated somewhat as he began pedaling. Sutherland was true to his word. The route was mostly flat pavement, and after playing with the gears, Milo found one or two that were his favorites.

He was pleased with his progress until Skyline drive began to narrow and hug the ridge line. Milo hadn't counted on the fact that he was now closer to the fast-moving cars on his left and the hundred foot drop off on his right.

"Oh, look there's a boat coming in! The bridge is going up!" someone shouted. Duluth's famous Aerial Lift Bridge was a great tourist attraction where the entire roadway of the bridge lifted up, letting the ships glide underneath as they entered the harbor. Of course, all of that was way off to their right and a long way down. Everyone looked except Milo who was trying to keep his front wheel from careening into cars or diving down the precipice. He had seen the bridge before.

After twenty minutes of tolerable biking and ten minutes of terror, Milo was wondering if they were ever going to turn around when Sutherland yelled back, "We're coming up to a hill Milo! Gear down."

Milo began fumbling with the gear levers but actually put the bike in a higher gear. He tried to gear back down but was not fast enough. The hill was upon him. He got about ten feet up. Pedaling became impossible, and he had to stop. "I didn't make it!" he yelled.

The others kept going, but Sutherland circled back and stopped in front of Milo. "Panicked, right?"

"I never panic; the bike panicked."

"I think it's the operator. Let's go down the hill a little so you can get into a lower gear." Sutherland once again reminded Milo about the levers and low gear. "You can only shift while moving, so you have to anticipate hills."

They started again, and this time Milo managed to get the levers right and the bike pedaled easily, but progress on Milo's part was slow. The rest of the group was waiting and applauded Milo when he arrived at the top. Milo feigned a bow and added, "Sorry for the delay. I had to save Sutherland's butt."

"He's always a problem," Larry said.

"My buddy," Sutherland joked good naturedly.

They rode for another twenty minutes, leaving Skyline drive and taking an easy trail before Milo began to recognize the parking lot ahead. *We've ridden in a circle and I never even noticed.* Milo chided himself thinking that a detective should notice these things.

The group gathered in the parking lot for post ride stretching, hydrating, and chatting. Milo allowed as to how riding in a circle was fun, and he should do it again in forty years.

"Oh no, no, no my friend," Sutherland chided. "We have Reggie and Megan next week and you need more practice. You're doing the paved areas pretty well. You can practice on Lakesong's roads, but we have to introduce you to the mountain trails. After all, they are here to do a story on the trails."

Milo groaned. He was hoping for one and done.

§

By noon, the warm eighties of the morning had become a chilly sixty-five as the wind shifted off the lake, air condi-tioning the city. After valet parking at the Nokomis Club, Agnes pulled her blue shrug around her shoulders to ward off the chilly weather and possible chillier atmosphere inside the club.

The front double door of the red-brick and white-stone building had been blocked but printed signs welcomed the

Thrana girls and directed them to the building's side doors. Agnes chose the left, entered, and looked down the Nokomis Club's long hallway with its barrel ceiling accented by carved wooden inlay. Raised oak panels covered the walls and leather seating arrangements dotted the windowed side of the hall. The Nokomis Club, like Lakesong spoke to Duluth's love of nineteenth century Jacobean Revival architecture.

Agnes slipped past groups of vaguely familiar women, smiling and nodding. She was having trouble seeing the girls she knew in the faces of the women they had become. With each group, her stomach tightened as she looked for the unwanted face, Jessica Vogel.

"Agnes! Agnes Larson! You have to sign here before you go anywhere."

Agnes startled, spun around, and saw a toothy, blue-contac- lensed, blonder-than-blond woman standing and waving at her. There was never a girl she knew with that face.

The frantic waver answered the confused question on Agnes' face with consternation. "I'm Maureen. Maureen! You know…Stobel, now Donahue." The latter was punctuated by Maureen shoving her oversized diamond rings in front of Agnes' still confused, now assaulted face. "You know my husband Cliff Donahue, city councilman, future state senator."

"Hello Maureen, I'm sorry I didn't recognize you." Agnes smiled and began to walk away.

"No, no, no! Come back! You have to sign in with me first!"

Agnes turned back to the table, eyeing the usual reunion paraphernalia, name-tags, lists, and handouts.

"I recognized you right away," Maureen said, picking up Agnes' name tag. "You haven't changed a bit. Still Larson

I see. Are you not married or are you one of those young moderns who keeps her own name?"

Had Maureen, the reunion chairwoman, set the tone? Agnes had not been verbally bitch slapped this much since she was in high school. She pinned on her name-tag, signed the arrival sheet, and picked up the schedule for the weekend. Absently, she thanked Maureen and turned away as the woman trilled on about an exciting reunion cornhole tournament to be held that afternoon.

With trepidation, Agnes scanned both sides of the hallway. She began to recognize groups of women, old high school cliques that somehow had picked up again after ten years, the former cool girls taking selfies, the tattoo piercing set comparing studs, and the out of towners. Of course, there was the new mommy group that crossed many boundaries sharing pictures of husbands, babies, and dogs. Floaters like herself moved about, saying hello but not sticking with any one crowd.

A fellow floater caught Agnes' attention. Her short cropped black hair was striking and her tangerine sleeveless blouse complemented tan defined biceps. Maybe it was the way the woman stood, but Agnes could not recall anyone in high school looking this fit. She struggled for a name.

The woman turned, looked at Agnes and smiled. Agnes squinted to read the name tag, but it was not necessary.

"Agnes it's me, Sophie. Sophie Moscatelli."

"Sophie! You look fabulous!" Agnes gushed as they hugged.

"Yeah, I know I look a lot different. Nobody here recognizes me."

"You're so tan and buff," Agnes said, flexing her own bicep in a weak comparison.

"Impressive, Agnes," Sophie said laughing. "My fitness is courtesy of the United States Army."

"Army? You're in the Army?"

"Was in the Army…flew helicopters…still do for a private company in Arizona."

Sophie was someone Agnes could call a friend at Thrana Hall.

"Agnes, you're different too…sophisticated. What are you doing these days?"

"Thanks. It's the hair. And what I'm doing? Right now, I'm a house manager for an estate owned by a couple of rich guys here in Duluth."

"Are they cute?"

Agnes blushed. "Well, one is…tall…handsome…charming…sometimes"

"What about the other one?"

"Short…shorter…a rugged face…funny, and… complicated."

"Short? So am I. This could work."

Agnes laughed. Sophie was still Sophie and fun to be around.

A tall, sandy-blond-haired woman left one of the mommy groups and joined them. "Agnes!"

"Oh, my goodness! Liz! It's so good to see you!" Agnes said, hugging Molly's sister, Liz Brooks.

"You're pregnant!" Sophie said as if she were disclosing a hidden secret.

Liz looked down. "Oh my god, you're right!" Then staring at Sophie, she blurted, "Someone as perceptive as you, I should know. Who are you?"

Sophie laughed. "I'm Sophie."

Liz looked at her nametag in disbelief. "No way!"

"Yeah it's me," Sophie assured her. "Would Maureen make a mistake and give me the wrong name tag? I just about had to show her my birth certificate to prove I was me."

"Isn't Sophie amazing?!" Agnes said, nudging Sophie's shoulder. Not wanting to leave anyone out of her lovefest she turned to Liz. "As are you Liz! Only you and your baby bump could look so cute in that snug, pink striped, knit dress."

"Oh, Agnes you are so nice," Liz said, touching her hand to her heart. "Thank you. I need to be told that these days."

"What is a gorgeous, pregnant lady doing these days besides growing babies? Where do you live?" Agnes was full of questions.

"I'm a California girl. My husband Bob, and I are on our second startup company—computer security."

"You're a geek? When did you become a geek?" Sophie questioned.

Liz laughed. "Bob's the geek. I'm the business side, MBA from Berkeley. This is my first time back since high school… you know since Molly." The mention of Molly brought the conversation to a screaming silence. Without meaning to, Liz's comment stopped the celebration of life's changes by reminding everyone of the friend and sister who would never get any older than fifteen.

As a way of apology, Liz said, "I didn't mean to bring you all down, but I came back to face Molly's death. I have never fully dealt with it."

"Losing a sister is hard," Agnes said.

Liz hugged Agnes. "You do understand. I read about Barbara. It made me so sad."

Agnes did understand. It was a club to which neither wanted to belong but did, anyway. "Thank you. I miss her. I know you and Barbara were close. I should have reached out, but that time is such a fog. She was murdered."

"Murdered…too," Liz mouthed in barely a whisper.

Agnes repeated, "Murdered too."

"When Molly died, I ran away." The happy California girl's face hardened. "I'm back to even up the score." She scanned the Nokomis Club's now loud and crowded reception area, "I wonder if Molly's murderer will have the guts to show up?"

Agnes looked pained at the thought. "I don't want her to be here."

Sophie's fists clenched. "Oh, I want her here. All the way through Army training, the face of the enemy was always Jessica Raymond!"

Their anger startled Agnes who had always felt powerless in the face of Molly's death and still did.

Liz glared beyond Agnes to the door. "Agnes, I read that the man who murdered your sister is dead. The woman who murdered mine is walking in the door."

Agnes' stomach clenched. She whirled around. There she was—fashionable, nose in the air, taking in the crowd much like one looks at lesser animals in the zoo.

Liz marched past Agnes shouting at Jessica. "Get out of here! Nobody wants you here!"

Jessica, hiding any hint of surprise at Liz's aggressive verbal attack, hissed, "Watch who you threaten little mama." Jessica pushed past her bumping Liz to the side, only to be hip checked and thrown off balance by a quickly arriving Sophie. Jessica stumbled but caught herself against a nearby wall.

Sophie was in her face. "She said no one wants you here, bitch!"

Many in the crowd turned at the raised voices.

"Who the hell are you?" Jessica shouted.

Sophie leaned in and menacingly whispered in her ear, "Molly's friend."

"Muskrat? Dreary mope! Get out of my way!" Jessica tried to push past but was no match for Sophie's strength and could not break free. Sophie's fingers tightened on her upper arm. It hurt.

Sophie leaned in and whispered, "How does it feel to be trapped and threatened? Scared?"

Jessica pulled her shoulder back expecting Sophie to let go. She didn't.

"Ladies! I see you're already getting reacquainted," Maureen Donahue chirped, coming between them touching Sophie's hand. Sophie let go abruptly, and Maureen led Jessica away.

Liz walked up to Sophie. "Thank you, but I don't want you to get into trouble for me."

Sophie turned. "It's not for you. It's for Molly."

Maureen was torn as she hustled Jessica over to the sign-in table and gathered her nametag and reunion schedule together.

Jessica watched Maureen flutter. "I suppose you think you saved me."

Maureen's toothy smile was beginning to hurt her face, but she had to give the impression everything was under control. "Somebody had to save you. You were getting your ass kicked."

"This doesn't get you off the hook. I still hold the cards and want my money."

Feeling a rush of false bravado, Maureen cautioned, "Don't underestimate me Jessica."

Jessica laughed. "Don't threaten me Momo. You're not like Amazon woman over there. It will end up costing you more, and we wouldn't want your slick willy husband to get clued in…would we?"

Maureen blanched at the thought of Cliff finding out anything.

Looking at the highlighted event on the reunion schedule, Jessica asked, "What's this 'Flowers for Molly BS this afternoon?"

"Just what it says," Maureen answered through her over-anxious smile. "We're going to lay flowers at Enger Tower in Molly's memory. If I were you, I'd stay away."

"Threatening me again, Maureen?" Jessica smirked. "Oh, I almost forgot, wish your husband well on his run for the state senate. You must be such an asset to him."

Maureen backed away from Jessica and raced to the safety of the back terrace where two bars were set up. Ordering a gin and tonic, she asked that the glass be filled to the top and easy on the tonic. With her back to the crowd she drained it to a polite level, a trick she had mastered.

Maureen had made one mistake in high school. She never told Cliff about it and couldn't afford to have him or anyone else find out now.

§

"Shall we take the stairs to the basement or the nonexistent elevator?" Milo teased.

Sutherland rolled his eyes. "Old joke! Let it go. Besides, I was told by one of my employees that the discovery of an unused elevator is not all that unusual in old mansions."

Milo opened the door to the basement stairs. "Oh look, stairs. Did you know those were here?"

"They're healthier," Sutherland persisted, sprinting down the stairs.

Milo muttered about how all this healthiness was killing him and followed Sutherland down the stairs, minus the sprint, past the furnaces to the vault.

"What are we looking for?" Sutherland asked as he opened the wide metal vault door.

"We should at least know Mr. Patterson's full name before we start asking questions and searching documents," Milo said. "Pictures would be helpful too."

Milo was introduced to the vault a few weeks after moving into Lakesong. As a child living here, he never knew it existed. An unusual walk-in room, it was far too massive and artistic for ordinary basement storage. Whatever the vault was meant to be was lost to history. The two began walking past drawers and shelves with intricate Scandinavian carvings of dragons, snakes, and men with swords. The hunt through the unexplored world of the Patterson's began with the careful removal of several tarps at the back of the room covering baby furniture, sealed boxes, and old steamer trunks.

They began opening the boxes and going through the contents. "It looks as if drawers were dumped into boxes," Milo said.

"Yeah, no organization. It's random," Sutherland added. "Old socks, paperclips, safety pins, bills…no rhyme or reason. Maybe it was done in a hurry." Sutherland pulled out a large leather tube with a strap. "This might be something?"

"I have an idea, why don't you open it up and see," Rathkey mocked.

Sutherland gave him a disapproving look but followed his instruction.

"Well?"

Sutherland loosened the tie. "It's blue prints! I bet for this house. I don't want to unroll them here. I'll take them upstairs."

"I found an ink pen," Milo said. "A real ink pen, not a ballpoint."

"Pictures!" Sutherland held up a drug store envelope with black and white photos and negatives. Milo came over and they looked together.

Most were of a family, could be the Patterson's, but there was no writing on the back. "Well, we have a young woman, a baby, a tall man, a dog, and a gruff looking woman." Milo pointed at her, asking who she was.

"An aunt? I have no clue," Sutherland said, quickly looking through the rest of the pictures. They were all variations of the same people taken on the back lawn of Lakesong by the now infamous wall. The only picture that had a notation was of the gruff looking woman by herself. Milo read, "Nanny Li…I can't read the rest of the name. It's been smudged."

"She's the nanny? Doesn't look friendly," Sutherland added.

"That dog's a water spaniel," Milo said.

"How do you know that?"

"When I was a kid, our neighbors had one."

They continued digging through the boxes and found a bill that gave Mr. Patterson's name as Henry James Patterson. At the bottom of one box, filled with bills and canceled checks, Milo found another clue. He showed it to Sutherland. "This is interesting."

Sutherland took it and read the note out loud.

Sir,

I have finished an exhaustive search for your family. I can find no trace of your wife Adeline, and child. They do not appear to be with family or friends. As you pointed out, your wife has not used her Diners Club Card, nor has she removed any funds from your joint checking account.

I understand your impatience at the lack of progress, especially because the police are pressuring you for answers. I am sorry that I was not able to help, and I feel that at this time a further investigation would not be worth my time or your money. Therefore, this will be the last communication from me. I enclose my bill for services rendered to this point.

Malcom Modine
Modine Detective Agency

"Pressure from the police? What is that about?" Sutherland wondered. "Was Mr. Patterson suspected of doing away with his wife and child? How grim! Is this what my dad suspected?"

Milo's brow furrowed. "Don't get ahead of yourself. All we know is the wife was missing, and she didn't use money or credit cards."

"She could have had her own money. My mother did."

"The letter doesn't mention that, but we don't know if this detective was any good or how long he looked."

"What's a Diners Club Card?" Sutherland asked.

"I think it was a credit card for rich people. I remember it from an old movie." Getting a surprised side eye from Sutherland, Milo explained, "My ex liked old movies."

"At least we have Mr. Patterson's full name, Henry James. So, what's next?"

"I have already started a computer search for Bennie Parsons and Susan Reading. I'll have my guy go to the library to check old newspapers on microfilm, and I'll ask Graham if police records go back that far."

"Do you think they do?"

"No, but we have to check."

§

Duluth was built on steep hills that descend into the tip of Lake Superior. On top of one of the hills rested Enger Tower, a five-story observation tourist attraction that had been the subject of ghost stories for decades. Each generation of Duluth children believed the cold, blue stone tower was a disguised grave stone where uneasy spirits walked the night.

In reality, the only death ever recorded at the tower was that of Molly Edwards who fell or was pushed down the stairs.

A small group of women, Molly's closest classmates, huddled inside the first floor of the tower, taking refuge from the lake wind. They watched as Liz placed flowers where Molly's body had been found. Clutching Molly's old teddy bear, through tears Liz whispered, "I'm so sorry."

Each friend placed a remembrance at the foot of the stairs. Inside the tower no one heard Jessica's Audi screech to a stop in the parking lot. Nor did they notice her edge behind the gathering. Shattering the respectful hush, she marched to the front and heaved twelve, black, long-stemmed roses onto the delicate bouquets, pictures, and hand-written notes, screaming, "Let her die! She was drunk. She slipped. She fell. End of story."

Maureen gasped. Agnes felt her breathing stop. Sophie's jaw clenched. There was silence.

"You're dead!" Sophie spat, charging and knocking Jessica backwards out onto the stone steps.

Stumbling, Jessica grabbed the handrail for balance as she inched down each of the fifteen steps with Sophie in slow motion pursuit. Reaching the bottom, she made her stand. Not for long. Sophie charged again knocking Jessica backwards. Both began to roll, as they struggled, stopped only by a boulder, mere inches from a steep thorn covered hill. Sophie held Jessica down, her hands around the woman's throat, squeezing hard, as if she meant to kill her. Jessica's eyes bulged. Her face distorted. She fought for air as Agnes and several other women came to her rescue.

"Stop it!" Maureen yelled. "You're ruining it!"

Liz stood watching in dumb silence not knowing what to expect.

Agnes ran down the stairs and pulled at Sophie's hands. "Don't do it, Sophie! No! Don't do it!"

Sophie's hands sprang open as she jumped off Jessica who rolled over coughing and choking. Sophie screamed, "I want you gone! It's your choice how you leave."

Jessica's face was red, and she was still gasping and coughing. Her damaged throat could only muster a whisper. "You tried to kill me! All you people are witnesses."

Sophie made a move toward Jessica who stumbled down the hill toward her car and safety. She peeled out, spinning and squealing her tires.

"You were choking her! She couldn't breathe!" Maureen gasped.

"I was under control. I know how far to take it."

Agnes sat on the hard stone step doubting it.

7

Mary Alice Bonner was going over several contracts in her sitting room when the house phone rang. The caller ID, *St. Louis County Jail,* filled her with dread. Her first thought was her son Richard had gotten into more trouble.

"Hello," she said, with an unsteady voice.

An automated voice told her this was a collect call from the St. Louis County Jail. Press one to accept. Press two to decline.

She held her breath and pressed one. "Hello."

"I'm looking for Richard," A man on the other end declared.

Mary Alice exhaled. She recognized the voice; it was so similar to her late husband's. "David?" she asked. "David Bonner?"

"Yeah. I want to talk to Richard," he said in a demanding tone.

"This is Mary Alice."

"I figured."

"Why do you want to talk to Richard?"

"I need to ask him something."

"David, I thought I was clear. I don't want to talk to you, and I don't want you talking to my son. If you call here again, I'll take out a restraining order."

"Calm the hell down! I just wanna ask him a question, but I can ask you."

Mary Alice said nothing.

"I have a friend who's getting out soon. He's looking to buy a condo."

Bonner's lie was so blatant, Mary Alice thought she should be insulted.

Bonner continued to prattle on. "He's been talking to a real estate woman but forgot her name. She's in her thirties, pretty, used to work in Atlanta. Do you know her?"

"David, I don't believe you. You don't lie nearly as well as your brother, and if I did know this woman, I would warn her."

Bonner let loose with several obscene comments.

Mary Alice was unfazed as she waited for silence. "David if you're finished, I have a question. Are you getting the monthly checks from the trust James left for you?"

"Yeah. What's that got to do with anything?"

"If you want those checks to continue, don't ever contact us again," She said, in a firm steady voice.

Bonner let loose with more obscenities as Mary Alice hung up. One Bonner was enough for a lifetime.

§

Safe in her hotel room, Jessica tried to stop shaking. She had always been the bully. The status quo had changed dramatically.

Moscatelli tried to kill me!

Jessica felt her neck, It was painful, and she was having trouble swallowing. She went into the bathroom and was shocked to see the red outline of Sophie's fingers on her skin. She shook out two prescription Motrin, carefully letting one at a time slide down her sore throat. Feeling light headed, she crept back to the bed, lay down, and closed her eyes.

Get it together Jessica. Don't let them win. No cops. It was assault but no cops. Get the money that's all. No cops, no crazies, just cash.

Her go-to day dream of azure water lapping against a yacht anchored among the Balearic Islands off the coast of Spain lulled her to sleep.

Waking several hours later, she showered and prepared for the formal reunion dinner. Her eyes were no longer blood-shot, and swallowing was easier, but the red, puffy marks on her neck remained. She used foundation and a Hermes silk scarf to mask the traces.

The light-headedness was gone. She clicked on Fitz and the Tantrums' "Handclap" as she shimmied into her drop-dead red dress.

As the music ended Jessica smoothed her dress, looked in the mirror, and mouthed, "I can do a lot more than hand clap. I can have a rewarding evening, with my favorite professor Paul Kendrick who has so much to lose." Jessica said to herself as she prepared to leave her room. "Focus. Remember what you're here for. Avoid the crazies. They will pay. Just not tonight."

§

Maureen, always more than punctual, arrived fifteen minutes early at the Hotel Duluth. She agreed to pick up her cousin and take her to the reunion banquet but now was regretting that decision.

She called from the lobby. Her cousin said she was running a little late and would be down in about twenty minutes. *I have so much to do. I don't have time for this.* Maureen went to the bar for a gin and tonic and sat down in one of the lobby's high-back chairs that face the wall.

Liz Brooks was also heading to the banquet. She walked through the lobby almost to the front door when her phone buzzed, her husband Bob returning her call.

Sitting down on the other side of ferns that separated her from Maureen, she answered. "Hi honey," Liz said with a sigh.

"What's wrong?" Bob asked.

"She's here. That bitch is here…now!"

"Do you want me there?"

"No. I know you're trying to be helpful, but I can do this. What I want you to do is go ahead with the plan."

"Are you sure?"

"Absolutely sure! I want her to feel pain…the pain I've felt every day since Molly!"

"I will make the phone call."

"Thank you."

"Love you, honey."

Liz ended the call, got up and walked through the door.

Maureen stood up in time to see Liz leave the hotel. *That had to be about Jessica! Feel pain? What's she gonna do?*

§

The evening event, cocktails and dinner, was being held at the former Moreland Estate, now owned by the University of Minnesota-Duluth. Located on London Drive, a mile north of Lakesong, it offered the same beautiful views of Lake Superior and featured an extensive flower garden and terrace, complete with a pedestal fountain in a large tiled basin. Tonight's dinner was set up in the basement ballroom which led out to a screened porch and the terrace. Two bartenders were at the ready on the porch.

Maureen had set up three heaters on the porch in case the wind continued to blow in from the lake. At five it shifted again and sixty-five degrees became eighty two. The heaters were never turned on.

Jessica ordered a Moscow Mule. Walking out onto the terrace, she bemoaned no flirting with husbands. They hadn't been invited. If not for the expected arrival of Paul Kendrick, her drop-dead red dress would be wasted.

He had gotten her email to come early. She was not going to endure this event any longer than necessary, especially with that psycho Moscatelli on the loose.

Jessica saw Kendrick open the large wooden door and scan the room. He still had his boyish good looks and tousled hair. His chocolate brown eyes sparkled like they had years ago. Too bad, all she wanted these days was his money. She noticed Maureen fluttering around him, and Jessica smiled. Maureen still had a prurient interest in Kendrick.

After extricating himself from Maureen's school-girl gushing, Kendrick spotted Jessica leaning seductively against a nearby oak railing. She was hard to miss.

"Hello Paul," she said smoothly as she sauntered up to him.

"Jessica." He greeted her with the familiar Kendrick charisma.

"Paul, you're late with your payments. We have to fix that."

"Not here," he said in hushed tones as if he were inviting her back to his place.

"Yes! Here! Now! Or you will be trashed to your precious tenure committee," Jessica cooed.

Kendrick manipulated women all of his life but being manipulated now by Jessica made him furious. "Down by the boat house."

"Lovely. After you." She gestured to Paul to lead the way. "I need another drink."

Agnes was enjoying her first dirty martini as she watched the pedestal fountain splashing water in the catch basin. This place was almost as nice as Lakesong but less intimate. It was built around the same time, with a long gallery, fancy gables, and carved woodwork everywhere.

Sophie had not yet arrived. Liz headed to the ballroom to save seats and say hello to the girls in her class. Since it was early, Agnes decided to wander down by the lake to enjoy the rest of her cocktail. She found a chair almost hidden in a clump of trees. To her surprise, a former teacher, Mr. Kendrick, was standing on the boat dock. He was one of her favorite teachers from high school. She remembered how his good looks fascinated all the girls, and she giggled a little at the thought. Agnes was about to get up and say hello when she saw a woman in a red dress march down and join him. It was Jessica!

I don't believe it! Agnes thought.

She shrunk back against the Adirondack chair hoping to disappear. At first, she thought it might be a tryst. In silent shadowed silhouette, Kendrick was holding Jessica by the shoulders looking down into her eyes. Their bodies were close but not tryst close. It was confusing. With a jerk and a shout, the situation changed.

"Let it go, Jessica! Forget it!" Kendrick yelled.

"I was sixteen. You were my teacher. It's called statutory rape, and I will testify it was only fun for you." Jessica laughed. "What you don't know is I have copies of the pictures you loved to take of all your little girls."

Kendrick backed away.

Jessica stepped toward him holding out her phone. "Remember this picture? It's me. I'm not in my school uniform, and we're not in study hall. Notice yourself in the mirror? Clear evidence."

Kendrick leaned in to see Jessica's phone and the picture. "Where did you get this?"

"From your computer…way back then. It's called me using a thumb drive while you were sleeping."

She had him. He was visible in the picture. It could ruin him. His right arm batted at the phone trying to destroy it.

"Oh no you don't," Jessica warned, stepping back and twisting before stuffing the phone down the front of her dress. "You are so pretty but so stupid? Destroy the phone? Dumb! I have copies in the cloud."

Kendrick took a menacing step toward her.

She squared her shoulders. "Back off."

He clenched and unclenched his fists but didn't move.

"Much better, Paul. You should have stayed with the original deal. The payments are now double. You get tenure. I get money. It's a win-win, charm boy."

They lowered their voices as the negotiation began. Agnes could not hear specifics, except a mention of Enger Tower tomorrow morning. She sat motionless until they both left. The overheard conversation made Agnes' stomach hurt. She always admired Mr. Kendrick but not now. It was quiet and dark. She took a large gulp of her drink. It went down hard. What should she do? What could she do? When she thought it was safe, she stood and slipped back to the Moreland House.

Jessica watched Kendrick return to the reunion. She headed for her car. She didn't need another episode with the lunatics, and besides, she had to get up early tomorrow. It was collection day.

§

Sophie and Liz saved Agnes a seat between them. "Where were you?" Sophie asked as the salads arrived.

"I…I…took a walk down by the lake. It was…eye opening."

"Is it anything fun?" Liz asked. "I could use some fun."

"I downed my drink in record time," Agnes said, feeling the effects of her vodka and vermouth. "I even went and got another one."

"I'm big on tomato juice," Liz said, patting her baby bump. "What's your record?"

"Record? I don't know. I never timed myself."

Sophie chimed in. "I can help with that. I'm an excellent timer."

Agnes laughed. "Have you ever timed the downing of martinis?"

"I've never timed anything in my life, but I know I'd be great at it."

They all laughed at the ridiculousness of their banter, and it set the tone for the night. It was carefree and wonderful.

After dinner, the three were alone at their table still laughing over coffee when Liz said, "Glad Jessica didn't show."

The bubble of the evening was broken. The laughter stopped.

Agnes whispered, "She was here. Earlier. Down by the lake."

"Did you have a run in?" Liz asked.

"No, she didn't see me, but I heard…" She stopped and looked to see if Kendrick was anywhere close. He wasn't.

"Heard what?" Sophie asked, moving in closer.

"Jessica is blackmailing Paul Kendrick. He's not what I thought he was. In high school, he and she…you know."

Liz grabbed Agnes' arm. "You're kidding!"

Agnes shook her head. "No. I wish I was. She has pictures he took of…"

"We get it," Sophie said.

"I thought he was one of the good guys. How disappointing," Liz offered.

Agnes nodded. "Jessica said there were other girls, and she has those pictures too."

The shattering of a coffee cup caused all three to start and look behind them. Maureen was ashen. For a moment no one said a word. "You have to go," she said in a monotone. "The wait staff needs to clean. We all have to leave now." Shaking, she bent down to pick up the broken cup. Agnes moved to help her, but Maureen stood up and walked away, leaving Agnes to pick up the pieces.

"That was odd," Sophie said. "So not Maureenie."

"Did she hear what I was saying?" Agnes asked.

Liz shrugged. "She was close enough."

"Why would she care about Jessica and Paul Kendrick?" Sophie asked. "She seemed upset."

Liz looked at Agnes. "You were talking about Jessica having pictures of Kendrick and other girls."

"Maureen?" Agnes asked.

8

Agnes had not been plagued with her recurring nightmare for weeks. She's rooted on a sidewalk. A car driven by her dead boss, James Bonner, races toward a woman standing in the road. Agnes struggles to warn the woman but can't. Blood pours from the car, down the street, threatening to engulf her. She wakes up in a sweat.

With effort, Agnes leaned over to check the time on her phone. It was still early. Dropping back down on the pillow, she closed her eyes and tried to shut her mind to the nightmare and the revelations of last night's banquet.

It wasn't working. She was awake but needed a large, strong cup of coffee to function. On her way to the kitchen, she phoned Sophie but got no answer. As her Keurig began to bubble and spit, she tried Liz with the same result.

Where is everybody? Was there a reunion breakfast I don't know about? Am I supposed to be someplace?

She sipped the hot coffee and checked her purse for the reunion schedule. There was nothing until a tour of the harbor on the Queen of the Lakes this afternoon. Relieved, Agnes stretched out on the couch, leaned her head back on the throw pillows, and closed her eyes. *Where was everybody?*

§

Sutherland wanted Milo to get in at least one more practice ride before the official picture with the newspaper people. Milo prayed for torrential rain but only got wind, gray skies, and a slight drizzle.

"Just kill me now," Milo said to Sutherland as he took his bike off the back of the SUV.

Sutherland sighed. "The mist has stopped. What's your problem?"

"I'm still stiff from the last ride. That's why I'm telling you to just kill me now. Why drag out this torture?"

"Take two of your magic Excedrin and you'll be fine. Besides, I'm trying to get you loosened up for tomorrow's tennis match," Sutherland lied.

"This is as loose as I get!"

"What a grouch," Sutherland said, removing his new bike from the rack.

Milo yawned.

Sutherland brought his bike over expecting Milo's attention. "In case you didn't notice, this is a new bike."

"The garage is full of bikes. Why would you buy another?"

"This is special. It's the G-trek Cyclocross!" Sutherland waited for Milo to be impressed.

Milo looked at the sleek, black machine. "Looks like a bike."

"It's a Steven Griffith design."

"Wow! Steven Griffith!" Milo mocked.

Sutherland, not picking up on the sarcasm added, "Do you know him? I'm impressed."

"Yeah, Steve owns a barber shop down on Lake Avenue… does a good job on my curly sideburns. He gets 'em straight."

"Heathen."

Larry Ashbach overheard the conversation and came over. "Where did you get that?" he asked, pointing at Sutherland's new bike.

"Bought it from G-trek. I would have bought it from you, but they don't sell retail…only take orders on line."

Larry crouched down to inspect it. "It's not Griffith's design. It's new. You know Griffith died years ago, ironically, in the water, not on the trail."

"Yeah, I know he's dead, but one of my virtual biking buddies said it was Griffith's design and well worth the money." Sutherland defended his purchase.

"This is crap!" Larry blew up. "No wonder you had to buy it on line. I wouldn't sell crap like this! Look, they've got you so far forward, you can't sustain the position. You'll fall back in the seat and cause drag. Griffith's partners were always idiots." He got up and walked away.

"Did he hurt your bike's feelings?" Milo asked once Larry was out of range.

"Naw, it's business. He'll get over it. He's upset because I didn't buy it from him," Sutherland explained.

Most of the group had arrived and were stretching, adjusting their bikes, and chatting.

Sutherland helped Milo set his gear for climbing and explained this morning was going to be off-road, trail riding. "Expect dirt and a few tree roots."

"What? I thought it was an asphalt trail with trees to stop the drizzle."

"The drizzle has already stopped and there are trees. Don't run into them."

While negotiating his first dip, Milo almost fell. "This is not flat! What happened to flat?" he yelled. Nobody answered back.

Larry, who was in the lead, stopped to take a phone call giving Milo a needed break. "Stay there, I'll be right home!" Larry said, looking at Sutherland.

"What's happening?" Sutherland asked.

"I gotta bail. Danielle says she found a dead woman, and she thinks she saw the person who killed her! She's really shook."

Sutherland called out to Milo. "Larry needs your help."

Milo laid his bike up against a tree and worked his way to the head of the line. "Please tell me this is over."

Sutherland urged Larry to tell Milo about the phone call.

"I need to get home to Danielle," he protested.

"Why?" Milo asked, ignoring his plea.

"She was at Enger Tower...found a dead woman...now she's home. That's all I know. I gotta go!" He jumped on his bike and headed back down the trail.

Explaining Larry's quick departure to the others, Sutherland said, "Go on without us, Larry has a family emergency." Turning back to Milo, he added, "We should to go up to the tower; it's a short way up the hill. We can bike there."

"Why?" Milo asked.

"What do you mean? Someone's dead. We should do something!"

"Why is it our business? Not to be too callous about it, people die all the time," Milo said.

"Danielle saw who murdered the woman."

"You didn't mention murder," Milo said. "I'll call Gramm and see what this is all about."

Sutherland began pacing. "Okay, that makes sense. If Ernie doesn't know about it, we'll alert him to it. He'd appreciate that."

Milo stared at Sutherland in disbelief. "It's Saturday morning; I bet he's with his grandkids. Do you think he wants this phone call?"

"I would."

"Yeah, I believe you would." Milo sighed as he hit Gramm's number on speed dial.

Sutherland stopped pacing to hover over the phone call.

"Yeah?" A gruff voice answered in a *this had better be good* attitude.

"It's Milo. There's a body up at Enger Tower, possible murder."

"Yeah, I know. How do you know?"

"A friend of Sutherland found it."

"Are you there now?" Gramm asked.

"No, none of my business."

"It is now. Get up there." The phone went dead.

Turning to an anxious Sutherland, Milo said, "Up to Enger Tower we go."

"We could ride the bikes up there."

"Not a chance."

§

Two squad cars blocked the entrance to the Enger Tower parking lot forcing Gramm and Sgt. Robin White to wait until one of the cars could be moved. The lot was sprinkled with cop cars, a few civilian cars, a forensics van, and one RV.

As she got out of her Kia, White gathered her long dark hair up in a ponytail. It was time to go to work. "It's Saturday. Saturdays are sacred to my people," she called to Gramm who was exiting his old Buick.

"Saturdays are sacred? What? You're not Jewish, you're Ojibway," Gramm objected.

"I could be both," Robin kidded.

"We're partners. I work; you work."

"Why didn't O'Dell catch this?" White asked, referring to Detective Doug O'Dell, Duluth's other homicide detective.

"He's off this weekend. He's moving into his new place at The Harbors," Gramm said. "I hear he has a great view."

"Good for him," White said sarcastically. "So, do we." She gestured to the panoramic view of Duluth and Lake Superior from their vantage point on the top of Enger Hill.

Gramm shrugged, put on gloves, and walked to the base of the cold, hard steps that led to the tower entrance. Medical Examiner, Dr. Cyril Smith was already crouching over the body which was lying face up about three-quarters of the way down the steps.

Smith acknowledged their arrival by unclicking his magnetic glasses. "Looks like she took a tumble down the stairs and broke her neck. I would say *accidental* except for the bruises around her neck, and the way she fell. From where she hit her head and where she landed, I would say she was pushed backwards."

"It doesn't sound accidental, but an accident would give us our Saturday back," White said with a sigh as she walked over to the parking lot where officers were standing by the RV and a green Jetta. Managing the witnesses was paramount. She didn't want them repeating their accounts too many times.

Gramm focused on the dead woman lying at the bottom of the stone stairs. Her eyes were open as if she had been surprised moments before death. Her head lay at an unnatural angle and there was blood seeping out of one ear. "Do we have a name?" he asked Smith.

"I found a driver's license in her pocket," Smith said, grabbing an evidence bag and reading off the license. "It's a Jessica Vogel, V-o-g-e-l. She's from Minneapolis."

"She came a long way just to die at Enger Tower."

Smith stood up. "That she did. Results sometime this afternoon."

Gramm was on his way to join White as Milo and Sutherland pulled up. On another day, Gramm would have a few comments on Milo's bicycle shorts, but it was Saturday, and Gramm was in a sour mood.

"How many cars do you own?" Gramm asked, eying the SUV.

"This one is for the bikes and camping," Sutherland said, innocently.

"Of course. I have one just to go to the Piggly Wiggly," Gramm grumbled. "So, tell me your tale before I hear their tale," he said nodding at the witnesses.

"Who's dead?" Milo asked.

"Some woman from Minneapolis. Who told you?"

Sutherland jumped in, over-explaining Larry's phone call from his wife.

Gramm raised his white bushy eyebrows and staring at the people in the parking lot, asked, "Which one is she?"

Sutherland not wanting to make a mistake, double checked to make sure that Danielle was not there. "She left. She's home. Larry said she was in shock. You know we civilians are not used to finding dead bodies all over the place."

Gramm sighed. "Give me an address; we'll have to go to her."

Sutherland checked his phone, gave Gramm the information, and headed back into the SUV.

Gramm walked away, called the number, and had a short conversation. Milo could tell he was talking to Larry, not Danielle.

Sgt. White had asked the RV couple to wait by their vehicle while she interviewed two people in a dark green Jetta. She introduced herself and asked the couple their names.

"I'm Reggie Cuff," the driver said, "and this is Megan Davis."

Megan leaned over to the driver's side window. "We're doing a newspaper story on the extreme sports in Duluth."

Milo and Gramm joined Robin who whispered to Milo, "Nice shorts."

"I lost a bet," Milo muttered, defending his choice of Saturday morning apparel.

"Milo!" Megan shouted as she emerged from the car. "What are you doing here?"

"I could ask you the same thing," Milo said.

Gramm was confused. "Is this the woman who called your friend?"

"No, that's Danielle. This is Megan."

Gramm shook his head in disbelief. "Do all of your friends attend murders?"

Milo didn't know how to answer that.

Megan explained how she knew Milo and Sutherland. "Reggie was using our drone by that Peace Bell back near the Japanese Gardens when we heard a woman scream."

"I don't understand," Gramm said.

Reggie explained further. "I use it to get an aerial view, so I can figure out the best place to get scenics. I can see it on my phone. As soon as I heard that woman scream, I brought the drone down and rushed over."

"Then what?" Gramm continued, still not completely understanding.

"She was head first on the stairs...not moving."

"Did you hear anything?"

"The scream," Megan said. "Reggie called 911. We packed up our gear and waited in the parking lot by the car."

"I was an EMT at one time," Reggie added. "I felt for a pulse but couldn't find one."

White broke in. "Did you touch anything?"

"Only her wrist."

"We'll need your prints," Gramm said. "Did you see anyone else?"

Megan nodded. "There was a woman on a bike talking to the people over there in the RV. She took off up the hill before you police arrived."

"Don't forget the jogger," Reggie said. "She ran past me by the Peace Bell."

"Can you describe the jogger, Mr. Cuff?" White asked.

"She had dark curly hair...ran fast. That's about all I remember."

Gramm had a few more perfunctory questions and then White took down the pair's contact information. The RV was next on their agenda.

A bearded man wearing a John Deere seed cap and a wide smile greeted them. "I'm Randy Sherman," he announced shaking hands with everyone. "My wife Erica. We're the Shermans from Ames, Iowa. We're on vacation. I sell these RVs." He handed each of them a card. "I can get you a good deal. Better than you can get here."

Erica nodded to the group and berated her husband. "Stop selling! These people don't want to buy an RV! There's a poor girl over there who's been hurt!" She took off her white visor and tousled her short blond hair with her fingers.

"Erica, you know I always say, ABC, always be closing."

Gramm introduced White and Rathkey and then asked the Sherman's if they had seen anything or anyone.

Randy was excited. "There was this gal on a bike..."

"She said her name was Dana, Danny...something like that," Erica interjected.

Randy added, "I think it was French."

Gramm ended the name game with another question. "What did she say?"

"She said she heard yelling in that tower over there and then a girl screamed. Like I said, this Dana gal was on a bike…"

"And she said a car came at her in the parking lot… tried to run her over," Erica finished Randy's thought once again. "We did see a sports car speeding up the hill when we first pulled in."

"It could have been the culprit," Randy guessed. "I think she was worried that hooligan was coming back. She took off on her bike right away. To tell you the truth, we were gonna take off too, but you guys blocked us in. I didn't really mind though. With all the police here, I knew we were safe."

"So, you're from Ames? What brings you to Northern Minnesota?" White asked.

"Well, we're primarily bird watchers," Larry said, reaching into the RV and pulling out a camera with a massive, white telephoto lens.

Erica added, "And we want to see all this pretty stuff, the tower, the view of the lake and city, some kind of garden in the back. People at the RV park told us all about it. Iowa's flat. Not many views like this one."

Gramm thanked the tourists and headed over to Sutherland's SUV. Sutherland rolled down the window. "I didn't do it."

"It's what you always say," White kidded. "That excuse is becoming a habit."

Gramm continued unfazed. "Okay, Sutherland, tell me your tale."

Sutherland got out of the car. "I don't know if there's much more to tell."

"Your friend said the woman was dead, and she saw the guy who murdered her? Go over that again."

"That's what Larry told me Danielle told him. Right Milo?"

White wrote the name in her notes. "Danielle could be the French name the RV couple was trying to remember."

Milo was looking around the parking lot. "What? Oh yeah, right."

Gramm stared at Milo. "I've seen this drifting act before. What's going on?"

Milo turned to the group. "Nothin'…I'm counting cars."

"Auditioning for parking attendant?" Gramm asked.

Pointing at the cars, Milo said, "Look, we have the RV people, the newspaper people, our SUV, and the four cop cars—that's seven. Robin's car and your car Ernie make nine. The forensic van is ten. Doc Smith is walking to his car. There are two left: that nice red SUV and the expensive but understated blue Lexus. If one belongs to the dead woman who owns…"

"Damn it!" Gramm shouted. "Hughes come over here!"

Officer Hughes, knowing the volume meant trouble, walked briskly to Gramm. "What's up Lieutenant?"

"Have we searched the grounds?"

"Not yet, sir."

"How many uniforms do you have here?"

"Four counting myself."

"Do a quick search now, include the tower!"

"What are we looking for?"

"The owner of one of these two cars. Wait a minute, Robin you move faster than I do. Go catch the doc before he leaves and ask him if he found the victim's car keys."

White jogged over to Doc Smith and held a brief conversation.

Gramm sighed. "Young legs."

White returned as quickly as she left. "The doc says the red SUV, the Audi, belongs to the victim."

"Let's run the Lexus plates, and Hughes get your people going."

They walked over to the Lexus and Robin called in the license plate. It wasn't necessary. Officer Butler, who had drawn the tower search, was escorting a person wearing a faded hoodie, jeans, and a blue, ball cap.

As they approached, Milo muttered, "Not very Lexus like."

"Lieutenant, I found her sitting on the second-floor stairs."

"I'm Lt. Gramm. Who are you?"

"I'm Maureen Donahue. Am I arrested?" Not waiting for an answer, she continued. "What for? My husband is Cliff Donahue...Councilman Cliff Donahue." She emphasized his title.

White rolled her eyes.

Gramm didn't react. "You're not being arrested...yet. How long have you been in the tower?"

"Why do you need to know?"

Gramm smelled a hint of gin. "Have you missed the fact that for the past two hours there has been a dead woman on those stairs?" he asked, nodding toward the tower.

"There was? I didn't know…I was coming here for the view…it calms me…I go sit at the top and read my book."

"Where's your book?" White asked.

Maureen looked at her empty hands. "I…I…forgot it today. I was looking at the view."

"When did you arrive?" Gramm asked.

"At eight…this morning."

"So," Gramm checked his watch. "you've been looking at the view for two-and-a-half hours?"

"Actually, I didn't sleep well last night. I may have sat down and dozed."

"The officer found you on the second floor, far from the top of the tower," White challenged.

"I…I was coming down when I heard noises and realized something was going on." She looked at the parking lot full of official vehicles and flashing blue lights. "I didn't want to be involved. My husband is running for the state senate. So, I sat down and waited."

"Do you know a woman named…" Gramm turned to White who checked her notes.

"Jessica Vogel." White said.

"Why?"

"Do you know her or don't you?" Gramm pressed.

"Yes! I went to high school with her. We are having a reunion this weekend. I planned it all," Maureen said proudly.

White wondered if the plan included a murder.

"What has Jessica done now? Did she push someone again?" Maureen asked.

The comment took Gramm off guard. "Again? She pushed someone before?"

"Twelve years ago, everybody thought she pushed Molly Edwards down the tower stairs. Molly died." Maureen gasped. "Oh my god! Who did she push this time? Sophie? Liz? Who's dead?"

White couldn't take notes fast enough.

"Vogel's dead," Gramm said, wondering if this was an act.

"Thank God!" Maureen exclaimed and then realized her gaff. "I mean thank God that it wasn't Sophie or Liz."

"You didn't like her?" White asked.

"No one did!"

"Who's no one?" Gramm demanded.

This sounds familiar, Sutherland thought, remembering his interrogation during the Bonner murder case. He turned his back on Gramm and whispered to Rathkey, "She's going down the rabbit hole."

Milo nodded.

Maureen answered Gramm's question. "Well, Sophie and Liz for two. Liz was Molly's sister, and Sophie was her best friend. In fact, Sophie beat up Jessica yesterday. Right here at Enger Tower where the flowers are! Almost strangled her! She would have if Agnes hadn't stopped her."

Sutherland looked at Milo and whispered, "Couldn't be."

"Agnes who?" White asked.

"Larson," Maureen said.

"And it is!" Milo whispered back.

White wrote down the name without giving away her thoughts. *Agnes Larson knows the dead woman. Of course, she does! Why not!*

Maureen filled in the rest of her information. Yes, she heard voices shortly after arriving. No, she didn't see anything. Brooks and Moscatelli were Liz and Sophie's last names.

Gramm told an officer to give Maureen a ride home.

"I have a car over there," she objected, thinking the last thing she needed was to be seen getting out of a police car.

"I smell alcohol on your breath. I'm cutting you a break here. I could give you a breathalyzer, or a ride home. Which would you and your councilman husband prefer?" Gramm asked.

Worried she would be over the limit, she took the ride home. "Can you keep my name out of this? My husband is running for state senator."

"You said that. Can't promise anything," White said.

Maureen looked frightened as she slid into the front seat of the patrol car.

Watching the car disappear up the hill, White said, "This could be an easy case. We may be giving the murderer a ride home."

"Early days yet," Gramm said. "Let's go talk to Sutherland's friends..."

"Larry and Danielle," White filled in the name.

"Do you need me there?" Sutherland asked.

Gramm shook his head, and Sutherland headed for the SUV with the thought of finding Agnes.

"That was quick," White said. "He didn't ask what was happening with you, Milo. I guess you're coming with us."

"I'll take the back seat," Milo said.

"Cuff him," Gramm said, gruffly, "for those silly ass shorts."

9

Martha's Saturday mornings were quiet this summer because Breanna, who could now drive, dropped Jamal off at swim practice and Darian at Lego camp leaving Martha to work in her vegetable and herb garden.

Earlier in the spring, she planted her usual lettuce, spin-ach, tomatoes, carrots, cucumbers, and beans. This year she added broccoli, cauliflower and pumpkins, along with basil, rosemary, and thyme, being a firm believer that home grown tasted better.

Martha hoped for a sunny, warm morning, but the clouds and slight chill refused to leave. As she pulled the weeds and watered, she was already planning meals around the fresh vegetables and herbs.

Breanna returned from dropping off her brothers and like most teenagers walked with her head in her phone. Unlatching the garden gate, she announced, "I got an email from the Patricia Lind Scholarship people."

Martha stood up from the weeding, stretching her back while waiting to hear more. She was a different person from her sister. If she had gotten the same email, the world would know whether she was excited or upset. With Breanna, you never knew. She had always been a serious child, but when Martha took over as Breanna's guardian, she worried that the seriousness was masking depression.

"So, what does it say?" Martha urged as she sat down on a bench and took a drink of water.

Breanna pushed back her coral head band and looked at her phone, scanning the email for information. "Well, I am one of three finalists."

"That's fabulous!" Martha cheered. "Get over here. Let me give you a hug."

Breanna, the only member of the family to wear glasses, adjusted them and continued to read the email around Martha's hug. "They liked my essay."

"What was it on again?"

"Me and math," Breanna said. "Like we were buddies. It wasn't a question, it was a statement. Tell me about you and math. So, I did. Now I have to go to an interview."

"Interview? With whom? Is there a panel? Do we need paperwork? How does this work? What do I need to do?"

"Let me read!" Breanna ignored the wave of questions.

While Martha waited for Breanna to finish the email, she went and closed the garden gate. She had given up reminding the sibs to do it.

"Well, there are two other finalists," Breanna said, redoing the clip that held her thin braids in a ponytail. "The interviewer is a university professor who is in charge of the scholarship."

"Only one, not a panel?"

Breanna shrugged. "I guess so. Dr. Bixby. He must be a math professor."

"What else?"

"It says I'll be asked to solve a math problem. Piece of cake."

"Are you excited?" Martha asked.

"I haven't won yet."

Martha knew math came easy to Breanna, but the competition was sure to get tougher. She hoped Breanna's unbridled confidence would continue even if she didn't get this scholarship. "Let me know the day and time. I want to go with you," Martha said.

"Thanks Martha. Don't worry, I've got this." Breanna stood, slipped her phone into her pocket, and walked out of the garden, leaving the gate open.

Martha sighed. *She may be a math maven, but she can't close a gate.* The deer and the rabbits who loved Martha's vegetables were on Breanna's side.

§

Larry and Danielle Ashbach lived in an upscale Woodland Hills, two-story, custom-built house that backed up to a park and nature preserve. Larry was out on the porch waiting for them. Gramm introduced himself and White, saying, "You already know Milo."

Larry seemed surprised. "I didn't know you were a policeman."

"Consultant," Milo corrected.

Not asking about the difference, he led them through the house to the glassed-enclosed, four-season room overlooking the nature preserve. He warned that Danielle was still upset. "I would appreciate it if you kept this short."

"We'll tread gently," Gramm said.

Danielle was sitting back on a green sofa looking out the window at a yearling deer munching on a cluster of tiger day-lilies. She was holding a half-filled wine glass. Milo introduced her to Gramm and White who sat down in nearby chairs.

"Would anyone care for a beer, wine, or a Coke?" Larry asked.

"I'd like a Coke," Milo said.

"What do we have, Danielle?" Larry asked, hoping to get her mind onto the mundane.

She continued staring at the deer. "I don't know, Larry, look."

Larry went into the kitchen and yelled back, "Let's see… Sprite, root beer, ginger ale, regular Coke and Diet Coke."

"Thanks, I'll take Diet Coke." Milo looked at Gramm and White who were busy conferencing over an email.

Larry brought a Diet Coke for Milo, a beer for himself, and a half opened bottle of wine for Danielle. She held her now empty wine glass up to Larry for a refill.

Finally, Gramm seemed ready to begin the questioning.

Danielle leaned back and began telling her story. "I was planning to go with Larry and our cycling group, but I needed to stretch my hammies and my calves, so I decided to work them out by running the steps at Enger Tower."

Larry was leaning against the kitchen door frame, scratching his beard stubble.

"Larry, you're making me nervous. Come sit down," Daniel ordered.

He said it was a nervous habit, apologized, and crossed his arms to keep from doing it again, but stayed leaning in the door frame.

"Did you drive to the tower?" Gramm asked.

"I wish I had, but no, I took my bike." Danielle managed a large gulp of her wine, put the glass down, folded her arms around herself, and leaned back. I was getting off my bike in the parking lot below the tower when I heard a woman scream, and a sound like something hitting stone, something hard. I got off my bike and ran toward the tower's the front steps. There she was, crumpled...not moving...eyes wide open...blood." Danielle drained her wine then looked up at Larry who filled her glass again. He asked Gramm and White if they wanted anything to drink. They declined.

"Then what?" Gramm continued.

"I couldn't help her. I didn't have a phone! I couldn't help her!" She looked at the police for acceptance of her plight.

White picked up the questioning. "So, what did you do?"

"I ran back to the parking lot to see if anyone there had a phone. I saw a car speeding around the parking lot. I tried to flag him down, but he came right at me! I ran to get out of his way. He swerved only at the last minute..."

Danielle took another healthy gulp of her wine and continued, "He took off up the hill. There was a dead girl…my mind went crazy. I thought he killed her and I was afraid he was coming back for me. I was scared out of my mind. I had to get away from there and go home. I was running to my bike when an RV pulled in. I raced over to them and banged on their door, yelling for them to call 911…there was somebody hurt, and I pointed to the tower." Danielle leaned back and closed her eyes. The wine was having an effect. She was a little tipsy, but mostly she was sleepy.

"We will want you to describe the driver's face to one of our artists," Gramm said.

"No…can't."

"Why not?"

She waved her hand around her head. "Hood. I didn't see his face."

White asked, "How do you know it was a man?"

Danielle opened her eyes. "I don't know. Do you think it could be a woman?"

Gramm jumped in. "What did you do once you left the tower?"

"Pedaled like hell until I got home, and then I called Larry. I was going on pure adrenaline. I couldn't believe any of it."

Gramm's stomach was beginning to growl. He appeased it by helping himself to a bright yellow and red wrapped candy sitting in a green leaf candy dish. "Describe the car."

Danielle's eyes closed again. "Sports car…blue… BMW…you know the cheap one."

Larry cut off the questioning. "She's been through hell Lieutenant. Can we end this? She needs to sleep."

"Certainly," Gramm said. His witness was sauced, and he was hungry. "By the way, these candies are delicious. I love cashews. Where did you get them?"

"Danielle gets them from Brazil," Larry said. "She found them on our honeymoon. They're called Serenata de Amor. I like them too." Larry rubbed his beard stubble. Danielle was sleeping.

10

Relieved to be released from the scene of his second murder investigation, Sutherland decided to take the sailboat out for the afternoon. He looked forward to the challenge of cold, choppy water and bracing winds. But before he could let thoughts of murder go, he needed to talk to Agnes. He was concerned about her involvement in the choking incident at her reunion, so he called her.

She answered in a hazy half sleep. "Sutherland? What do you want?"

"Did I wake you?"

"Yeah, I sort of dozed on the couch. I didn't sleep well last night."

"Because of that choking thing at your reunion?"

Agnes' fog was retreating. "How do you know about that?"

"Because of the dead body."

She was now fully awake. "Mr. McKnight, what are you talking about?"

Sutherland filled her in on Danielle's phone call to Larry, Milo's phone call to Gramm, and how they ended up at Enger Tower.

"What does any of that have to do with me, and how you know about Sophie choking Jessica?"

"The dead body is that Jessica person."

She was trying to make sense of what Sutherland said. "I'm confused."

"I'm sorry. I'm being my usual muddled mess. Where does it get confusing?" Sutherland asked.

"At the beginning. Start again." Agnes walked into the kitchen to make coffee.

"A woman named Jessica was found dead on the steps leading to Enger Tower this morning. Police suspect murder. They found a woman in the tower who mentioned the choking incident yesterday and your involvement."

Agnes shuddered. "Sophie? Was the woman in tower Sophie Moscatelli?"

"I don't remember her name. Blond, baseball cap, wearing a hoodie, driving a Lexus."

"I don't know who that is, but it's not Sophie." Agnes relaxed then she remembered Liz. "Was the woman pregnant?"

"I don't think so, but I'm calling to let you know Lt. Gramm is interested in your knowledge of the people involved. Like I said, I was concerned. It's your second involvement in a murder investigation too."

"Actually, it's my third, Sutherland," she whispered.

Sutherland stopped talking and closed his eyes. Her sister Barbara. He wondered how he could be so dumb.

"I'm coming to Lakesong this morning to meet my wedding assistant, Margaret Brune. I'd rather talk to the police there," Agnes said.

"I'm going out on the sailboat for an hour or two. Can we talk this afternoon?"

"Sure."

§

The Chinese Dragon catered to government workers, journalists, and business people, leaving empty lunch tables on the weekend. Henry Hun, Milo's boyhood friend, whom everyone called Hank, met them at the door. "Lt Gramm, Sgt. White welcome! I see you brought Mr. Egg Foo Young with you." Hank's reference was to Milo's permanent order.

"I may order something else today, thank you," Milo said.

"And I'm playing first base for the Twins tomorrow," Hank retorted as he twisted his way past the huge gold Buddhas to Gramm's preference, a table in the back. As per their usual banter, Hank handed menus to only Gramm and White, ignoring Rathkey.

"The special today is a Szechuan spicy tofu with mung bean noodles, ground pork, and scallions."

"I don't know that one," White said.

"It's called Mapo Dofu. It's spicy but light, a great dish...."

"...Mapo Dufus?" Milo interrupted. "Come on what the hell is Mapo Dufus? Didn't the bullies call the kid who ate paper Mapo Dufus?"

"Every class had a kid who ate paper, Milo. But the kid we knew who ate paper now owns a bank in Wichita." Hank directed a server to come over with water and a pot of tea.

"As amusing as all this yakking is, can we order? I'm hungry!" Gramm demanded.

"I'll have the special," White said, handing back her menu.

"I think you're going to like it, Robin," Hank offered.

"I'll have broccoli beef with an egg roll," Gramm said.

Hank looked at Rathkey as he collected Gramm's menu.

"I'm going to play tennis," Milo said.

Hank stared at Milo. "Perhaps you're confused. This is where you order egg foo young with extra gravy."

"I'm just sayin'…it's been a while. I'm gonna play tennis again."

Curiosity got the better of Hank. "Singles?"

"No. Mixed doubles."

Hank laughed. "You would need to find a woman to be your partner."

"I have one," Milo said, grabbing a menu from his friend.

Gramm and White looked on in heightened curiosity.

"Someone I know?" Hank asked.

"Maybe…Mary Alice Bonner," Milo said looking at the menu.

Gramm choked on his tea.

"Are you kidding me?" White asked. "You're gonna play tennis with the lying widow? Do you even play tennis?"

Milo's phone began to vibrate, and he turned in his chair to take the call.

"Milo sucked at baseball," Hank jumped in. "Couldn't catch a football and forget about dribbling a basketball, but for some odd reason, he was the monster of the tennis court."

"Life is full of surprises," White said.

"Mary Alice Bonner and Milo?" Gramm shook his head, remembering the beautiful blue-eyed widow who for a long time was a suspect in her husband's death. "Talk about out punting your coverage."

Milo's call ended, and he turned back to the group. "I choose to ignore that punting remark…besides it was her idea." Looking up at Hank as if this had never happened before he said, "I'll have the chicken egg foo young, and don't skimp on the gravy."

Hank snatched Milo's menu and walked away muttering to himself.

"Once again you're antagonizing people who are going to be feeding us," Gramm admonished.

"Don't be fooled," Milo said. "He enjoys our little game."

While they waited for their food, White pulled out her pad and began her process of going through her notes. Gramm and Rathkey talked about the record number of lake trout this year.

"We could go fishing on the motorboat one of these weekends," Milo offered.

"Sounds great," Gramm agreed.

White looked up from her work. "Am I invited?"

"Of course," Milo said. "Do you fish?"

"Only since birth."

"What size is your boat?" Gramm asked.

"I have to remember. I think it's around fifty feet," Milo said.

Both Gramm and White laughed. "Among us peasants," Gramm said, "a fifty-foot boat is a yacht."

Rathkey shrugged. "John McKnight always called it a motorboat, so I call it a motorboat."

"Can you pilot a fifty-footer?" White asked.

"I was in the Navy." Milo seemed offended.

"You were shore patrol!" Gramm challenged.

"John taught me well. Trust me."

White waved her note pad. "Putting our recreational activities aside, let's get this case in order. We have one dead body, and three possible suspects…"

"For now, and it's only been four or five hours," Gramm added. "If this is like the Bonner murder, we could have six more by dinner."

White gave him a sidelong glance. "Let's hope not. My money is on gin girl." She checked her notes. "Maureen Donahue."

"Yup. I don't buy that sightseeing stuff. She lives here. Locals never go sightseeing. What was she doing up there?" Gramm questioned.

Rathkey picked up the discussion. "She was quick to mention the choking incident, taking the focus off of her, somewhat suspicious."

Enjoying the sweet and sour cucumber appetizer that always came before the meal, Gramm added, "I almost forgot. When we were at the Ashbach's, Doc Smith texted us about the choking marks on the victim's neck. They were a day or two old, not connected to being pushed down the stairs. That fits with what we know about the attack by um…Robin?"

"Sophie Moscatelli."

"Yeah, her. We definitely need to talk to her. Smith also said she had cuts and bruises on her leg and shoulder."

"Dead woman was unpopular, or a poor roller derby girl," Milo said. "Choked and now pushed down the stairs, plus other cuts and bruises."

"Was it one someone who wanted her dead, or multiple someones?" White added.

The food arrived. Hank placed the entrées in front of White and Gramm and plopped Rathkey's food down with little care. Milo checked the gravy. "Good, you didn't skimp on it this time."

Hank walked away shaking his head.

As they dug in, White brought up one more curious fact. "Let's not forget Agnes Larson who once again seems to be at the center of a murder."

"She works for me you know," Milo said. "Actually, me and Sutherland, she's our house manager. As your consultant, it's part of my full disclosure."

Gramm sat back. "Robin take notes on this please. Milo, you are canoodling with Bonner's widow, and you've hired Bonner's administrative whatever. Have you also adopted his kid…what's his name?"

"Richard," White said.

"Yeah, Richard."

White put down her note book and continued eating.

Milo sighed. "Canoodling? How old are you? I haven't heard that word since…ah…never."

"I will Google canoodling later under, what—old guys speak?" White joked cutting off a Gramm rant. "In all seriousness, I think we need to talk to Ms. Larson before we do anything else."

Gramm agreed. "Good idea. We need to know as much about that choking incident as we can before we talk to…"

"Sophie Moscatelli." White sighed.

Gramm gave her a stare. "I knew it this time! You didn't give me a chance."

White smiled.

"That was Sutherland on the phone earlier," Milo offered, "saying that Agnes was at Lakesong. I think that's your next stop. You have to drop me off anyway."

"The manor. I've never been to the manor," White said.

"It's no big deal," Gramm added. "A lot of rooms, a lot of land, on the lake…never mind."

§

Jamal took only a few minutes to master the drone and was now expertly hovering it over the back lawn of Lakesong. His younger brother Darian was bellowing about not getting a turn.

"It's not our drone. You could break it," Jamal reasoned. "It belongs to Mr. Rathkey. He's letting us use it. Watch me first then maybe you can try."

Lt. Gramm took off his jacket and eased himself into a cushioned rocking chair on the back terrace as he watched the boys play. Despite the forecast of all-day gray skies and windy weather, the clouds dispersed, and the temperature was on the rise. As Gramm took a sip of coffee, he said to the group, "The department is going to get drones like the one the kids are playing with. I've never seen them in action."

"That one's mine, a new toy from Ed Patupick," Milo said. "I'm letting the kids figure out how to fly it, and then they can show me. With that wind this morning, I would have flown it into a tree. I do know how the phone app works however, here's the picture from the drone's camera."

While Gramm and White both looked at the wide-angle, high-def picture of Lakesong, Agnes slipped into a chair around the table. Helping herself to coffee and one of Martha's chocolate chip cookies, she watched Sutherland hike up from the boat house and talk to the kids about the drone.

Still looking at the video being sent from the drone, Gramm exclaimed, "That's us!"

"The quality is great!" White said. "We could use it for surveillance. When do we get ours?"

Gramm was pleased that White seemed eager to take on this latest piece of hi-tech equipment. "They're looking at vendors."

"They should talk to Ed. He's my go-to guy for all things technical," Milo said reminding Gramm that it was Patupick who helped them get the pictures from James Bonner's safe camera, and in fact, it was Patupick who invented the device.

White typed Ed's name into her phone.

Sutherland finally made his way up to the terrace, grabbed a cookie, and sat down next to Agnes. "Great sailing today!"

"The lake's kinda choppy, isn't it?" Gramm commented.

Sutherland smiled. "I prefer to call it challenging, refreshing, and mind clearing."

Gramm cleared his throat and looked at Agnes. "Well, Ms. Larson, this is becoming old hat."

"It seems so," Agnes said, not rising to Gramm's attempt at humor.

"So, tell me what you know."

"What I know about what?" Agnes felt stronger than she did after her sister's murder and the death of her boss James Bonner, but the nightmares were back. She was feeling confused. *You can do this Agnes…just do it.*

"Do you know that a Jessica Vogel was murdered this morning at Enger Tower? I understand she was attending your reunion," Gramm explained.

"The only Jessica I know is Jessica Raymond," Agnes said.

White checked her notes. "Five eight, brown hair, ombre highlights, brown eyes, about a hundred and thirty pounds."

"That sounds like her…Jessica Raymond. Maybe she got married and changed her name," Agnes suggested.

"There was a woman in the tower this morning named…" Once again, Gramm looked at White.

"Maureen Donahue."

"She told us that today's victim may have pushed a classmate down the tower stairs a number of years ago. Tell us what you know about that."

Agnes took a deep breath. "It was twelve years ago. My friend Molly Edwards died at Enger Tower. We were sophomores in high school. The official report was she fell down the stairs and broke her neck. I was there. I never believed it."

"What did you believe happened?" White asked.

"I thought Jessica pushed her."

"Why?"

"Because she was mean. I don't think she meant for Molly to die…but she did."

"What happened yesterday at the tower?" Gramm asked.

"We had a small ceremony in memory of Molly, a laying of flowers. Jessica interrupted the ceremony, disrespecting Molly and everyone there. You have to understand. Liz Brooks was Molly's sister. Sophie Moscatelli, and I were Molly's best friends."

"Understood," Gramm said. "I know that this Sophie Moscatelli was choking the victim, and you stopped it."

"That's technically true, but Jessica attacked us. Sophie came to our defense. She's ex-military."

"Was Moscatelli angry?" Gramm asked.

"We all were. I was," Agnes said.

Angry and trained in combat tactics with a motive sounded like a prime suspect in Gramm's mind, not Agnes' intention.

"There's more you need to know about Jessica," Agnes said.

I may need a new notebook, White thought.

"Do you want the history or the present day?"

"Let's start with history," Gramm said.

"In high school, Jessica got girls to do things for her. It was small stuff, like homework, buying her makeup, a new CD. It was rumored she would find dirt on them and then threaten to tell people, expose them, unless she got what she wanted."

Agnes paused and pursed her lips together as she decided how to tell the last part of this seedy story. "I think her schemes escalated. Last night, at our reunion banquet, I overheard her blackmailing a former high school teacher, now a college professor, named Paul Kendrick. Apparently, she and Mr. Kendrick were a…couple…when she was still in high school…too young for a teacher. I heard her say she had pictures, not only of her, but of his other girls too. You need to look at her phone."

"How did you come to overhear this?" Gramm asked.

"I was there, enjoying a drink, looking at the lake. They didn't see me. They were over at the boathouse. First, I couldn't hear them, but when they started shouting, I could hear almost every word." Agnes paused and thought about what she was going to say next. "You need to understand, I didn't want to know any of this."

Sutherland looked at Agnes. He was concerned but didn't know what to do.

"Are these people local?" Gramm asked.

"Kendrick lives here. He's a professor up at Le Caron."

"What about Sophie?"

"No. I think she lives in Arizona."

"Where is she now?" White asked.

"The reunion had a harbor cruise scheduled this afternoon. I don't know if she's on that or if she already left town. Yesterday was an awful day."

"Who would know if they were going to take the cruise?"

"Maureen. She knows everything. She planned the weekend."

White got up to make the call.

Gramm thanked Agnes and changed the conversation to a personal tone. "So, you're working here these days."

"Yes, I'm the house manager."

"It's a big house," Milo said.

"There's a lot to do," Sutherland jumped in.

"Absolutely. Hell, Ernie, we have a lot of employees. I even have two drone testers out there on the lawn." Milo moved the conversation away from Agnes.

Gramm looked out at the boys. "I wonder if a recording device can be hooked up to those things."

Rathkey consulted his phone once again, showed it to Gramm, while rewinding the video. "Already there."

"Wait a minute!" Gramm interrupted. "Those things record?"

"Yup."

"I love technology. We have to check with that photographer from this morning to see if his drone was recording. He might have recorded our murder scene."

White returned and said Moscatelli was on the boat. "I think we should be down there. Maureen Donahue is also on the boat."

Gramm pulled out his phone. "First give me the number for that photographer. Those flying things record what they're looking at."

White flipped through her notes, showing Gramm the number.

The conversation was short. Gramm asked Reggie to bring the video into the police station either this afternoon or tomorrow morning. Reggie agreed, but said all police requests had to be accompanied by a subpoena. For Gramm that wasn't a problem. Hanging up, he looked at his watch. "Look, Robin, could you handle that boat? I promised my wife I'd at least make an appearance at the family picnic."

"Yeah sure, I don't have a life," White said, sarcastically.

"Good. Now I don't have to feel bad."

"Did you feel bad before?"

"No."

§

Liz Brooks and Sophie Moscatelli had been enjoying the warm breeze created by the motion of the double decker cruise boat. A tour guide—talking over the cry of the gulls—was highlighting points of interest along the harbor, but neither woman cared.

"I forgot about Duluth weather," Sophie said.

Liz echoed her thought. "I was wearing a sweatshirt this morning, and now it has to be in the mid-eighties."

Sitting with eyes closed, soaking up the sun, their relaxation was broken by the ringing of Sophie's phone. The conversation was short. Sophie put her phone down, sat up, and straddled the lounge chair. "That bitch filed a complaint against me!"

Liz looked up. "What?"

"Jessica! That was a cop, and she wants to talk to me when the boat docks."

"Why?"

"She didn't say, but why else? Jessica wants me charged for assault. That's my bet."

"Ugh. Will we ever be rid of her?"

Sophie's phone rang again. This time it was Agnes. The conversation was longer. "What? Are you kidding?"

Liz struggled to sit, listening, trying to figure out who was calling and what was going on.

Sophie continued her phone conversation. "That's not good. No wonder the police want to talk to me. I thought Jessica had filed a complaint. How do they even know about me and Jessica?"

Liz wished the call was on speaker, especially because there was a long pause as Agnes answered Sophie's question.

"Are you kidding me? If she was there, why do they want to talk to me?"

Another pause, not as long as the first.

"Well this is a shit show. Thanks for the warning." Sophie clicked off.

"Well?" Liz asked.

"That was Agnes. Jessica did not file a complaint."

"Good."

"Bad. She's a cold crumpled corpse. The cops think she was pushed down the main Enger Tower Steps. That's why they want to talk to me, and that's the shit show."

"I'd say how ironic, but this doesn't look good," Liz said. "Do they know about yesterday?"

"Oh yes they do because your friend and mine, Maureen, told them all about it!"

"How does Maureen get in there?" Liz asked.

"She was there. According to Agnes, she was *sightseeing* at the crack of effing dawn."

Liz sat back. "Jessica died just like Molly. What a coincidence."

"I didn't kill her," Sophie said. "Did you?"

"About a million times."

11

A series of loud plaintive meows announced Annie's displeasure at no morning bacon. Martha tried to placate her majesty with a few commercial bacon bits, but Annie turned up her nose and strutted out of the kitchen toward her Guiana Chestnut tree in the gallery.

"Your lack of bacon is upsetting the cat. What are you eating?" Sutherland asked Rathkey, not seeing his usual breakfast.

Milo looked at his plate. "It's a peanut butter, jelly, and banana sandwich."

"He made me make it!" Martha shouted from the kitchen.

"Why the change?" Sutherland asked.

"Tennis. This is what I eat before tennis."

"Oh sure. I'm supposed to believe it's what you always eat before your many tennis matches," Sutherland chided.

"Trash talking from the green goop drinker? Being a tennis ace, it's my preferred fuel."

Sutherland laughed and said under his breath, "Tennis ace. Right." He went back to reading his paper.

Between bites, Milo held out his right arm, stretching his hand downward, and then turned his hand around repeating the movement.

Sutherland looked up. "I thought you weren't a stretching kind of guy!"

"Where did you get that from? I stretch every chance I get. Currently I'm preventing tennis elbow. Stretch the wrist and upper arm one way then the other. Not too much, warming things up, getting the blood flowing."

Sutherland went back to his paper convinced Milo found stretching exercises on the internet, a sign he was desperate.

Milo stood up, put a dish towel under his arm, and pressed the outside of his hand against the wall, keeping the towel from falling.

"Now what are you doing?" Sutherland asked.

"Rotator cuff. Warming up the shoulder."

"You're being silly. We're not even on the court yet." Sutherland shook his head and snapped his paper to make his point.

Milo finished his exercises and his peanut butter, jelly, and banana sandwich, satisfied he had created enough doubt to mess with Sutherland's head.

§

Gramm knew the patrols would be out with only a handful of office staff in the building. He hated coming into the near-deserted office on weekends. Sitting down he threw his

142

cooling coffee in the trash, reached for a box of latex gloves, and began to go through Jessica's iPhone.

"I had to give up my sailing lesson for this," White complained as she arrived at Gramm's office thirty minutes later.

"Sailing?" Gramm questioned.

"Yeah. It's fun, and my instructor is cute."

Gramm smiled. "Some of that no life?"

She pursed her lips to avoid a smile.

"Speaking of no life," Gramm said, "the family thanks you for taking those interviews yesterday. I was able to enjoy the tail end of the picnic. So, what did you get?"

White sat down and folded back her notebook to yesterday's interviews. "Sophie Moscatelli admits to choking the dead woman but says she was just trying to scare her."

"Pretty much matches what Agnes Larson said yesterday. How big is this Moscatelli?"

"Tiny, about five-four."

"Does she have an alibi?"

"Yes and no. She says she was jogging alone along the Lakewalk."

"We can check cameras."

"I also interviewed Molly Edwards' sister, Liz Brooks. She believes Vogel killed her sister."

"Strong motive. Alibi?"

"Was eating breakfast alone but talking to her husband by phone."

"What restaurant?"

"The hotel's. I know…more cameras to check."

Gramm held up Jessica's phone. "Speaking of cameras, take a gander at Vogel's phone. I looked at it this morning."

White put on gloves and took the phone. "Let me *gander* at this. I assume that means look at the pictures."

"At least use it right, *take a gander* which means look in the folder labeled, *PAUL*."

White scrolled through six pictures of teenaged girls in suggestive poses. She recognized Jessica but none of the others jumped out at her. Scrolling back, she paused at another picture, enlarged it, and handed the phone to Gramm. "Did you notice this girl?"

"What am I looking at here?"

"Make her hair blond, take a few pounds of teenage weight off and put a ball cap and hoodie on her head."

Gramm looked again. His old partner Jablonski would have never spotted her. Gramm didn't. "We must have another conversation with Maureen *my husband is a city councilman* Donahue."

"And a first interview with this sleaze ball Kendrick," White added. "I'll print these pictures to jog his memory."

§

Leroy Thompson sat in the prison common area reading the morning paper. The room was empty as the other prisoners were outside in the warm sun, playing basketball or milling around. Leroy, short and slight, didn't do basketball or milling with fellow prisoners. A small guy could get hurt.

He read the sports section first, thinking he'd go back to book making when he got out of jail. He had to keep up. After the sports section he picked up the newspaper's front page. The headline, "Minneapolis Realtor Found Dead" caught his eye. After reading the first two paragraphs he figured this was the woman Bonner was looking for. *How do I play this? Gotta be careful. Don't know who's calling the shots.*

Leroy got up, eyed the cold, empty cinderblock room, and deemed it safe to make a phone call.

§

The gates were open and welcoming as Sutherland glided his Porsche into the Bonner estate, parking on the left side of the front entrance. He was walking towards the tennis courts when Agnes arrived. She jumped out of her new silver Mitsubishi Mirage and smoothed her aqua tennis dress. She was excited and craved a bit of fun after Jessica.

Sutherland enjoyed her curves, especially her long legs. He waved. Agnes didn't seem to notice as she pulled her tennis bag out of the back of the car. She debated taking her sweater, but as the day was sunny and warm, she left it in the car. Sutherland started to call her name when a familiar Bentley cruised in front of him.

At Lakesong, Milo said he was running late and told Sutherland to go on without him. Now he showed up in the Bentley. Agnes smiled, wondering if the Bentley was part of Milo's little game. He joined Agnes, and the two walked toward Sutherland.

"The Bentley?" Sutherland chided.

"Doesn't it need to be driven? I'm trying to be helpful," Milo said as he and Agnes strolled past him.

Sutherland looked doubtful and fell in a couple feet back.

"Nice messing with his head," Agnes whispered, and quickened her pace toward the court. She couldn't wait for this match to begin.

Mary Alice was on the court looking amused as Milo entered. Unlike their singles match in traditional white, Milo now sported a faded t-shirt advertising a long-past Metallica concert which he personally never attended. The shirt, however did go with the brown cargo shorts, but not the black tennis shoes. The only tennis whites were his socks, except they had two Kelly green stripes. He was not her usual GQ cutout.

After dropping his bag, Milo crouched and shuffled sideways, football style, down the baseline, first in one direction then the other.

"What's that?" Sutherland yelled as he slid his tennis bag under a nearby bench to watch this side show.

"My hips are a little tight," Milo said.

Agnes couldn't stop snickering. *Sutherland you're such a nice guy but so in for a shock.*

Mary Alice walked over to her. "You know what's going on here? Right?"

Agnes whispered, "I do. Sutherland doesn't think Milo knows how to play." She could have added, "he doesn't think I can play either," but held her tongue. This farce was just beginning.

Sutherland walked over and picked up Milo's racket. It was a couple years old but expensive. *Unusual for Milo*, he thought. "What are you doing with this racket?"

Milo stopped stretching. "Playing tennis. What do you do with your racket?"

Ignoring Milo's snide remark, Sutherland advised, "You have too much racket for your game."

Agnes glanced at Mary Alice and admired her ability to keep a straight face.

"And the strings? What are these strings?" Sutherland continued.

"I don't know, came with the racket."

"I think they saw you coming. You got taken."

"You think so. I got it on this Craig's List thing. Ed Patupick helped me out. It seemed reasonable."

Not sure if Milo was kidding, Agnes asked Mary Alice, "Craig's list? Really?"

"Not a chance. Custom made. He told me," Mary Alice said smiling.

The four took their places and started warming up with Milo acting the rube.

The warm up took about ten minutes then Milo served first, hitting a simple popup to Agnes. She drove it down the alley with a well-practiced, two-handed backhand.

Sutherland nodded to Agnes. "Great shot! You can play tennis!"

"How nice of you to notice," Agnes mocked.

Getting ready to receive serve, Sutherland decided Milo needed a tip. "You should throw the ball up higher to hit it with more force."

Milo looked a little puzzled and asked, "Up higher? Are you sure?"

"And snap that wrist," Sutherland said, waving his hand around.

"Okay." Milo said. "Throw the ball up high and snap that wrist."

"Yup."

Knowing what was going to happen next, Agnes called over to Sutherland. "You may want to step back."

Sutherland smiled at her naïve suggestion and didn't move.

Agnes wondered exactly when Sutherland caught on to the farce. Was it the toss, three times higher than before? Maybe it was when Milo's feet left the ground? Or was it his racket blurring through the ball with a snap that could be heard four houses away? Without a doubt, it was when the ball hit the service line, chirped, and slammed into Sutherland's stomach. His racket remained useless by his side.

Mary Alice came up to Milo. "Nice serve partner," she said, as the two clicked rackets.

"Maybe you were up too close?" Agnes questioned, batting her eyelashes.

Sutherland seemed a bit dazed. "What the hell was that?"

"Sorry, didn't mean to hit you," Milo lied.

Agnes was by now laughing so hard she almost dropped her racket.

Sutherland noted his opponent's congratulatory racket click, and his partner's laughter. "I've been had, haven't I?" He turned to Agnes who was still laughing, "And you knew."

"Yes, I did," Agnes said, with indignation. "I saw Milo practicing on Thursday. I tried to tell you, but you were...um..."

Sutherland sighed. "Yeah, I know. Sorry...I was a real butt-head."

"Are we playing or talking?" Milo asked, bouncing a ball off his racket, clearly in control of the tennis court.

Sutherland asked one more question. "That racket…"

"Yup…love the strings…love how they're strung."

"No Craig's List?"

"Never heard of it."

The first set was quick. Milo always seemed to put the ball out of Sutherland's reach. Even Sutherland had to laugh and at one point, Agnes asked Milo for one of his hard serves. She managed to hit the ball into the net, something Sutherland was unable to do. "I got a piece of it," She crowed. "Not bad for someone who's just gravy."

Sutherland grimaced in mental pain but couldn't help but enjoy the sparkle in Agnes' brown eyes as she chided him. Those long legs weren't bad either.

After the first set—which Milo and Mary Alice won six-love—Milo took something off his serves, so everyone could have a fun match.

When the match was over, Mary Alice put her arm through Milo's, leaned in and whispered, "You are fun." Walking off the court, Mary Alice did not remove her arm.

§

Paul Kendrick was worried. Jessica's death showed up last night on the local news but details were sparse. The Sunday paper didn't have much more, her name, Jessica Raymond Vogel, the fact she died, and police were investigating.

No more payments! Then the doorbell rang.

Before opening the door, he glanced out the window but didn't recognize the car in his driveway. *Who would come this early?*

Gramm introduced himself and Sgt. White at the door. "We have questions about Jessica Vogel."

Showing them into the older craftsman house, Kendrick said, "Why do you want to talk to me? I was sorry to hear about her accident. She was a student of mine years ago."

Standing in the entryway, Gramm got right to the point. "We know you had an affair with her when she was under age, and she was blackmailing you."

Kendrick began to answer, thought better of it, turned and walked into the kitchen. He closed the kitchen door as they sat down on benches next to the wooden table where he launched into his defense. "You know we weren't that far apart in age. I was in my early twenties and she was I think seventeen going on twenty-five."

"She was sixteen, and you were twenty-five," White challenged.

Kendrick put his head in his hands. "It was a mistake. A serious, serious, mistake."

"Tell us about the blackmail," Gramm demanded.

Kendrick sighed, moved his hands to rub back of his neck then sat back in his chair. "She demanded money after I ended our relationship. I paid for a long time, but I got tired of it. I stopped paying and hoped she would forget about it."

"She wasn't happy with that. Right?" Gramm asked.

"No. I ignored her emails, but on Friday she emailed me, told me she was in town, and demanded I come early to the reunion dinner."

"Why?"

"She said she wanted money but wasn't staying for the banquet."

"Why did you agree to talk to her?" White asked.

"To tell her, in person, I wouldn't pay anymore."

"What was her reaction?"

"It was good. I called her bluff. I mean she had no proof. It was her word against mine."

White pulled out a glossy eight by ten from her file.

Gramm jumped in. "That's your first lie. Make it your last."

"You should recognize this. After all, your reflection is in the mirror," White said as she laid the photo on the kitchen table. "It's from her phone, and we have a witness that can testify the victim showed you this picture on a boat dock Friday night."

Kendrick put his hand on his forehead and closed his eyes. "I never knew she had those pictures. I had no choice."

"So, you killed her," Gramm said, hopefully.

"No, no, no. I had no choice but to keep paying. I didn't kill her!"

"Where were you Saturday morning?"

"I was here, doing yard work, I think."

"All morning?"

"Yeah. I was home all day."

White removed the picture from the table. "Well Mr. Kendrick, you are mixed up in murder and statutory rape."

Gramm stood up. "Don't leave town and get a lawyer. You're in trouble Mr. Kendrick."

"Why? I told you what happened."

Gramm said nothing as he and White walked to the door.

A female voice from the top of the stairs asked, "Paul are you making breakfast?"

Both White and Gramm looked at Kendrick.

"She's twenty," he said defensively seeing the cops out, slamming the door behind them.

"Where should we put this creep on our list of suspects?" White asked as she got into the car.

Gramm sighed. "I don't know. It's a tossup between the professor and the ball cap lady. He's got a great motive, but she was in the tower."

"If he was paying the dead woman, could Maureen have been there for the same reason? Her glossy is in my file too."

Gramm sat back and buckled his seat belt. "I knew I kept you around for a reason."

"Only one?" White kidded as Gramm's phone rang.

"Hmm interesting," Gramm said looking at his phone.

"Who's calling?"

"Frank Ugger, ambulance chaser and favorite attorney to low life criminals."

White waited for the phone call to end.

Gramm shook his head as he hung up. "You're not going to believe this one. Our good buddy Leroy Thompson wants to trade information about our dead woman for a few months off his sentence."

"You're right. I don't believe it. What would Leroy Thompson know about a realtor from Minneapolis?"

"Don't know, but I am going to find out. He wants to talk to me alone, so you have the rest of the day off."

"I have a life for a whole afternoon. Whatever will I do?"

"Put a sail on your kayak, save money on those lessons."
"I think you missed the point—the instructor's cute."

§

Toweling off, Mary Alice said, "Cook has left us refreshments. Let's go get them and bring them out here. The lake breeze feels good after tennis."

They entered the house through the library and were beset upon by three large dogs, two of uncertain breed, jumping up and begging for attention.

"Big dogs!" Sutherland said, while petting the greyhound whose paws rested against his shoulders. The other two danced around the group waiting for someone to pet them.

"Yes, three large rescue mutts. The largest they had. James would have hated them," Mary Alice said, letting them out to run on the back lawn. "In fact, I converted his study into a doggie spa." Noticing Milo's perplexed look, she explained. "It's where they get rinsed or dried off after being outside. Again, James would have hated it."

Rathkey looked around the library. Last January when he entered the room for the first time, it was stark white, filled with unread books sitting on Lucite bookcases. All that was gone. Pain-spattered tarps were everywhere, and the walls were covered with sample colors.

"Be careful where you step, this is a construction zone. Everything in here is going to be changed. I haven't decided on a final look," Mary Alice said, leading them into the main gallery.

It too was under construction. All of James Bonner's ugly artwork was gone.

Sutherland asked, "What did you do with the um…"

"Crap? I had Jules, my art person, sell it all and donated the proceeds to the local ASPCA. James would have hated that too," she said with a lilt in her voice.

I sense a theme, Milo thought.

While everyone was taking refreshments out to the library terrace, Milo hung back to take a tour of the repurposed, James Bonner study. It was where Rathkey saw the boastful Bonner last, and the place where the real estate developer met his grisly death.

Milo opened the door. The blood-and-brain littered Lucite desk and three computer monitors had been replaced by a large subway tiled shower-tub combo, an adjustable grooming table, and multiple food and water dispensers. The wall safe was now colorful shelving which held shampoos, ointments, and medicines. Milo especially liked the huge pet door that allowed access to the outside.

"Well, Bonner, you've been erased, and I kinda like what she's done to the place."

Milo didn't know much about doggie spas, but he did know moving the plumbing and installing a floor drain had to cost a pretty penny. This room would have been easier to create in other parts of the house. By putting it here Mary Alice was making a statement.

As Milo joined the others at the terrace table, Agnes was telling Mary Alice about Jessica's death. "There was supposed to be another event last night, but it was canceled. I guess no one was in a party mood…I wasn't. As a matter of fact, I need to call two friends and say goodbye before they leave town."

"The ones involved in the fight with the dead woman at Enger Tower?" Milo asked as he sat down.

"Yes," Agnes said.

"Don't bother saying goodbye; they aren't going anywhere. I'm sure Gramm has asked them to stay in town until he figures this out."

"Stay in town? Why?"

"They're witnesses, but I think they're suspects too," Milo explained.

"Oh my. Liz's pregnant."

"I think she can be pregnant and still be a witness or a suspect," Sutherland snarked.

Agnes shot him a look.

"What! I'm learning to be sarcastic from Milo."

"If you're going to pick up something from Milo, make it tennis," Agnes blurted.

Mary Alice smiled. "Good line."

A voice in Agnes' head reminded her that Sutherland was her boss. Agnes stood up and excused herself, half wondering if she still had a job. "I need to phone them and tell them to stay with me. It's friendlier, and they can't afford a hotel indefinitely." She walked over to the tennis courts to make her call.

Milo helped himself to several small sandwiches and refilled his lemonade from a fancy tall glass dispenser with a spigot in its very own ice bucket.

As Sutherland reached for a cookie, Mary Alice asked, "Are you happy with the progress of our Miller Trunk development?"

"I haven't checked with Piper in about a week, I'm on a forced vacation…don't ask…but last time I talked with her it seemed to be going well."

Mary Alice nodded. "I think so too. Richard told me he's about to sign the first anchor."

Milo interrupted. "Wait a minute. Are you two in business together?"

Mary Alice smiled. "Why does that surprise you? I told you we're trying to change our image."

Milo laughed. "Well, you couldn't get more squeaky clean than Sutherland."

"Thank you…I think," Sutherland said.

Mary Alice nodded in agreement as she reached for one of the small sandwiches. "I got a strange call yesterday from my brother-in-law, David Bonner."

"Isn't he in jail?" Sutherland asked.

"Inmates can make phone calls," Milo said.

"I did not know that," Sutherland said looking at Mary Alice. "What did he want?"

"He asked me if I knew of a realtor, a woman, who used to sell condos in Atlanta. He made up a silly story about a friend wanting to buy one and forgetting her name."

"Why is that strange?" Sutherland asked.

"He's a thug who worked for James. He has a quick temper, and I doubt he has any friends…at least none who are in the market to buy a condo," Mary Alice explained. "What do you think, Milo?"

"I don't know him," Milo said. *David Bonner is looking for a realtor, and now there's a dead realtor. I hate coincidences.*

"On a more pleasant note," Mary Alice said, "Milo, what do you think of the doggie spa?"

"The residents are friendly, unlike your late husband."

"That's what I think too," she said as the greyhound rested its long slender snout across her legs. She reached down and petted the dog's head as it closed his eyes to nap.

Milo watched Mary Alice, still beautiful, same memorizing blue eyes, blunt and funny but somehow more relaxed. So far he enjoyed being her tennis partner. The greyhound wasn't the only lucky dog at the table.

12

Officially, Leroy Thompson was being taken to a doctor for evaluation of an undisclosed medical problem. In reality he arrived at a conference room in the cop shop where Gramm could question him without alerting other prisoners.

"You've shaved," Gramm quipped, as Leroy was led into the room by two guards. He was in his orange prison outfit with handcuffs but no leg shackles. They were joined by Frank Ugger, Leroy's attorney.

Gramm nodded to the guards who took off Leroy's cuffs and left the room. Leroy ignored Gramm's comment concerning the loss of his goatee.

"So, Leroy why am I here?"

"My client has information about that dead woman you found yesterday, but first we want a deal," Ugger demanded.

Leroy sat rubbing his wrists as if the cuffs had been on for days rather than the five minutes it took to get from the county jail to the police station.

Gramm sighed. He was tired; he didn't get much of a weekend, and doing this dance with Leroy Thompson was old. "What sort of information?"

"What about a deal?" Ugger asked.

"Leroy already got a deal, that's why you're only inside for six months."

"I want out now, and what I got, you want," Leroy pushed.

Gramm sat back. "I tell you what. If your information checks out, I will talk to the DA about letting you out for good behavior. You have had good behavior? Right?"

"Like a friggin' choir boy."

"So, sing choir boy."

Leroy looked around as if there was someone overhearing what he was about to say. He leaned into Gramm. "Some people, dangerous people, were asking about a good lookin' skirt with dark hair who sold stuff in Atlanta, you know condos." He paused waiting for a reaction. Receiving none, he continued. "I don't think they were lookin' to buy."

"Yesterday's dead woman was from Minneapolis."

"Yeah, yeah, now. Maybe she moved. It's the same one, I'm tellin' ya."

Not buying what Leroy was selling, Gramm continued. "You said some people? Who are some people?"

"I don't know. All I know is…people, dangerous people, were lookin' for her and then I read she's dead. I figured they found her."

"How do you know about it?"

Leroy raised his voice, objecting to the question. "I'm Leroy Thompson. People talk to me."

Gramm stifled a laugh. "So, someone—you won't tell me who—was looking to find a female realtor from somewhere, and because we have a dead woman who checks a few of the boxes, you're connecting the dots. I don't think you got much here Leroy."

"I'm telling you, you should be looking for a hitman. If you're lookin' at anyone else, you're wasting your time."

Gramm called in the guards who put the cuffs back on Leroy. "How are you doing without your partner?" Gramm asked referring to the late Stan Shultz.

Leroy stopped without turning around. "I'm Leroy Thompson, I got friends."

Gramm seriously doubted it.

§

The Sunday night poker game originated when Gramm and his buddies were rookie cops. Over the last thirty years, several moved, one died, and one retired, all replaced by civilians. For Gramm the game had always been about camaraderie, relaxation, and good natured competition. It still was.

The round card table was set up for five in the not-spacious-but-cozy living room of Gramm's clapboard three story duplex. The tall, squared-paned, screened windows were open allowing the lake breeze to cool the heated nickel, dime, quarter poker game.

When Gramm bought the duplex twenty-five years ago, the neighborhood was sketchy, but it had seen a revival. Back then, it was close to work, but was no longer as the station had moved up over the hill. Still, nothing in Duluth was more than fifteen or twenty minutes from anything else

Amy's poker snacks were stick-to-the-ribs food. Winter was chili, but summer was hearty cheeses, a meat platter with salami, prosciutto, country ham, toasted salted pecans, and her signature buttermilk corn bread. The setting wasn't as classic as Lakesong's billiard room but was always comfortable and welcoming.

The current five poker players had been together since January. Sutherland, and financial advisor Creedence Durant, joined the veterans of the game, Milo, Gramm, and Feinberg. As they were settling in, Creedence, living up to his cherub like face and body, innocently asked what was new.

Milo was silent, but Sutherland blurted, "Milo beat me at tennis this morning wearing a black Metallica t-shirt!" It was as if he had to get this shame out in the open.

"Thrashed by a thrash metal band. It has a nice symmetry," Creedence mused, popping several salted pecans into his mouth.

"I've been told one never plays Milo in tennis," Gramm informed Sutherland.

"Never…ever…ever play him in tennis," Feinberg echoed, slathering a thick slice of corn bread with soft butter. "He pulverizes me, leaves me for dead."

"How does everyone know this but me?" Sutherland demanded, rolling the salami and prosciutto together like a cigar.

"Now you know," Milo said. "And I'll beat you at poker too. Someone deal."

Feinberg, the big winner at the last game, dealt first, calling for traditional five-card draw. Gramm beamed, being the hater of all gimmicky, wild card games. After a count of two Feinberg added, "Duces wild," just to see Gramm's curmudgeon face scowl.

To heap coal on the fire, he added, "Ernie, the dead woman at Enger Tower, was it murder?"

Ernie picked up his cards and rearranged them in his hand. "Saul, you usually wait a hand or two before asking questions you shouldn't ask."

"Business is slow...I'm bored," Saul said waiting for Rathkey to finish his ham and cheese combo and begin the betting. Milo tossed in a dime chip.

"Same deal as always, information for information?" Gramm offered.

Saul shook his head. "I've got nothing, Ernie. I read she was from Minneapolis."

Gramm added his dime.

Sutherland raised a dime.

Gramm muttered about being surrounded by millionaires.

Sutherland laughed to himself. This old house, nicely updated, was now in a prime neighborhood. Ernie could grumble all he wanted to, but he was house rich. "It's a dime, Ernie!" Sutherland said, having become comfortable with the group and their eccentricities.

"Where were you on Saturday morning?" Ernie countered.

"I told you before, I didn't do it," Sutherland said, raising his hands in mock surrender. "Besides, Milo's my alibi."

"Ugh! Weak. Even I couldn't defend you with that," Feinberg joked.

Creedence put in his twenty cents and pushed up his glasses. Was it a tell or ill-fitting glasses? Milo still didn't know. "The only way I can afford this game is by embezzling all your money," Creedence said. "And Sutherland, you can afford the game because you're flipping condos, and laundering money, on top of being a murder suspect. I read it in the paper."

"You got me. Up to my eyeballs in drug money because that's the way I roll," Sutherland kidded. "By the way Creedence, I read that same article in the Journal."

"It's reached Duluth. Wow, we're big time. I thought it was mainly Miami, Atlanta, and Dallas," Feinberg said. "Yeah guys, I too read the same story."

"Even I might be involved," Gramm added. "Amy found a ten-dollar bill in my pants after they went through the wash."

"That makes Mrs. Gramm the true money launderer," Creedence pointed out.

Gramm shook his head. "I'm not arresting her or my laundering will end."

Feinberg, Rathkey and Gramm added one more dime to the pot.

"Ernie, I agree with you about Amy, but Creedence admitted to embezzling," Feinberg pointed out.

"Don't care. I'm a homicide detective. Give me better cards. These suck!"

Rathkey took three cards as did Gramm. Sutherland took one. Creedence took two, and the bidding began again.

Milo tossed in his cards. "I'm out."

"Ernie, as fun as locking up Creedence and Sutherland would be, you're avoiding my original annoying question. Was it murder?" Feinberg asked again.

"Could be. Could be an accident. Are you looking for paying clients?"

"Paying clients would confuse the king of pro bono," Rathkey said.

"Would screw up his taxes big time. Trust me, I know," Creedence added.

"Thank you, gentlemen, for piling on," Feinberg chided. "I like to be well informed, especially since I heard there was a Koz sighting."

"Koz?" Gramm questioned.

"Kozlov...don't know the first name. Have you never heard of him?"

"Nope. Do I want to?"

"You may. Let's say...several of my clients mentioned his name. From what I gather, he's kind of a fixer for...individuals who have a *problem* that need fixing."

Gramm played with his chips thinking about this afternoon and Leroy Thompson's insistence that the murder of Jessica Vogel was a contracted hit. He wondered if he was getting Rathkey's *coincidence* itch.

"Ernie? Are you with us?" Feinberg questioned. "Murder or an accident?"

Gramm grabbed the last piece of cornbread. "Okay, okay. The Enger Tower thing is murder. We have a couple of suspects but we're always looking for more to join the party."

The bidding continued amid discussions of murder with Creedence and Sutherland pushing the pot to a lofty dollar and a quarter. Creedence's full house wowed the table as he raked in the winnings.

The evening progressed with banter, bidding, and beer and a timeout or two for more meat and cheese. After the final hand, Creedence and Feinberg were the first to leave, with Feinberg telling Milo he should throw that Metallica t-shirt in a landfill.

"Never. It's how I bag all you guys the first time we play."

After Creedence and Feinberg departed, Gramm invited Milo and Sutherland to have a brandy out on his deck.

The view from Gramm's Observation Hill neighborhood had changed—fewer gritty industrial grain elevators and rusty cranes more, parks and sailing friendly resort hotels. The June evening wind had shifted off the lake. Ernie lit the portable fire pit in the center of his deck to take the chill off.

"Ernie, this view is fantastic," Sutherland said, looking at the lights of the harbor.

"We like it," Ernie said. "The salties down by the grain elevators usually keep their lights on all night which adds to the view."

"All we get is the lake and a passing ore boat by Lakesong," Milo said.

"Aww, don't tell me that. I'll feel bad for you all night," Ernie chided. "But we need to talk business. Let me tell you where we are with this case."

"Should I be here?" Sutherland questioned.

"Absolutely not, but you are, so everything you hear is confidential," Gramm gruffed. "You kept your mouth shut during the Bonner case, so I think I can trust you."

Sutherland was pleased.

"Moscatelli admits choking the victim. She doesn't have an alibi...says she was jogging. We also talked with that teacher, Paul Kendrick. He admits to having an affair with the dead woman when she was a teenager. He also admits to being blackmailed by her."

"Alibi?" Rathkey asked.

"None."

"My money's on him," Sutherland said.

"Don't get ahead of yourself," Milo admonished, something he did often with Sutherland.

"But my latest concern is a brief visit with Leroy Thompson. Remember him?" Ernie sipped his brandy and sat back waiting for a reaction.

Milo stared. The fire crackled. Sutherland was quick to react. "Leroy Thompson knows something about this woman's death? How? Isn't he still in jail?"

"He is. He wanted to bargain."

"With what?" Milo asked.

"According to Leroy, the woman's death was a hit—you know a contracted murder."

"How would he know?" Milo asked.

"He wouldn't say."

"A hit? Like in the movies? Was it this Koz guy?" Sutherland guessed, enjoying the hitman theory.

Milo shook his head. "Both you and Thompson need to stop watching too many bad movies. Hitmen do not come to Duluth, but I do have another piece to your puzzle Ernie."

Gramm was interested. "Do tell?"

"After the infamous tennis game," Milo said looking at Sutherland, "Mary Alice told us about a call from David Bonner asking about a realtor from Atlanta."

Without comment, Gramm picked up his phone and called White. She was less than pleased to receive a call at this hour. "Yeah?"

"Tomorrow check to see who has called or visited Leroy Thompson and David Bonner in jail. It could be tied to the murder. Also, does our victim have any ties to Atlanta?"

"Couldn't this wait until morning?" White questioned.

"It's important. Now we both know it's important."

White yawned. "I have to teach you how to text." She hung up.

Gramm turned back to his guests. "Forgetting the hitman theory, what are your thoughts about the regular old-fashioned motives for murder—the councilman's wife, the ex-army woman, the sister, or the teacher?"

"It's a tossup," Milo said, "but there's something nagging at me—something that doesn't add up. I can't tell you what it is. It's been there for a while."

Ernie was used to the way Milo's brain worked and knew he had to be patient. "When the back of your brain talks to the front of your brain, let me know."

"I still like the hitman theory!" Sutherland persisted.

13

Gramm poured himself a second cup of coffee from the break room. His routine afforded one cup per day except Mondays, the result of his weekly, late Sunday night poker game.

"How'd you do?" Sergeant White asked as she came into his office.

"Do?"

"At the poker game?"

Gramm sighed. "Won some. Lost some. Lost some more."

White smiled. "Isn't that what you always say?"

"That's pretty much what always happens. I think those millionaires cheat."

"Millionaires?"

"You know, McKnight, Rathkey, Feinberg. I don't know about that Durant guy, but I know he handles the millionaires' money."

"I've got answers for you," White said sitting down.

"Already?" Gramm question.

"Some of us were not up all night losing seventy-five cents."

"A dollar ten, if you must know."

"Tragic, but let's get down to the questions from your much-too-late phone call."

"I don't think you're afraid of me anymore," Gramm complained.

"Never was," White answered. "As for our victim and the city of Atlanta, the answer is yes. She used to sell real estate in Atlanta."

"How do you know that?"

"I called her boss in Minneapolis."

"When did she work in Atlanta?"

"She left about ten years ago."

Gramm sighed. "What about visitors to Leroy and Bonner?"

"Leroy is blank. No incoming phone calls, no visitors. Bonner has had one visitor, a guy named Ron Jones. According to the sign-in sheet, he stayed for about ten minutes."

"Ron Jones? They're not even trying. Why not Jack Smith?" Gramm complained.

"Okay, now tell me what this is all about," White said.

Gramm filled her in on Leroy's claim of a hitman killing their victim and then Feinberg's mention of a fixer named Kozlov. White seemed doubtful before Gramm added Milo's information about the Bonner call to Mary Alice.

"What the hell is going on here?" White asked.

"We may be adding two and two and getting five, but our victim comes from Atlanta, is a realtor, and seems to fit the description except for the hair. It's not totally dark."

White laughed. "Those are ombre highlights. They're added at the salon. Her roots are dark, her hair is dark."

Gramm lifted his arms behind his head and stretched out his back, which these days always seemed to be stiff. He added a yawn. "Okay, we can add a hitman to our list, but we have no motive. Also, since when do murder-for-hire guys push their victim down the stairs in a public park?"

White smiled, watching her boss try to wake up. "Could be he wanted it to look like an accident."

"Not on Doc Smith's watch. He says murder. He has yet to be wrong," Gramm said. "Let's not abandon our other suspects, number one being the sleeping sightseer in the tower."

"Maureen Donahue," White responded.

"Yeah, her. She has means, opportunity, and after you spotted her picture in the victim's phone, she has motive. I think we should invite her up here for a formal interview. I never bought her excuse of enjoying the view."

"She does have the magic three."

§

Milo was awakened early to the sounds of motors, clatter, and shouting. Peering out the window he saw a delivery truck positioned precariously on an angle while sections of decking were being piled up by workmen pulling handcarts. Milo couldn't see her, but Agnes was on the terrace pointing while a man next to her shouted directions through a walkie-talkie.

Milo hadn't figured the wedding would cost him sleep.

Realizing the noise wasn't going away, he dressed and headed for breakfast. His usual breakfast companion, Annie, was nowhere to be found. Milo thought all the clamor may have thrown her off her bacon.

"Where's the cat?" he asked Martha as he entered the kitchen.

"She's over at my place. Today's going to be noise, open doors, people in and out—hubbub and chaos—not conducive to a cat that sleeps twenty-three hours a day in peace and quiet."

"Did she tell you that?" Milo asked.

"She did. When the first truck arrived, she meowed at the basement door, and trotted her butt down to the tunnel. She wanted to go to my house. She's been there before. As a kitten she followed the sibs from time to time to get a second breakfast, or to escape construction when the house was being remodeled. She'll be back this afternoon. The sibs call me and let me know Annie is coming through the tunnel. I go down to open the door for her."

"Wedding week has descended upon us," Sutherland called from the morning room.

Milo joined him, poured a cup of coffee and asked, "Other than losing sleep, what does that mean for us?"

"It means we stay out of the way. Agnes and Martha have this; we're excess baggage."

"Good to know. I think my ex-wife referred to me as excess baggage more than once."

"You're used to it. Good," Sutherland said. "I'm not. I'll be glad when it's over."

"You both understand that it hasn't even started yet," Martha said from the kitchen. "This is just one delivery truck. Agnes has a schedule. They'll be arriving all week."

"What will be arriving all week?" Milo asked.

"Trucks today. Electricians tomorrow."

"Electricians? It's a wedding. What do we need electricians for?" Milo complained.

Martha rolled her eyes. "Oh, I don't know, lighting, sound systems, you know stuff like that."

"I thought it was an exchange of I do's and a few flowers. You know, a wedding."

"Don't go there," Sutherland admonished. "I said that to Agnes."

"Bad?"

"She gave me a look that took two years off my life."

"Okay then," Milo agreed. "What does excess baggage get to eat?"

"I figured a half lumberjack because of your tennis workout," Martha said, handing him his eggs, bacon, and hash browns to which Milo added two Excedrin.

Sutherland laughed. "I knew I ran you all over the court."

"No, I'm stiff from standing still."

Sutherland smiled but side stepped Milo's criticism of his game. "How are we doing on the Annie Patterson front?"

"Calling my guy this morning."

"Good," Sutherland said, going back to his paper.

Something big fell off a truck with the crash, followed by swearing.

Milo winced. "I've gotten used to Lakesong's peace and quiet. I'll be glad when this wedding is over."

"Incredible!" Sutherland said, shaking his head. "You're grumbling? This wedding is all your fault."

§

After breakfast and before his swim, Milo called private detective Joe Ripkowski, a colleague who took over most of Milo's clients. He had already hired Joe to research the disappearance of Annie Patterson.

After the hellos and thanks for the work, Joe gave Milo the scant news. "There was nothing about a missing daughter in the newspaper files. Patterson was mentioned a number of times for business and stuff like that, but nothing about a missing daughter. Then I checked with the cops. You must have a lot of pull, Milo, because they let me go through their old boxes of files. It was dusty."

"Did you find anything?"

"I did. The police investigated the disappearance of Patterson's wife and child after her sister filed a missing person report. The cops back then were suspicious of Patterson… you know…like maybe he offed them."

"Really?"

"Lt. Gramm let me take the box to give to you. Oh, before I forget, with all that work you sent me when you left the business, I'm taking the family on vacation this week!"

"Good for you, Joe."

"Yeah, the kids are excited. I hate to ask this, but would you follow Heidi for me while we're gone? It's summer, and Heidi is rockin' her bikini. Harry's going crazy. Good for business, but I already booked a cabin in Moose Lake."

Harry Reinakie, the Cadillac king of Duluth had been Milo's bread and butter client. He was always suspicious of his much younger wife, Heidi, and wanted her followed. It was an easy gig. She never cheated.

"Sure. It will be like old times. Is she still as predictable as she always was?"

"Pilates, the nail place, the coffee shop, and an occasional dry-cleaning pick-up on wild and crazy days. I'm not complaining mind you."

"Good to know. Some things never change."

"I'll pay you what Harry pays me."

"Don't need it."

"Yeah, I heard about your inheritance. Thanks, that is generous of you. Oh Milo, there's one more thing."

"What?"

"One of the cops that investigated Patterson back in the day was named Karl Rathkey. Any relation?"

Milo was silent.

"Milo?"

"Yeah, Joe…thanks for the info. Have a good trip with the family. Oh, and drop the box by the house before you go."

"It's that Lakesong estate on London Road…right?"

"Yeah that's it."

"So, who's Karl Rathkey?"

"My father."

§

Cliff had been silent all through breakfast. Maureen had made his favorite: blueberry pancakes with fresh blueberry compote. He accepted a second cup of coffee and added his cream and two teaspoons of sugar while Maureen poured herself a cup. Cliff pushed his empty plate toward the middle of the table. She removed it and put it in the dishwasher.

"Your hair looks awful. Get it done," Cliff ordered as he drank the last of his coffee and pushed it toward the center of the table.

Maureen said nothing as she went to pick up the cup. Cliff slammed his hands on the table and stared at her. She knew that look. Her heart pounded.

In measured tones Cliff began, "Why do you keep sabotaging my life! All you have to do is stay sober and look as pretty as my money can buy! It can't be that tough!"

"I…I'm sorry," Maureen whispered.

His measured tones became louder and his eyes colder. "You were drunk at Enger Tower Saturday morning! My wife was so damn drunk she had to be taken home by a cop!" Cliff stood. "Did you think I wouldn't find out?"

Maureen, cowered, remained silent, and held her breath.

Cliff stormed out. Maureen reached for a bottle she hid behind the cereal. She poured the gin into her empty juice glass and was on her second gulp when Cliff barged through the door from the garage. "I forgot my damn speech!" he yelled. "You've got me so damn mad, I'm making mistakes."

Maureen tried to hide the drink, but it was too late. Cliff saw it and knocked the drink out of her hand, the glass shattering against the wall, shards flying onto the counter and floor.

"What did I do to be cursed with you!" he screamed, grabbing her by the hair on the back of her head. Throwing her aside, he threatened, "Get it together Maureen!"

She backed away and put the marble kitchen island between them.

"Pick up all this damn glass!" Cliff yelled, grabbing the bottle and smashing it against Maureen's prized porcelain farmer's sink. "This isn't over!"

Maureen ducked, her arms shielding her head as the ricocheting glass exploded out of the sink. Cliff snatched his speech from the island, his feet crushing broken glass as he stomped out the door.

The kitchen was silent.

§

Breanna and Martha waited in the hallway of the mathematics building at the University of Minnesota-Duluth. The previous applicant emerged looking dejected. Martha glanced at her younger sister, trying to gauge any dropping in confidence. There was none.

The office door opened again. A young teaching assistant peeked out. "Breanna? Dr. Bixby will see you now."

Martha and Breanna entered the office. Bixby, a seventy-something math professor, was sitting behind her desk. Breanna offered a handshake. It was ignored.

"Breanna Gibbson?" Dr. Bixby asked.

"Yes," Breanna said, starting to sit.

"Don't sit!" Bixby ordered.

Breanna bounced up.

"There is a mathematical proposition on the white board. Prove it true or false. You have thirty minutes."

Martha watched as Breanna wrote and erased, wrote and erased. Dr. Bixby paid no attention. Martha's stomach was tight. She had worked under various types of executive chefs—good, bad, and ugly. The verdict was out on Dr. Bixby. Maybe Breanna was being ignored because she didn't fit the criteria. Martha gathered her courage, got up, and softly spoke to Dr. Bixby not wanting to interrupt Breanna's thinking. "Professor, I hope the fact we live on the Lakesong estate doesn't influence your decision. I work on the estate. I do not own the estate."

Dr. Bixby looked up and spoke in a loud voice. "It doesn't matter."

Breanna glanced at the duo. Martha sat down with no more information, but Dr. Bixby taught her not to interrupt the process. Martha settled in to watch Breanna work, serious to a fault, the image of their mother. She even touched her temple with her fingertips when thinking.

After thirty minutes a simple kitchen egg timer rang. "Time's up," Bixby called, turning around.

"I didn't solve it yet," Breanna complained.

Bixby glanced at the white board. "No, you didn't."

Breanna kept working.

Martha stepped in. "Breanna, Honey, the time is up."

Breanna turned around. "I know that Martha. I want to solve it."

Martha looked at the professor who appeared to be reading a journal. "Is it okay if she continues?"

Dr. Bixby didn't look up. "Of course."

Martha stood. "Breanna, I'm going to the student union to get something to eat. Join me when this is over."

Breanna waved.

"Did the other two applicants solve the problem?" Martha asked the professor.

Bixby didn't answer.

Martha left shaking her head. *Dr. Bixby failed courtesy*

§

"I told Donahue we want to see her today," White said, sitting down in Gramm's favorite booth at Gustafson's. "She either just woke up or was drinking her lunch, so I told her not to drive…to take a cab or Lyft…whatever."

"I think the lady has a problem," Gramm shouted over the lunch crowd noise.

"Is it me or is this place getting louder?" White shouted back.

"It's you," Gramm said, grabbing a sliding menu Pat, the waitress, threw across the table on her way past.

"Be right back," she shouted. "New deal, specials are written on the inside."

Gramm looked offended. "She doesn't tell us? Where's the personal touch?"

White chided. "Is this a big change for you? Do you need time to process it?"

Gramm laughed. "My whole world has been shattered."

"While you're healing, I have another revelation for you. Moscatelli does not show up running at Lakewalk Saturday morning, and you can add to that, Brooks wasn't in the restaurant," White said.

Gramm bushy eyebrows became one. He didn't like lies.

Pat returned. "Where's Milo?"

"Busy I guess," Gramm said.

"Too bad. His is one order I don't have to write down," she said, referring to Rathkey's constant order of hot meatloaf sandwich, mashed potatoes, green beans, lots of gravy.

White ordered a Cobb salad and iced tea.

Gramm smiled. "I've never tried it. Give me the Milo special but not so much gravy."

Pat stared at him. "Diet Coke, like Milo?"

"Naw, just water."

Pat put her hands on her hips. "Are you going to eat the green beans or push them to the edge of the plate like Milo?"

"I'm sorry he does that. I eat my green beans, honest."

Pat left.

"Why are you apologizing for Milo's eating habits?" White asked.

"Anything connected to Milo and restaurants...I don't know...I feel I have to apologize."

White laughed.

"While you were talking to Donahue, I talked to the FBI in Atlanta. In fact, they called me," Gramm said.

"The Atlanta FBI? Why?"

"They are investigating money laundering and are looking for several real estate people who participated in this scheme ten...fifteen years ago. One of them was a woman named Jessica Berg, also known as Jessica Raymond."

"Didn't Agnes Larson say our victim's name was Raymond?" White asked, checking her notes. "Yes, I got it here. In high school her name was Raymond."

"I told them the name Raymond was familiar. The agent said Raymond and Berg were the same person because Jessica Raymond married a man named Phillip Berg while in Atlanta. I sent them a copy of our victim's fingerprints to be sure."

"Do we need to talk to Phillip Berg?" White asked.

"I already did it. He told me he was only married to her for a year. Here's why the Feds are interested in her. Berg thought she was making a lot of money, more money than her job paid, but she refused to talk about it."

"He thought?" White asked. "Don't you know if your spouse is bringing in a lot of money that wasn't there before?"

"Not in their case. He said she refused to combine personal bank accounts. All he knew was she sold condos especially for one developer. When they were getting divorced, there were two suspicious deaths in that company that freaked her out, and she left town."

"Who died?"

"I've got the names in my notes. One was the main financial guy who died from a fall at a construction site. The other was the company president who died in a boating accident," Gramm said.

"Our victim was involved in money laundering, freaked out over two deaths, left town, and changed her name to Vogel. I hate to say this, but the hitman theory is becoming a real possibility."

Gramm sighed and shook his head. "Once again we have good, solid suspects with motives, and we're chasing shadowy bad guys."

The food arrived, and Gramm dug into his Milo special. After a few mouthfuls, Gramm offered his critique. "It's good, but it's heavy. I prefer my Reuben and fries."

Between bites of salad, White asked if Berg and his wife had remained in contact. Gramm said Berg didn't even know Jessica was in Minnesota. "He said she called only once asking if anyone was looking for her."

"Was anyone looking for her?" White asked.

"Not that he knew…green beans are good."

"Milo would not agree," White laughed.

§

Danielle barged in, letting the screen door slam as she headed for the refrigerator and a cold energy drink. Sweat was still beading on her upper lip and forehead. She had finished an intense five-mile ride but was upset at not beating her best time.

Grabbing the drink and wiping her face with the front of her shirt, she walked through the kitchen to the four-seasons room. Larry was deep into his computer. There was a time when they first met in college, Larry was the most exciting person in her life. Not anymore. The future they planned was not the life they were living, and she was sick of Duluth and Larry's withdrawal. "Larry, what are you looking at?"

Larry looked up. "Nothing. Just looking."

Danielle walked over and sat down next to him. "Looking at the G-Trek website? So, Sutherland's new bike does bother you."

"Look at that price! Over charging for crap! It's not worth it!"

Danielle slammed his computer shut. "Stop! Just stop! You're sitting on your ass upset because your millionaire friend bought a damn bike. I'm trying to get enough endorphins to erase the trauma of Saturday!"

Larry put the computer aside.

Danielle ignored the gesture. "My brain is going numb. In fact, I wanna get out of here. I'm beginning to hate this town. I want bigger."

Larry rolled his eyes. They've had this fight so many times, it was like following a script in a bad play.

"Did you hear me? I said I want to leave."

"I like it here. I have the shop and you have your interior design business."

Danielle walked over, looking down at him. "So, my trauma Saturday morning doesn't bother you?"

"Of course, it bothers me, but it was a onetime thing. What are the chances of it happening again?"

"What were the chances of it happening once?" Danielle shot back.

14

aureen was more careful this time. She heard the garage door open, Cliff's car start, and the garage door close. She crossed to the dining room window and watched as the car disappeared down the street. Waiting a few more minutes to make sure he wasn't coming back, she bolted into the laundry room and unearthed another bottle to steady her nerves. Her hands shaking, she gulped the piney liquid, sliding down to the floor, her back supported by the drier.

She wished she could take the bottle upstairs, lie down, and make the day go away, but she couldn't. The police called earlier. She had to go and talk about Saturday. What a joke. If she could remember what happened Saturday morning, this would be easier. Was it the gin or cold fear that gripped her stomach as she lurched to the laundry sink and threw up?

Her phone chirped. The Lyft driver was in her driveway. She stashed her bottle for later, grabbed her purse and extra breath mints before heading out the door. Appropriate makeup repairs could be made in the car.

They need me to fill out a report. What do I say? Can I make it up?

§

Sergeant White spotted an out-of-place memory card on her cleared desk when she returned from lunch. She held it up. "Anybody know who this is from?" she yelled to the room.

One of the IT techs stood up. "It was from a photographer. He said you owe him a subpoena."

"Thanks, but next time put a label on it," White said, sitting down and putting the card in her computer.

Gramm, having heard the exchange, came out of his office and looked over her shoulder.

Watching the drone camera's high, wide shot, White said, "We've got to get one of these."

They watched as the drone flew toward the harbor, dipped down, turned around and came back before gaining altitude and making one loop around the tower. The drone picked up speed, flew over Reggie and came straight down. They could see him operating the controls. Then the video went black.

"I'll play this again in slow motion; I saw two people besides Reggie in that video," White said.

"Do it. Let's see if we can identify anyone."

White played the video at half speed. When the drone came back up the embankment a jogger could be seen running between a clump of trees. The drone was climbing, but White paused the video on the best frame. The jogger appeared to be female with short, dark hair, wearing a bright orange jacket and shoes.

"I wonder what Moscatelli wears when she runs?" White mused "It kinda looks like her."

Gramm agreed. "It's worth an inquiry. Can we stop it on the other person, the one by the tower?"

White started the video and stopped when the shot was coming around the tower. The drone was much higher now, and the person could be seen running toward the parking lot.

"Is that our witness?" Gramm asked.

"The drone is up so high it's hard to tell. All I see is what could be a dark pony tail—could be me, you in a wig, or my brother. He has long hair too," White joked.

She continued the video. The drone jerked, turned around, and came at Reggie. The video went off as it landed.

Gramm looked upset. "If he hadn't called back the drone right after the scream, we might have video of the murder. Have a tech make stills of the two people we found and check for anything we may have missed."

"We have to check Moscatelli's running gear," White added.

"While we're casting a wide net, see what your brother was doing Saturday morning."

"Can't be him. He doesn't run—bad ankles."

§

Pre-inheritance, Milo made a portion of his living searching for people, usually wayward spouses. Men were easier than women because they rarely changed their names. Bennie

Parsons, the young boy on the wall with John McKnight, died in 2009 but a more extensive search found Susan Reading, now Gordon, alive and living in Albert Lea, Minnesota.

Milo called her and introduced himself. "I am trying to find a girl you knew as a child—Annie Patterson. We have a picture of you sitting on a wall with her at her home called Lakesong, on London Road in Duluth. I think you were eight or nine."

She paused. Milo wasn't sure she was still on the phone until she said, "I don't remember. Why are you looking for her?"

"My client, John McKnight, wanted me to find her."

"Oh, I remember John. I grew up with John. It would be fun to see that picture and it might help me remember. Wait, I have my son here, he can tell you how to send it to me."

After a few minutes of following her son's directions, the picture appeared on Susan Gordon's phone. "Oh, I remember this!" she said. "That's Bennie Parsons, me, John and... that girl."

"That girl?" Milo asked.

"Yeah, I can't remember her name, but I do remember my parents making me go and play with her. I thought she was strange. You know kids can be cruel and I was no different, I'm sorry to say."

"How do you mean strange?"

"She liked boy stuff. Rough and tumble. More of a tomboy than I was. Bennie and John liked that, but then she would start to cry for no reason. Bennie hated that. She wasn't hurt. We hadn't been mean to her. It was odd and confusing to us. We played board games, but once she started playing, she wouldn't let it end. She kept playing the same game over and over again. We would get bored and want to go home. I only played with her a few times. I think John played with her more. Why does John want to find her?"

"She disappeared, and he wanted to know what happened," Milo explained.

"I didn't know she disappeared. It was so many years ago. I tell you one thing I remember, she never played with us alone. Either her father was watching or the nanny. Neither seemed very friendly. The nanny took her away every time she got upset. I was never happy when I was over there…kinda scary. When I stopped having to go. I didn't mind. She had a lot of toys, but it wasn't worth it."

"What about her mother?"

"Hmm, now that you mention it, I don't remember her mother. She was never around, only the father and the nanny. By the way, how is John?"

"I'm afraid he died last year."

"I'm sorry to hear that. I hear it a lot these days."

Milo hung up with more questions than answers. *Could Susan's childhood memories be trusted? Was it a scary place? If so, why did John continue to play there? Why did he buy Lakesong? Why would he ask me to find Annie?*

Sutherland came into Milo's office carrying the blueprint tube they had found on Friday. "These blueprints are of this house," he announced.

"Anything interesting?" Milo asked.

Sutherland unrolled them and flipped to the drawing of the basement. "Yeah, look at this."

Milo was not a student of architectural drawings. "A lot of white lines. Fascinating."

"Lucky for you, I know how to read these."

"A man of many talents. I'm impressed."

Sutherland pursed his lips in a half smile. "With these you will not be able to surprise me about things in my own house. Over here," Sutherland pointed to the right corner of the blueprint, "is the now infamous elevator I knew nothing about."

"I knew about it."

"Nearby is the hidden kitchen, which looks like it was meant to be the main kitchen when the house was built. Another interesting item is on the other side of the house." Sutherland moved to his left and pointed to a large room.

"A big blue blob. What makes this interesting?"

"This is the vault, only it wasn't the vault then. It was only a large room but follow these dotted lines leading from the vault to the lake." Sutherland looked pleased with himself.

"Oh my god!" Milo exclaimed. "Dotted white lines. Why didn't you say so earlier! I am overcome with joy. Is joy the right emotion?"

"Maybe, but it's my joy. The dotted lines indicate a tunnel which looks to have been added at some point in time. I didn't know it existed, and you didn't know it existed either. So, I've got one up on you, Detective Rathkey!"

"Actually, I'm ahead. I had both the elevator and the kitchen but go ahead, enjoy your moment."

"I am. Thank you," said Sutherland. "The tunnel leads to a boat house and dock which no longer exists. The current boat house must have been built much later a little north of this tunnel."

"All this blueprint stuff is fun, but I actually did some work today," Milo said, filling Sutherland in on Susan Gordon's recollections of Annie Patterson.

As Milo spoke, Sutherland's face became serious. "What you're telling me is disturbing. Mrs. Gordon thought the father and the nanny were scary?"

"She was a child. All adults are scary when you're a child."

"My adults weren't." Sutherland combined his tunnel discovery with Susan Gordon's information. "We may have a grim reality here. If her father or nanny murdered her, Annie's remains are in the tunnel."

Milo stared at him. "What did I just say that would lead you to child murder?"

"What do you mean? Her father was scary. The Nanny was aggressive. Mother and daughter disappeared. It all fits! We have to find that tunnel!"

"Of course. One plus one equals twenty-two. Let's go!"

"Great!"

"I'm kidding! Do you expect to find dead bodies in this make-believe tunnel?"

"It's all possible!"

"Stop, Nancy Drew! Before we settle on your theory, let's look through the police file from that time."

"You have it?" Sutherland was surprised.

Milo reached under the desk to retrieve the box supplied by Joe Ripkowski.

Opening it up, Milo lifted up three thin files. He was surprised it was so sparse. "This is it? Not much."

Sutherland took one, and Milo looked through the other two. "These are the reports of the three investigating officers," Milo said.

"Three? Isn't that a lot?" Sutherland asked.

"It is these days. Maybe this Patterson guy was a bigwig, and they were making sure they covered their bases."

Sutherland began looking through his file. "Milo?"

"Yeah?"

"This file is signed by a Detective Sergeant Karl Rathkey. Any relation?"

"Yeah, my father."

"Oh. I didn't know—you never mention him."

"He died when I was eight. He was shot," Milo said not looking up.

"How horrible. Who shot him?"

"Don't know…never solved."

"Milo?"

"Yeah?"

"You're a detective. Shouldn't you solve it?"

"It was a long time ago. I was a child. I've been busy."

Sutherland let it go. It was a discussion for another time. "Your father says Patterson's wife, Adeline, and child were last seen by a friend in October 1954."

"Yeah these other reports say the same. The detective in charge indicated he thinks it could be foul play but nothing could be proved. He repeats what we read earlier, no money was missing, and she didn't use credit cards."

"It's time to go to the tunnel," Sutherland urged.

§

Maureen's confidence returned as she sat in the police interview room. Her makeup was free of tear stains. The blond tendrils shaken loose by Cliff this morning were smoothed back in a sophisticated pony tail with a pink ribbon. Her fingers moved up and down the straight, narrow crease in her white summer slacks. She felt public perfect.

Gramm was about to enter the room when White handed him a sheet of paper. "I was right," White said. "Mrs. Donahue was being blackmailed by the victim. Vogel had protected her email with a common encryption which forensics broke this morning."

Gramm looked at the emails and nodded. "This may wrap it up."

"There's more. Kendrick also threated our victim recently by email."

"Of course," Gramm muttered, seeing his easy case once again getting murky.

Maureen smiled as the two cops walked in. "Good afternoon," she said, with as much cheer as she could muster. Her stomach began to burn again. She reached into her purse for an antacid.

Gramm and White sat down opposite her with White placing a manila folder on the table.

"I've come in to write my report as you requested, but I don't know how this works. Do I write it long hand, or do I dictate it to someone?"

"Thank you for coming in," Gramm said. "We'll get to that report, but first, we have a small problem you can help us with."

"Certainly. What do you need?"

White opened her folder, took out the picture of young Maureen and slid it over to her. "We need you to explain this."

Maureen's stomach clenched. She spun around and threw up into a nearby waste basket.

Gramm looked shocked and attempted to stand, but White put her hand on his shoulder and said, "Wait she's not finished."

Maureen continued to heave. After several minutes she apologized and said she was ill. White pushed a box of tissues to her, picked up the waste basket, and left the room. Maureen wiped her face and took two breath mints from her purse.

White re-entered the room with a fresh waste basket and placed it closer to Maureen who apologized again. "I must have the summer flu."

White offered her a bottle of water, which she accepted and took a small sip. Taking a tissue, she dabbed at tears which had rolled down her face and tried to push back the hair that had escaped from the crisp pink-ribboned pony tail during the convulsions. Her public perfect persona had taken a hit.

Gramm, who doubted the summer flu theory, continued the interview. "What can you tell us about that picture?"

Maureen glanced at it before turning it over. "Nothing. It's a young girl…looks pornographic…why are you showing me this?"

White scanned the ceiling, took a deep breath, stared at Maureen and continued calmly. "It's a picture of you, Mrs. Donahue. A picture taken by your teacher, Paul Kendrick, and used by your classmate, Jessica Vogel, to blackmail you."

"That's preposterous! I don't look anything like that poor girl," Maureen complained, adjusting the collar on her pink and white striped blouse.

"But you did," White countered, sliding another picture across the table. "This is your yearbook picture, Mrs. Donahue. Do you see the resemblance?"

Maureen closed her eyes. *This has to end. I want to get away.*

"We don't fault you. You were a victim," White said. "But in trying to hide this picture, you have motive for killing someone who threatened to make it public."

"Blackmail? That's ridiculous!"

Gramm jumped in. "We have the emails Vogel sent you and your responses. In one you threaten her. Can we please stop with the lying?"

White read a portion of one email. "If you keep threatening me, this will end badly for you."

"Sounds like a threat to me," Gramm said.

Maureen looked around the room like a caged cat. "I didn't come here for this! I want to make my statement and go home!" She started to rise.

"Sit down!" White yelled. "We are not done!"

Maureen flinched and sat down.

Gramm came forward in his chair. "Mrs. Donahue, you were at the scene of a murder. You could have pushed Ms. Vogel down the stairs and then walked back into the tower. And with the blackmail, you have a serious motive."

Did I push her? I can't be arrested. Cliff will kill me! "I'm not the only one!" She blurted. "I overheard Liz Brooks arranging to have Jessica killed."

Gramm and White were silent.

Maureen continued manically, "She was on the phone. She said she wanted to go ahead with the plan. She wanted Jessica to feel pain. Jessica killed her sister! Liz hated her!"

Gramm got up and motioned for White to join him in the hall for a conference. "Another hitman? How many damn hitmen can go after one woman? I'm surprised they didn't kill each other in the crossfire."

"Brooks and her husband run a software company. I doubt either of them knows how to hire a paid assassin," White said. "Still, we'll have to check it out."

"She already lied about where she was Saturday morning. Can we trust her?" Gramm asked.

"Absolutely not."

Gramm laughed at White. She was picking up his distaste for people who lie. "For the moment, let's get Maureen's statement—the true statement—on the record."

Maureen agreed to give a corrected statement of Saturday morning's events to include the fact that she was there to meet Jessica Vogel. She stuck to her story that she was at the top of the tower waiting, and Jessica never showed up. She failed to mention that after arriving at the tower she began to drink and remembered nothing until she was found by police.

15

As Martha predicted, Lakesong was host to trucks, equipment, and workers all day. Not predicted was Linda Baer, the bride's grandmother who showed up unannounced stopping Milo's and Sutherland's tunnel hunting. Both men were somewhat annoyed but played perfect hosts to the petite lady who resembled a teamster.

"So, which one of you is Raymond and which one is Saturday?" Linda asked.

"Ah neither," Sutherland said, a little confused by the question. "I'm Sutherland McKnight and he is Milo Rathkey."

Linda eyeballed them without apology before sitting down in the Gallery and accepting a cup of coffee, cream, two sugars. "Looking at you two, I would bet that you," pointing at Milo, "know my ex-husband."

Rathkey laughed and nodded at Sutherland. "Why not him?"

"Looks too innocent."

Sutherland was not pleased. Why couldn't he know a mobster?

"Let me get to the point, and I'll get out of your way," Linda said. "I want to thank you both for helping my granddaughter. I want to make sure that my ex-husband does not touch Brittany or Joe's life in any way."

"What exactly are you worried about?" Sutherland asked. "From experience, I know Morrie has a knack for dragging people into his dark world."

"Morrie told me he's showing up to the wedding and leaving. There will be no dragging," Milo said.

"Yeah right," Linda said, not believing it for a minute. "Don't play me for a sucker, Buster. You and I both know Morrie is constantly followed by cops, and anyone associated with him is also followed by cops. When I remarried and started the trucking company, the cops were sure it was a front for Morrie. We were followed for years. I want to make sure neither of you guys work for Morrie or are associated with his illegal business."

"Neither of us works with or for your ex-husband. Milo assured me we are simply doing your granddaughter a favor," Sutherland said.

"Besides, like I said, Morrie's coming to the wedding and then leaving," Milo repeated.

"So, no Morrie money is exchanging hands?" Linda asked.

"Not a penny."

"I don't believe you." Her look was frightening. If she had been Morrie, both Sutherland and Milo would be on their way to the trunk of a car. "Why is catering suddenly costing much less than it did at the other venue?"

Sutherland shrugged. "If that's true, then I would say Martha, our chef, isn't charging you a fee. However, a nice tip might be in order."

"And the wedding planner? That bill's half."

"That's our house manager, Agnes. She may not be billing you either, only charging you for her assistant Margaret. Another nice tip perhaps," Sutherland suggested. "If you want to know for sure, Agnes and Margaret are in the back supervising. You can ask them."

"I will," Linda said getting up. "I don't mean to be ungrateful, but Morrie's influence is already popping up. Brittany and Joe went to talk to financial aid at the U of M. They're entering medical school in the fall. Their tuition has already been paid—four damn years—all of it. No loans, no financial aid will be needed. Where do you think that money came from?"

"Isn't that a good thing?" Sutherland questioned.

Milo knew it wasn't. "I understand your worry. I do. If I had to guess, I would say the tuition was a wedding present."

"A useless silver tray would have made me feel better."

"Why don't you ask him if the tuition payment was a wedding present?" Sutherland suggested.

Linda looked at him. "Do you like to talk to Morrie?"

"I've never met him," Sutherland blurted.

Linda laughed. "Where's your back door? I have to go talk to Angie and Maggie."

§

Sutherland handed Rathkey one of two flashlights—big ones that used dry cells and gave off wide beams of light. "We are going to need these," he said to Milo.

"For what? I have a cell phone. It has a flashlight. Where'd you even get these?"

"Dad's emergency stash. You know, in case the lights go out, or if the world ends. He has stuff in the garage."

"You're thinking we're going to find this imaginary tunnel, aren't you?"

"It's not imaginary. It's on the blueprints. Blueprints don't lie." Sutherland was adamant.

"I'm thinking they closed it off years ago. The original boathouse is gone. I bet the tunnel is too."

"We've already had this conversation. Let's go."

Milo spent the walking time turning his flashlight on and off to annoy Sutherland. It worked.

After about ten SOS flashes he heard, "Stop that! You'll wear out the battery."

"In five hundred years, maybe! This puppy is huge and heavy. It could replace Split Rock lighthouse," Milo complained.

Sutherland typed in the code on the vault door keypad, waited for the familiar click, and opened the thick door. The light came on. "I'm hoping the tunnel has these automatic lights."

"The imaginary tunnel has imaginary lights now!" Milo laughed.

At Sutherland's direction, the next thirty minutes were spent in the Patterson area of the vault, moving two small tables, a cabinet, a child's rocker, and two steamer trunks along with various boxes.

"This is part of the 'get Milo to exercise' plot, isn't it?" Milo again complained.

Sutherland was busy looking at the recently revealed wall. He was hoping to find a door. No such luck. The wall was a continuation of the rest of the vault, floor to ceiling cabinets and drawers decorated with Scandinavian wood carvings.

"No door," Milo stated the obvious. "Good plan, enjoyed the exercise, let's get a snack."

"Wait a minute, there could be a secret latch." Sutherland began opening the drawers and cabinets.

"Try your secret decoder ring," Milo snarked as he sat on one of the Patterson's tables, dangling his legs.

"You sit there being all smug. When the door to the tunnel opens, you'll drop that pompous attitude," Sutherland said, rifling through the drawers.

"Are you going to go through each drawer?" Milo asked, noticing they were floor to ceiling.

"Yup."

"Anything interesting in them?"

"Most are empty, but several are filled with wooden toys, silverware, clothes—mainly thick sweaters." Sutherland paused. "I should let the Duluth Playhouse know. They could use these things for props and costumes."

"Get back to it. The sooner you open them all, the sooner we can go upstairs. Did I mention my snack?"

"You could help."

"I wouldn't want to take away your discovery."

Sutherland shook his head and was about to chide Milo as he opened a tree-carved cabinet door. It was unusual as the other door carvings were animals and mythical creatures. Both men heard the click, and an entire section of wall popped out about an inch.

Milo opened his mouth, but nothing came out.

Sutherland turned to stare at Milo, a million comebacks flooding his mind. He settled on, "Looks like an imaginary door to my imaginary tunnel. Come follow my decoder ring into the…"

"Yeah, yeah. You got lucky."

"Blueprints never lie."

"Words to live by," Milo said standing up. "Don't gawk. Open the damn door."

Sutherland took one side, Milo the other, and they pulled back the section of wall that had popped forward. There were no hinges on the wall. It moved with ease on hidden rollers. "Someone put their engineering know-how into this," Sutherland admired.

Both men edged their way around the section of wall and entered the tunnel. They were greeted with dark, damp, dead air.

"What's that smell?" Sutherland asked.

"Dampness and rot," Milo said.

"Ewww. Could it be a rotting body?"

"No. The body you're looking for would be nothing but bones by now."

"I'm not sure that makes me feel better."

"Let's get this over with."

Sutherland turned on his flashlight but was disappointed at how ineffective it was. Dark stone lined the walls and seemed to eat the light. Even when Milo turned on his flashlight, doubling the glow, the tunnel remained dark and gloomy.

"These walls are not like the other tunnels on the estate," Sutherland said as they progressed down the narrowing tunnel. "The floor is dirt. I'm starting to hit my head on the ceiling."

"Not a problem for me. I suggest you stoop," Milo said, asking if Sutherland wanted to lead the expedition. He declined. Milo advised, "I'll be careful to avoid the quicksand. I'm sure it's waiting at every turn."

"We're not zoned for quicksand," Sutherland shot back. "Maybe not quicksand but we are zoned for big rocks. I just passed one. Watch out!"

The warning didn't work. Sutherland tripped on a large stone sticking out of the ground, catching his balance against the wall. "This wall is uneven and slimy!"

Milo turned his light on the wall and ceiling. "Tree roots," he explained. "They've invaded the tunnel and water is trickling down them."

Sutherland eased his handkerchief from his pants pocket and wiped the slime from his hand. "There's no air down here. It's getting hard to breathe, and that smell is getting worse."

"Tunnel maintenance is not what it used to be," Milo said. "Did your blueprint show side tunnels?"

"No. Why?"

"There's one to my left, see," Milo said, shining his light to show a shadowy opening leading off from the main tunnel. "You stay here; let me see where it goes."

"Don't get lost," Sutherland warned.

Milo disappeared into the entrance and then screamed, "Ahh, quicksand!"

"Stop it!" Sutherland snapped.

Milo re-emerged after a minute. "It's a room, nothing in it."

"Let's keep going," Sutherland urged.

"Lead on."

Sutherland went another hundred feet before stopping. "I hear water dripping."

"So?"

"Why is water dripping?"

"I thought I covered this. See the roots..see the water… bigger roots…more water. Drip, drip, drip."

"Thank you, Professor. I see another one of those open-ings. It's off to my right. Do you want me to check out this one or do you want to do it?"

"This one's yours," Milo said, with a sweeping gesture.

With some trepidation, Sutherland entered the room. "Hey there's something in here! Oh God!"

"Nice try. Is it quicksand? Use your decoder ring."

Sutherland quickstepped out of the room. "I'm serious. It looks like a coffin in there!"

Milo edged past Sutherland into the room. The beam from his flashlight fell on a long narrow wooden box, large enough to hold a body, maybe two. Rough rope handles were nailed to either end. "Son of a bitch," Milo said sweeping the room with his flashlight, seeing nothing more than the box.

"What do you think?" Sutherland yelled.

"I'll tell you in a second," Milo yelled back, walking to the box and noticing that the lid was nailed shut. "We need a crow bar."

"No, no, no!" Sutherland protested. "This is where we call Gramm. He brings his crowbar. This is a police matter!"

Milo trudged back to Sutherland. "It's a wooden box, in an old rotting tunnel."

"We have to call Gramm!" Sutherland persisted.

"You make the call but put it on speaker. I wanna hear Gramm's reaction when you explain how you discovered an old box in your magic tunnel and want a homicide detective to open it."

Sutherland's excitement waned. "Well, when you put it that way."

"I saw a crow bar in the maintenance shed last winter. I'll go get it."

"What do I do?" Sutherland asked.

"Explore, count the water drips." Milo turned and headed back to the vault.

Not sure how he felt about being left alone in a rotting tunnel with dead bodies, Sutherland's aching back decided movement was the best option. He proceeded, one slow step at a time, still stooping, sidestepping the water dripping from the ceiling in three places. As he crept along, the air became warmer and less foul smelling. After several minutes, he reached a vine-covered dead end. Even Sutherland knew vines don't grow in the dark. Pulling at the vegetation and pushing his way through, he stepped out onto the shore of the lake. The bright sunshine hurt his eyes. Putting his hands on his back, he stretched from side to side, the first relief he had gotten since entering the tunnel.

Why would someone make such a horrible tunnel from the vault to a boat house? If the weather was bad, going out on a boat would be suicide. It makes no sense.

Sutherland opted to wait on the beach rather return to the cramped ante room and the wooden box. Ten minutes passed before he heard Milo shouting about a crowbar and a hammer. His muscles having rested, he crouched down, re-entered the tunnel, and made his way back past the dripping water to join Milo.

"This tunnel was made by short people like you," Sutherland complained.

Holding his tools up, Milo asked, "Do you want to do the honors, Tall Guy?"

"Are you kidding? You're used to dead bodies and blood all over the place. I'm not. But before you begin, I was thinking that this tunnel is misplaced."

"How so?"

"I found the end of the tunnel. It ends where the old boat house used to be, like the blueprints indicated. Why would they build a tunnel from the vault to the boathouse? If they were trying to avoid bad weather, they still couldn't sail."

Milo smiled. "You've got it backwards," he said as he disappeared into the alcove.

"Backwards? What's backwards?"

"Give me a second," Milo yelled as he began to pound on the crowbar with the hammer, forcing it between the box and its cover.

The banging and squeaking drove the *backward* question out of Sutherland's brain. Here he was with another dead body—maybe two—a common occurrence with Milo Rathkey living in the house. Nervous sweat dripped down his back.

Milo came out wiping dust off his pants. He looked grim.

Sutherland looked at his face. "Oh my God. I was right, wasn't I?"

"The contents are old. Tests will have to be performed before we can fix a date."

"Now we have to call Gramm."

"I don't know. I'm not in a sharing mood."

"What? You can't keep dead bodies to yourself!"

"Who said anything about dead bodies?"

"You did!"

"No, I didn't." Milo held up a dusty bottle. "I think this is at least eighty-year-old Scotch…Macallan single malt."

"What?" Sutherland grabbed the bottle holding it up to his flashlight. "My God, the whiskey is up to the top of the bottle; none of it has evaporated!"

"Why do we care?" Milo asked.

"You don't understand. This whiskey looks to be in a pristine state. This bottle is worth thousands."

Milo laughed. "What about the other forty-seven?"

Sutherland stared at Milo. "We have forty-seven bottles of eighty-year-old Scotch?"

Milo sighed. "Forty-eight, counting the one your hand."

"This could be half a million dollars in Scotch!"

"No bodies though. Good thing we didn't call Gramm," Milo said.

"Yeah, that would have been embarrassing," Sutherland agreed. "Wait, a minute. Why is the whiskey here?"

"Still don't get it?"

"No."

"Like I said, you're looking at it backwards. The tunnel doesn't lead to the lake. The lake leads through the tunnel to the vault. This is a smuggler's tunnel. I'll bet somebody smuggled liquor into the country from Canada back in the thirties. This crate was left, and no one ever came back for it."

"A smuggler's tunnel right under our feet! Dad would have loved this! We discovered another mystery, but not the one we came for. We're no closer to finding Annie."

"You can drown your sorrows with a good Scotch."

"A great Scotch," Sutherland corrected.

16

Agnes was up early making breakfast for Sophie and Liz. Not knowing exactly what they liked, she set out berries and yogurt, got the coffee going, and dragged the toaster from its hiding place in a low cabinet.

Liz came in first. "Oh breakfast! Great!"

"How do you like your eggs?" Agnes asked.

"I used to like poached eggs, but baby bumpkin here has changed my appetite," she said, patting her belly. "We don't eat eggs at all."

Sophie chose to sleep on the screened-in porch, so she wouldn't disturb anyone when she left for her early morning run. Agnes and Liz were surprised when Sophie opened the back door. "Morning all."

"Oh, I thought you were still sleeping," Agnes said. "Were you running already?"

"Early morning runs happen in the early morning," Sophie joked. She stretched and left her orange shoes and jacket on the back porch.

"Coffee?" Agnes asked.

Sophie gave a thumbs up and sat down at the table. "Let me know if I should take a shower. I'm not used to company after my run."

"You're downwind. It's fine," Liz quipped as she spooned yogurt into a bowl and sliced several strawberries to put on top.

"That yogurt looks good, but I could also use carbs," Sophie said.

"Toast?" Agnes asked.

"Great. Thank you for doing this, Agnes," Sophie said as she reached for the yogurt. "When cops strongly suggest we stay in town, they don't provide money to stay in town. I thought I was going to have to stay in a cheap motel somewhere."

"That's awful. I mean that they suspect you," Agnes said.

"Well, I did choke Jessica—not my brightest move—but can't say I'm sorry about it."

"I'm glad you did," Liz said. "I wish I could say I'm sorry she's dead, but I'm not."

Agnes and Sophie looked at her in surprise.

"That's not a confession. I just didn't want her to enjoy life. Molly can't."

Handing Sophie her toast, Agnes changed the subject not wanting talk of death to overtake breakfast. "How was sleeping on the back porch, Sophie?"

"Great. Crisp enough for a second blanket, like camping without mosquitos."

"How about you Liz? How did you sleep?"

"It was fine which is tough these days. In fact, I'm going to move out of the hotel today."

"You didn't move out last night?" Sophie asked.

"I wasn't sure if I could be comfortable, and I didn't know if my many trips to the bathroom would bother you two."

"Didn't bother me. Didn't even know you were up," Agnes said, sitting down to join them for breakfast.

"So, you could afford to stay in a hotel for a week or more?" Sophie asked.

"Yeah, I could," Liz admitted.

"I should have gone into computers. Flying helicopters is fun but not quite as lucrative."

"So, Agnes what do you do?" Liz asked.

"Don't you know Liz?" Sophie joked. "She works on an estate. Could be she owns it."

"Yes of course," Agnes cooed. "This is the guest house. The mansion is in the back, or is it in the front? I forget. The estate is so sprawling."

Liz and Sophie laughed.

"In reality I work for two rich guys who own the estate," Agnes admitted.

"I already called dibs on the short one," Sophie challenged.

"There's a tall one?" Liz asked.

"Yeah, but Agnes already has that one taken."

Agnes was shocked. "I do? I don't remember saying that."

"So, I take it these two guys living together are not gay?" Liz asked.

Agnes laughed. "No, they're kinda brothers. Sort of brothers who never met before."

"Okay that's strange," Liz said.

"That pretty much describes it," Agnes said as she explained how Rathkey came to live at Lakesong.

"Amazing,' said Liz, shaking her head.

"Which one is cutest?" Sophie asked.

"Sutherland!" Agnes blurted far too quickly and then countered, "Well, both are in their own way."

"Sutherland, huh? Got a last name?" Sophie asked, grabbing her phone.

Agnes blushed. "McKnight."

Sophie did a Linkedin search. Grinning, she showed Liz a picture.

"Oh, he is cute!" Liz exclaimed.

"We have an employer-employee relationship," Agnes asserted.

"Yeah, right," Sophie said, not believing it for a minute, "but if you kick him to the curb, let me know. I enjoy short and funny but I'm a sucker for tall blonds with dimples."

Agnes put an end to the conversation about her and Sutherland by getting up, collecting the breakfast dishes, and offering her friends a second cup of coffee.

"I hate to be a downer again, but I do need to talk about Molly and Jessica," Liz persisted. "Sophie, why did you phys-ically attack Jessica last Friday?"

Agnes looked at Sophie. She had to admit the same question had gone through her mind.

Sophie folded her arms and sat back. "I never said this out loud. Molly's death was my fault."

"Your fault?" Liz was shocked. "What did you do?"

"Nothing. That's the problem." Sophie used her paper napkin to blow her nose. "Sorry...allergies. Molly and I were sort of partners...to fend off the bullies, especially Jessica. We noticed they weren't so quick to attack us if we were together." Sophie jumped up, leaned on the back of the chair, and stretched out her left leg behind her. "Sorry, I started to cramp."

Agnes wasn't sure if it was a cramp or Sophie needing time not to cry.

Sophie continued. "When I realized that Molly had been taken up the tower by Jessica, I should have raced up to protect her, but I didn't. That's what I've been carrying. When Jessica yelled 'let her die' I exploded."

Without a word, Liz stood up and hugged her. "Molly is not your fault. It's Jessica's fault. We were all there that night. I felt the same guilt, but it's not our fault. It's taken a lot of therapy for me to say that, but it's true."

Sophie reached for another paper napkin.

§

Milo hated to admit it, but he missed Annie accompanying him to breakfast. She was still spending mornings at Martha's cottage. He hoped she was getting enough bacon.

This morning's delivery trucks were carrying food. Martha and Agnes directed the delivery guys to the basement kitchen where new refrigerators and two freezers had been installed. Martha was beaming—it was the first use of the massive mystery kitchen.

"Your breakfast is in the warming drawer," Sutherland said. "Martha's busy."

"Got it," Milo acknowledged, removing the plate full of eggs, and bacon.

"Use the hot pads and don't forget to turn it off," Sutherland ordered.

"Doing it, Mother," Milo said, shaking the oven mitts in Sutherland's direction.

"I think we need to check the grounds," Sutherland suggested as Milo sat down.

"For anything in particular?"

"For the bodies! We didn't find them in the tunnel yesterday."

"Good plan. I'll rent a back hoe."

Sutherland took a slice of bacon from Milo's plate. "I didn't say we dig up the yard. We can use GPR."

"I just learned what GPS means and now you hit me with GPR. Is there a relation?"

"Absolutely none. I'm talking about ground penetrating radar. It's a way to see under the ground without the backhoe. My company uses it before we start digging foundations."

"There's no stopping you and your theory is there?"

"It's not my theory. Your dad's investigation years ago said so."

Milo laughed. "No, it didn't. It said foul play was a possibility. It didn't say GPX should be used in backyard to delay a wedding."

"GPR, and we have a window of time before the plat-forms and tents go up. We have to find somebody who can do it. Unfortunately, the company I use needs at least a two week lead."

Milo reached for his phone thinking he could get Sutherland's far-fetched theory behind them. "Okay, Joe Hardy, I'll call Patupick."

"Now I'm one of the Hardy Boys? So long Nancy Drew. Why would Patupick have a GPR device?" Sutherland asked.

"I have no idea. He seems to have everything," Milo said as Ed answered his phone.

"What now, Milo?"

"I'm putting you on speaker. I need…" he looked at Sutherland to fill in the blank.

"Ground penetrating radar." Sutherland over enunciated sure Patupick wouldn't know what he meant.

"Yeah, what he said. We want to run it over the back lawn," Milo explained.

"Whaddaya looking for?"

"Dead bodies!" Sutherland shouted.

"Milo?"

"I guess," Milo said, without enthusiasm.

"I'm in. I can come over tomorrow morning with my gear, but I've gotta warn you, trees are a problem."

Sutherland shook his head. "There's a huge grassy area before we get to the trees."

"How do you know the bodies aren't buried in the front?" Ed asked.

Sutherland was surprised. He never thought about bodies being buried in his front yard. *Aren't bodies always buried in the back? Who buries bodies in the front?* Sutherland pondered this for a few seconds before realizing what he was thinking. *Wait, a minute! Who buries bodies at all? This is what my life's become.*

"Let's rule out the back before the wedding," Milo suggested.

"You want to rule out buried bodies the back yard before a wedding? I've never heard of that tradition," Ed said as if he was serious.

"Yeah, it's different."

"See you tomorrow, eight sharp."

"Thanks Ed." Hanging up, Milo said to Sutherland, "Easy peazy."

"We want to check the back before the wedding? Why would you say that? That sounds like we're crazy."

Milo dabbed his eggs in ketchup. "And dead bodies in hidden tunnels sound sane? I'm just saying out loud all the squirrely ideas floating in your head. I like facts. Here's one. You get to tell Agnes that the tent can't go up tomorrow morning as scheduled. It needs to be done in the afternoon."

Sutherland grimaced.

§

White, waving a piece of paper with a flourish, announced to Gramm, "I have Kendrick's motor vehicle information in my hand."

Gramm took a sip of his coffee and wished he had added more cream. "And it's interesting?"

White sat down. "Creep Boy got a speeding ticket on Arrowhead Drive the morning of the murder."

"Funny place to do lawn work. That puts him close to—but not at—Enger Tower."

"True. But let's check report number two," she said, with a Cheshire Cat grin, flipping to a second piece of paper. "Kendrick drives a 2015 BMW, M4 convertible, dark blue."

"Our witness described a cheap BMW. Is that considered a cheap one?"

"Not in my budget, but I'll check. If it's Kendrick's car that would put him at the scene. It clicks the opportunity box." "Either way, Kendrick's another liar. Let's call him in for a more formal chat."

"Don't forget Liz Brooks and the 'hitman' phone call," White reminded Gramm.

"And our favorite jogger, Moscatelli. Load up on the coffee. It's gonna be a long day."

§

Milo pulled up to the rambling Reinakie ranch house in Woodland Hills a few minutes before ten. To Milo's surprise Heidi backed a sporty red Cadillac convertible out of the garage. This was new. The old white SUV had been replaced.

Oh man, Heidi's gone sporty. This has to have Harry absolutely vibrating. Lots of pay days for Joe.

Milo followed a safe distance behind. The car may be different, but the destination was pretty much the same. Heidi was heading into the Hu's Nail Emporium as Milo drove his car into the parking lot. He thought he should feel nostalgic following Heidi again, but he didn't.

Milo thought the sporty Cadillac looked good on Heidi. Now and then Sutherland suggested Milo get a new car, but Mr. Anderson, Lakesong's car guy, resurrected his old Honda and it seemed a shame to get rid of it now. *One of these days I have to meet Mr. Anderson and thank him,* Milo thought.

Before John dumped millions of dollars on his head, Milo spent his 'Heidi' time hustling for other jobs. Today, he spent it waiting. He unfastened his seat belt, reclined his seat one notch, and wished he had taken a book from the library. His thoughts drifted to the Enger Tower murder. Something about the description of events bothered him. He closed his eyes and spent Heidi's mani-pedi time trying to figure it out. Nothing.

Red was the color of the day. Milo guessed she did her nails to match the new car. Hu's Nail Emporium was usually followed by coffee in the same shopping center with a friend but not today. Heidi headed down the hill to the Fitger's building, the old brick brewery which now housed restaurants, shops, and a hotel.

He parked and watched her long blond curls bounce into the building. *Is this a rendezvous? Should I follow her? Oh, come on Milo, it's Heidi. I'm getting as bad as Harry.*

He decided to give her fifteen minutes, two for each of the years he had been following her. His faith in Heidi's character was rewarded. She returned to the parking lot with a boutique bag proclaiming *The Snow Goose*—a purchase not a rendezvous.

Back on the street, Heidi zoomed up the hill to the Woodland area but not to her house. Instead she parked near a similar house a couple of blocks away. By the number of cars in the driveway and on the street, Milo assumed this was a party, and the Snow Goose bag held a present.

He parked within eyeshot of Heidi's convertible. Milo had always kept a journal in his glove compartment where he wrote down notes when he was tailing people. Because her routine hadn't changed until today, the last Heidi entry was a year ago. Milo began to jot down today's trip. "Up to Hu's, down to The Snow Goose, and back up to…" The cloud in his brain vanished. He knew what had been bothering him. All he could say was, "Curious."

17

Paul Kendrick paced in the sterile gray interview room. He had decided against a lawyer hoping to keep this interrogation uncomplicated and quick. His affairs with students occurred ten years ago, beyond the statute of limitations. Of course, this could be about Jessica, but Kendrick was sure the police couldn't place him at the scene.

As lunch was looking doubtful, White offered Gramm part of her protein bar. He declined, saying he was going to hit the vending machines.

"Liz Brooks and Sophie Moscatelli have checked out of the hotel," White added.

Gramm looked up and drew his white bushy eyebrows together in a frown. "Are they still in town?"

"Oh, they're in town. They're staying with Agnes Larson."

The eyebrows rose to the occasion in surprise. "Of course. Agnes Larson…of course. We can't have a murder without her. Do we know what she was doing Saturday morning?"

"Already went there. She was riding her bike on a trail with Rathkey and McKnight."

Rolling his head from side to side, loosening up his neck, Gramm said, "Pretty solid alibi. Let's set up the ladies once we finish with Kendrick, unless of course he does us the honor of confessing."

"If only."

Kendrick checked his watch. He was looking forward to his twelve-thirty lunch date with a captivating co-ed for 'tutoring' and whatever came afterward. This was a momentary delay.

Gramm and White entered the room and Kendrick began to complain. "I have a lunch meeting at noon."

"When this conversation gets around to where we should care, you let us know," White said, in a hostile manner.

Gramm smiled. His Sergeant had staked her claim to bad cop.

"I told you everything I know. Why am I here?" Kendrick demanded.

"You told us you were doing lawn work Saturday morning," White said.

Kendrick was silent as White picked up the copy of the speeding ticket. "Officer Drummond would beg to differ with you. He clocked you going fifty-three in a thirty on Arrowhead Road at 8:23 in the morning."

Kendrick broke into his boyish dimpled smile, but his hazel eyes looked worried, as he ran his fingers through his wind tousled hair.

The son of a bitch is handsome, White thought.

"I forgot about that. I went out to get things for supper. I was having company."

"You went shopping for dinner at 8:23 in the morning?" Gramm questioned.

"I'm an early riser. Besides, I was going to smoke a butt in my egg. It takes all day."

White picked up her pen. "Give me the name of the grocery store. You know they all have cameras these days."

"It's a butcher shop. I don't remember the name."

Gramm folded his hands and placed them on the table. "I hate being lied to. I don't think you went to a butcher shop. How about this scenario? You drove up to Enger Tower Saturday morning to have it out with your blackmailer, Jessica Vogel. You two fought, and you pushed her. Then you hopped in your car, pulled out of the parking lot, and almost hit a witness on a bike who gave us a description of your car."

"I never came close to hitting her!" Kendrick erupted before realizing his mistake.

White smiled. *Gotcha! Handsome but dumb.*

"You just admitted you were up at the tower," Gramm insisted.

Kendrick dropped his head, rubbing the back of his neck. "No, I was confused."

"Then how did you know our witness was a she? This hole you're digging is getting deeper. I can already arrest you for obstruction."

"Okay, I was up there! Happy?" Kendrick spat.

"Ecstatic," White said. "Start at the beginning."

"With the truth this time," Gramm jumped in. "No BS about butt smoking."

"I went up there to pay the bitch, not to kill her."

"Why Enger Tower?" Gramm asked.

"That was her idea. She was psycho."

"Go on," Gramm urged.

"Go on with what? Nothing happened. I parked, got out of my car, and started toward the tower when I heard a scream."

"Was it Jessica?" White asked.

"I don't know," Kendrick said, with exasperation. "A scream is a scream. I'm up for tenure. I didn't need to be around any drama. I jumped back in the car and took off. I saw that woman on a bike, but I didn't come close to her. I wanted to get out of there."

"You heard a scream and didn't bother to see if anyone needed help?" White asked.

"I told you, I'm up for tenure. I don't need problems."

White stared at him.

Gramm leaned back and folded his arms. "Here's what is going to happen Mr. Kendrick. You are going to make your lunch, but right now, you're suspect number one."

"I told you, I didn't do it."

White continued being the bad cop. "The next time we bring you up here, come with a lawyer."

§

Breanna was heading out the door, keys in hand, to pick up her brothers from their camps when her phone rang. "Hello?"

"I am looking for Breanna Gibbson," a male voice said.

224

"What is this in reference to?" Breanna asked, thinking this could be a robocall. Martha trained her to never give any information over the phone unless they knew the person calling.

"I'm Dr. Bixby's teaching assistant, Tom Rodgers. I need to talk with Breanna Gibbson about the Lind Mathematics Scholarship."

Breanna's stomach clenched. *I never solved the problem. This has got to be a rejection.* "This is Breanna Gibbson."

"Congratulations, Ms. Gibbson. You are the winner of the scholarship."

Breanna was confused. "I…I didn't solve the proposition."

Rodgers laughed. "No one does, Ms. Gibbson. No one except Dr. Bixby. She's quite famous for having solved it."

"Oh," Breanna said, wishing she had known that.

"Dr. Bixby would like to visit you tomorrow."

Breanna didn't even think to ask why Dr. Bixby wanted to come to her house rather than have her go up to the University. "Does she know how to get in here?"

"She told me she does."

"I live in the cottage on the back of the estate. I'll tell my sister. Thank you."

"Again, congratulations, Ms. Gibbson."

§

Upon returning to Lakesong, Milo found Sutherland in the gallery hanging the gold, art déco framed picture of his father and Annie sitting on the wall.

"I like it," Milo said.

Sutherland turned. "Me too. I thought this would be the best room because we can see the real wall on the back lawn and the picture of the wall. It's sort of symmetry, but I'm bad at these things. I might ask Danielle if it needs a different frame."

"Danielle?"

"Danielle Ashbach. She's a designer," Sutherland explained. "She designed my rooms upstairs and did a ter-rific job. During the process, we got to talking about cycling, and she mentioned her husband owned a bike shop. That's how I met Larry."

Milo walked up to take a closer look at the picture. "You're still convinced Annie is buried out there?"

"Well, I don't know where she's buried, but I do believe she was murdered. Everyone thought so. Besides, I owe it to my dad to try to solve this mystery." Sutherland knew that last statement would keep Milo on board. He had come to know that Milo could be outrageous and cantankerous, but he was loyal to a fault.

Milo sighed. "Well, when Ed gets here tomorrow, we'll see."

"Are you sure your guy knows how to use GPR?"

"He knows how to use everything. Speaking of knowing everything, I need to pick your brain about cars," Milo said, adding, "You want a beer? We can go outside."

Sutherland brightened up. "You're finally getting a new car!"

Milo strode into the family room and grabbed a couple of beers from the bar. He yelled back, "I was thinking of a sports car?"

Sutherland, on his way to the terrace, stopped dead in his tracks. "Did I hear that correctly? My Porsche would welcome the company." Sitting down on one of the padded wrought-iron chairs, he wondered what model sports car would fit Milo. He couldn't picture Milo Rathkey behind the wheel of a single one. Seeing him drive the Bentley was shock enough.

Milo handed Sutherland an IPA, sat down, and opened his Pabst.

After sampling his beer, Sutherland asked, "You want a sports car?"

Milo said if he did buy a sports car, he didn't want to spend a lot of money.

"You have money. You have 'I want to buy a Ferrari' money."

"But I don't have a 'spend Ferrari money' brain. What sports car doesn't cost a lot?"

"It depends on your definition of a lot."

"What's yours?"

Sutherland explained he paid a hundred and thirty grand for his Porsche last year, and he considered that to be expensive. He added, people who were driving the two hundred thousand dollar Porsche would call his cheap.

"Let's leave out both the Porsche and the Ferrari as too much for me. What are the names of other sports cars that would be considered inexpensive by you?"

Sutherland laughed, wondering if Milo would ever be comfortable spending any of the money his dad gave him. "I think you can get one for around sixty grand. That's cheap."

"Give me names."

"I know Mercedes has a cheap one, so does BMW, Audi, or you could go American with a Corvette. There's a lot more. I'd have to do research."

Milo moved on. "We should invite Gramm over tonight for some Scotch, you know—the tunnel Scotch." Milo said.

"Wait a minute; aren't you going to buy a car?"

"Not today. I'm doing my research."

"So, years and years ago, research led to your trusty Honda."

"No, my bank account led me to my trusty Honda—which still runs thanks to Mr. Anderson. But a new car might happen."

"Your new bank account should lead you to something better. You know you can still keep the Honda. There's plenty of room in the garage."

"Something to think about. What about Gramm tonight after dinner?"

Sutherland checked the calendar on his phone. "I'm good."

§

Gramm took two antacids, trying to mitigate the damage done to his stomach by two spicy vending machine burritos. He loved them when they never talked back. It was time to retreat to the blander sandwiches and chips.

Returning to his office, he found White sitting in a chair finishing a large Nicoise salad. Gramm stopped and stared at her. "Where did you get that?"

White looked up. "I had it delivered from that new French restaurant by the gun range."

"They deliver?" Gramm asked, sitting down.

"No, there are a couple of companies that deliver lunch. I got an app here on the phone."

Gramm sighed. "I don't want an app. Next time let me know. You'll be my app."

"Giving up the burrito delights?" White teased.

Gramm touched his stomach. "They attacked me. I thought we were friends."

White was leaving the room to toss her empty salad container in the garbage when her phone vibrated. She looked at the screen. Moscatelli and Brooks had arrived. She went back to Gramm's office to discuss strategy. To her surprise, he suggested splitting them up, giving her Liz Brooks while he took Sophie Moscatelli. This was the second, much less friendly interview, and White was pleased Gramm trusted her to do this interview alone.

§

Sophie looked around at the bare institutional gray walls, metal chairs and table. The waiting room was bright and inviting, but this room felt dark and menacing.

Gramm came in, sat down, and set a closed file on the table. "Ms. Moscatelli, you lied to us," he began. "I don't like being lied to."

Sophie fell back on her military training on how to behave if captured. She remained silent.

Gramm, hearing no pushback, continued, "You told us you were jogging on the Lakewalk last Saturday morning. You weren't."

"You're right. I wasn't."

So much for my surprise attack. "Where were you?"

"I suspect you know."

Gramm opened the folder and showed her a still picture from the drone video. "Is that you?"

Sophie looked at the profile picture of a jogger with an orange jacket and shoes. "It looks like me," she said.

"Do you know where this picture was taken?"

"If it was Saturday morning, I would say near the Japanese Peace Garden behind Enger Tower."

"I can see why you lied," Gramm said. "This picture puts you running away from the scene shortly after the murder of Jessica Vogel. Would you like to confess to pushing her now?"

Sophie did not rise to the bait. "No. I didn't even know she was there. I was jogging. Clearly, I picked the wrong place."

"Why did you lie?"

"It looks bad for me to be at Enger Park. That's why I'm here, right?"

While she was still a prime suspect, Gramm had to consider the possibility that she was innocent, and, if so, could she provide information about the murder? "Okay, let's say you didn't push her," Gramm continued. "Did you hear a scream?"

"No. Here…look," Sophie pointed to her picture. "I have my earphones in. I didn't hear a thing but my music."

"Did you see anything?"

"Just the park."

§

Liz Brooks smiled as Sergeant White entered the room. "Can I clear something up for you?" she asked.

White sat in the chair opposite Brooks and matched her smile. "Yes you can. But first are you comfortable? Do you need anything?"

"No, I'm good. I brought my own water," she said pointing to her purse which was sitting on a nearby chair.

"Good. If you need anything, ask," White said.

"Thanks. So how can I help?"

"When you told us you were having breakfast in the hotel restaurant Saturday morning, you weren't."

Liz's smile was frozen on her face. "Um…I…must have gotten confused."

Another confused and flustered suspect. How original.

"I've eaten at the restaurant most mornings. If I wasn't there, I must have been in my room. I honestly don't remember."

"Did you order room service?"

"Room service? Let me think. You know we had that late dinner celebration at the reunion Friday night. I think I fell back to sleep Saturday morning."

White nodded, dropped that line of inquiry, kept her smile, and moved on to the phone conversation overheard by Maureen Donahue. "We have another problem. A witness has come forward telling us about a conversation between you and your husband early Friday night."

Liz tilted her head. "I'm confused. Yes, I talk to Bob most days."

"You were heard," White checked her notes, "*planning pain* for the deceased. Our witness says you told your husband to go ahead with the plan. Considering Ms. Vogel died exactly the same way as your sister, we're thinking your husband hired someone to kill her and that was the plan."

Liz laughed. "Oh no, no no. The plan was about suing Jessica for wrongful death. It certainly wasn't about hiring someone to kill her. Why would you think we would even know where to find such a person? We're geeks not goons. Gees."

"A lawsuit? Why now?"

Liz looked down, put her hands on her baby bump, and then looked up at White. "One last thing to do before I moved on. Suing Jessica was a way to mess up her life like she messed up all of ours."

"I'll need the name of your lawyer," White said.

§

Gramm not only accepted the invitation for a drink but invited himself to dinner. Amy was out of town. Milo's invitation had included Robin, but she had a sailing lesson. Gramm wondered if 'sailing lesson' was millennial code for 'date.'

Sutherland and Rathkey didn't see the necessity of Gramm knowing anything about Morrie Wolf and the wedding. They dropped the electric shades in the gallery to hide the wedding prep on the back lawn and had dinner in the family room.

After a dinner of grilled, mustard-glazed pork tenderloin, with a side of summer vegetable gnocchi, they retired to the billiard room where Milo teased, "This house has many secrets and we are going to share with you a deep, dark, dusty…"

"Dram," Sutherland added.

With that Milo produced the tunnel bottle of Macallan, wiped off the dust, and showed it to Gramm. Ernie stared at it in wonder. "Where did you get this? How old is it?"

"We think it goes back to the thirties," Milo said.

"The bottle was upright and tight, no evaporation," Sutherland added.

"Macallan is not for sissies," Gramm, a long time Scotch drinker marveled. "What a taste this would be!"

Milo shrugged, opened the bottle and began to pour.

"What the hell are you doing?" Gramm jumped out of his chair. "Do you know how much that bottle was worth unopened?"

Milo looked at him. "Did you miss the day I was given a lot of money?"

Sutherland piped in. "If you can't drink it, why own it?"

Gramm accepted his glass, shook his head, and toasted, "To rich, crazy friends."

They each sipped. Sutherland and Gramm closed their eyes as they savored the biting liquid. Milo, a vodka drinker, did not like Scotch Whiskey and tried to hide his displeasure at its taste.

"Smokey…rich!" Gramm exclaimed.

"It is!" Sutherland added.

Overrated, Rathkey thought.

Sutherland suggested a couple of games of eight ball. Gramm complained that Sutherland was a shark, remembering the last time they played. He sunk two balls, missed on the third, and never got another shot. Milo suggested Sutherland be required to hit at least one bank shot with the eight ball. Gramm agreed.

Sutherland broke. Gramm pocketed the one and six ball before missing on the two. As before, Sutherland dispatched all of the striped balls, called the eight ball with, not one, but two banks into the side pocket.

Gramm glared at Rathkey. "You set me up!"

"Let's see if he makes it."

Sutherland took his time pretending to eye the shot and figure out the angles. He was having fun. The shot was quick. The cue ball struck the eight ball which ricocheted from one cushion to the opposite cushion to the center of the middle pocket.

"Like I said, you set me up," Gramm complained.

"Who knew he could make it," Rathkey shrugged.

Milo watched as Gramm and Sutherland savored another shot of Scotch until Gramm broke the reverie. "So, you guys invited me over to sip incredibly rare, expensive whiskey and humiliate me at pool. Right?"

"That, and find out more about the dead woman at Enger Tower." Sutherland jumped in once again, like a puppy. "It's kind of like…our murder!"

Milo shook his head.

Gramm held up a thumb drive. "I'll see your Scotch and raise you drone video recorded at the time of the murder. You guys got a computer?"

"In the office," Milo said, getting up, leading the way to his office.

"This was shot by a photographer…Reggie…um…"

"Cuff?" Sutherland offered.

"Right. Good memory," Gramm said, not knowing if he was forgetting names or White's notes were so good he was beginning to rely on her.

The trio watched the video several times before Gramm said, "The jogger is Moscatelli. She admitted it this afternoon."

"Is she jogging or running away?" Sutherland asked.

"Good question." Gramm went through the afternoon conversations with the suspects before realizing Milo had yet to comment on the drone video. "What did you see in that drone video? Did you see anything we didn't?"

"I saw Reggie and the jogger," Sutherland offered.

"Milo?" Gramm asked.

"Yeah, Reggie and the jogger," Milo said without conviction. "But…"

"Damn it!" Gramm almost yelled. "We went through that video frame by frame. What did we miss?"

"It's what you don't see," Milo said.

Sutherland looked puzzled.

Gramm said, "I'll bite. What don't we see?"

"I'm wondering why she isn't there."

"Who?" they both asked at once.

"Megan, the reporter. She's not in the shot. Where is she?"

Sutherland laughed. "Megan? Why would she kill the victim? She didn't even know her."

"Well, you don't know that. She was at the scene. Everyone who was there is a suspect."

§

Agnes couldn't remember laughing as hard as Liz continued to regale Sophie and her with stories from their high school years. "We thought you guys were such dweebs."

"Oh yes, because you were two years older than us and sooooo sophisticated," Sophie mocked.

"Of course. Still am," Liz joked.

"Barbara never told me that your crowd made fun of us," Agnes said, thinking of her older sister who was part of Liz's group in high school.

Liz reached across the table and patted Agnes' hand. "It was done with love. Besides, Barbara was the nice one."

Agnes put her free hand on Liz's. "Barbara would have loved this."

Liz slapped her hand on top and they played slap hands for a few seconds, laughing at their own childishness. Liz looked down at her baby bump, "You know I'm not too far from having to do games like that again."

"Peekaboo, Pattycake, Itsy Bitsy Spider," Agnes chimed in.

"Thumb Wars, Jacks," Sophie added.

"I think I'll start with Peekaboo before Jacks or Thumb Wars," Liz laughed.

"Suit yourself," Sophie said, "but I hear Thumb Wars is all the rage this year with the diaper set."

Liz tried thumb wars with herself, and then confessed, "Sophie, you'll have to teach her Thumb Wars. I suck at it."

"Her?" Agnes asked.

Liz broke into a big smile. "Yeah, her. You're the first to know…after Bob of course."

"Good of you to let him in on it," Sophie said.

"I'm nice that way." Liz flipped her hair teasingly.

Agnes stood and started clearing the dinner dishes. "Well, this calls for an all-girl celebration, baby included." She put the dishes in the sink and opened the freezer door. "What do we like? Rocky road, mint chocolate chip, chocolate chip cookie dough, or pralines and cream?"

Sophie and Liz both blurted, "Yes!"

"Yes? Which one?"

"All of them!" Liz exclaimed.

"Bring spoons," Sophie demanded.

"Big spoons!" Liz added.

Agnes grinned as she slid all the ice cream cartons to the middle of the table along with spoons and napkins. This was fun.

When most of the ice cream was a memory, the three retired to the living room. "If you're the pregnant one, why am I waddling?" Agnes asked.

"You hogged the pralines and cream and half the mint chocolate chip," Sophie complained.

"Oh yeah, I forgot. I do love pralines and cream," Agnes confessed.

Liz sat down on the sofa, flipped off her shoes, put her feet up, and patted her bump. "Molly is saying whatever that stuff was, she liked it."

Both Agnes and Sophie looked at Liz, wondering if they had heard correctly.

"Yes, you heard right. I'm naming her Molly."

Sophie responded at once. "Yes! Molly's name should go on. Molly would like that. I like that!"

Agnes fought tears, both for her friend, and for the fleeting thought that raced through her mind. If she ever had children, could she name one Barbara?

Liz whispered, "Agnes? Is that a problem?"

"Oh no. My tears are the happy-sad ones. I'm happy that Molly's name will go on in a brand new person, but I'm still sad the old Molly will not be here to enjoy her."

The room fell silent for a moment as each woman felt the soft cool breeze off the lake waft through the opened windows, each of their thoughts following a different direction.

"This is so nice," Sophie sighed. "I hope you two will visit me when I'm in prison."

"Before you get your heart set on doing hard time, Maureen told the cops I had hired a hitman," Liz laughed.

"Where did she get that idea?" Sophie asked.

"She misheard a phone conversation I had with Bob."

"Well, Maureen shouldn't be pointing fingers. Remember I told you, she was in that damn tower when Jessica was killed!" Agnes said.

They all agreed.

18

Gramm sat at his desk, closed his eyes, and shook his head. This Thursday morning was not beginning well. He and Robin had discussed charging Maureen Donahue with Jessica Vogel's murder, but a quick call to the district attorney told him otherwise. The DA's position was that despite Maureen's being in the tower and having a motive, her defense attorney could point toward Kendrick or Moscatelli as having the same opportunity and motive. He added that the fact that there was no weapon further complicated the case. Any one of three could have pushed Vogel.

After that disappointment, Gramm's boss added another problem. Councilman Cliff Donahue, a man with friends in high places, was demanding the police wrap up their investigation and leave his wife alone. The mayor was pressuring the police chief, and it flowed downhill from there until it landed on Gramm's desk.

The Lieutenant's back was tightening. He tried to stretch it out as he flipped through the Vogel file, hoping something new would pop out at him. Several minutes later White checked in.

"From the look on your face, and the back stretching, I would say the DA is a no-go on arresting Donahue," she said, sitting down, taking the lid off of her coffee.

Gramm looked up and explained the DA's position as well as the concerned phone call from their boss.

White shrugged. "He's catching crap and throwing it at us."

Gramm smiled. "Interesting visual, but the clock is ticking."

"I got ahold of Brooks' husband and the lawyer," White said. "Her story checks out. She was planning to file a suit against Vogel for wrongful death."

"At least that's one hitman we can scratch off the list." Gramm tapped the file. "I've been rereading this material and rethinking our suspects. Could Donahue and Kendrick have been in it together? They had the same motive; they know each other. Can we find a current connection?"

"Moscatelli was up there too, but I can't see her colluding with either one."

"No sign that Vogel was blackmailing her, but she did attack the victim, and she lied." Gramm closed the file. "This is worse than the Bonner murder. They all were there and they all could have done it. We need to make one of them crack."

"What's Milo doing?" White asked.

"I don't think much of anything...exploring tunnels and drinking fine old Scotch."

"Tunnels? What tunnels?"

"Their house has tunnels," Gramm explained.

"Doesn't everyone's?"

§

Agnes patrolled along the terrace of Lakesong, sitting for a few minutes only to jolt up and begin pacing again. She watched Sutherland and a tall, skinny guy with a bandana around his head, inch along pushing a lawn mower with wires. Her well-planned schedule for the wedding was now in disarray. The deck construction had to wait until afternoon.

Sutherland kept glancing in Agnes' direction. Her disapproval loomed over his dead-body search. "Can we go a little faster?" he asked Ed.

"No," Ed responded.

Milo, who had finished his morning swim, stepped onto the terrace to observe the activity on the back lawn. He greeted an agitated Agnes with hesitation. "Morning."

Agnes marched over to him. "I was told to move back my schedule for this? What's going on? What are they doing?"

Milo sighed. "It's a long story, but here's the quick and dirty version. We are trying to find out what happened to several people who used to live in this house but disappeared in the fifties."

Agnes' face was not encouraging nor engaged.

Milo tried shock and awe. "Sutherland believes they were brutally murdered, and buried in the back lawn. That gadget Ed's using can find bodies."

Agnes whispered through clenched teeth, "If they're dead and buried, can't this wait until after the wedding?"

"Yeah. That's a good point." Milo looked at Ed pushing his device back and forth across the lawn as Sutherland pirouetted around him, turning to peer up at Agnes, down at the machine, running ahead to remove debris, and then rejoin Ed's side. This dance repeated itself several times. He knew Ed didn't like to be crowded while he was working; if Sutherland continued his dance, this would not end well.

Milo said to Agnes, "Let me get Sutherland out of there. This may go faster."

"Please."

Milo strolled out on the pretense of taking an interest in the GPR screen. Looking at the worthless jumble of horizontal lines, he asked, "When do we get a picture?"

Looking down on Milo, Ed said, "You're looking at it."

"I can't see anything."

Sutherland pointed to the screen. "Lucky for you, I can. I've been taking lessons from my tall friend, Ed, here. See that long white spot there?"

"Yeah."

"That could be a buried pipe."

"It's a white blob."

Ed stopped and looked down at both of them. "I'm not holding GPR school. Nice place you have here. Both of you go enjoy it and leave me alone."

Milo grabbed Sutherland by the arm and pulled him toward the house. "But what if he sees something?" Sutherland protested.

"He'll let us know," Milo said.

Agnes met them at the top of the stone stairs. "How long will this take? Peggy, my wedding assistant, is due any minute. She charges by the hour."

"Peggy?" Milo questioned.

"You know, Margaret…Peggy…it's the same person." Agnes explained. "Is Ichabod Crane gonna pick up the pace?"

"I asked. I did," Sutherland asserted. "He said 'no.' I guess it's a slow process."

"One way or another, we will be done by noon," Milo said.

Sutherland was a little taken aback. "You can't promise that."

"If he isn't done by noon, we'll do it another day," Milo said, still not convinced any of this was necessary. What was necessary was getting Morrie Wolf's granddaughter married, or he and Sutherland would be buried in the lawn.

§

Martha was pacing by the intercom in her cottage. It buzzed exactly at ten. She pushed the talk button. "Yes?"

"I'm Professor Bixby here to see Breanna Gibbson."

Martha pushed the *Gate Open* button. "Follow the lane to the left around the main house; it will lead you to our cottage. There's a small parking area next to it."

"Thank you," Bixby said.

Martha and Breanna went out to greet her as she parked her green Chevy Volt, stepped out, and looked around.

"We're very pleased to see you again," Martha said, "and pleased that Breanna won the scholarship."

"I'm pleased as well. I don't give the prize every year, only when I find someone who loves math as much as I do," Bixby explained.

Martha reached over to Breanna and gave her a small hug. Breanna smiled back.

Professor Bixby's attention was given to Ed on the back lawn.

"I have no idea who that is, or what he's doing," Martha said.

"It's ground penetrating radar. He's looking for something buried in the yard using sound waves," Bixby explained. "It's physics, math and science."

"I've seen them since early morning, but I didn't know what they're looking for. Would you like to come in, or should we have coffee and cookies out here?" Martha asked.

"Out here. It's a nice day," Bixby said. "But no coffee for me. I'm driving, and coffee makes me nervous. Water would be good."

They sat at the round, umbrellaed patio table and talked about the scholarship. Dr. Bixby explained that the scholarship paid for tuition, books, and living expenses for four years. She added Breanna would be expected to pursue something in math or science.

"I'm interested in astrophysics," Breanna said.

"That would be acceptable."

"That's a lot of money," Martha said. "Where does it come from?"

"Come from? Me of course."

"But it's called the Patricia Lind Scholarship. Who is Patricia Lind?" Martha asked.

"A friend. She died," Dr. Bixby said, biting into a cookie. "I like these cookies."

"Thank you," Martha said. "I'll give you some to take home."

Bixby stood up. "I would like to go down by the lake. I always like to look at the lake."

"It's beautiful," Martha said, preparing to go with her.

Bixby turned and said, "You don't need to come."

Martha watched Bixby stride down the path to the lake. "She's...direct." Martha said to Breanna, thinking rude might be more accurate.

"She's a math person. We like to get to the point."

§

Agnes' construction people were due in an hour. Her old schedule had built-in problem time. This new schedule, brought to you by nonexistent dead bodies, needed everything to work exactly as planned which rarely happened. To calm her mind, she took a brisk walk to the lake. When she arrived at the shore, Agnes was surprised to find a white-haired woman sitting in one of the Adirondack chairs facing the water.

"Hello?"

Dr. Bixby turned around. "Hello."

"I'm Agnes Larson. Can I help you?"

"No. I'm Professor Bella Bixby."

"Oh, Breanna's scholarship! How wonderful! We are all so proud of her! It's nice to meet you!"

"Why?"

"I'm sorry?" Agnes said, somewhat thrown by the abrupt question posed by the older white haired woman.

"Why is nice to meet me?"

Agnes was at a loss.

Dr. Bixby continued. "I like this view. I live up the shore now, but I don't have this close-up view of the ore boats. I always liked the ore boats. They don't seem to be moving, yet they make progress."

"I like them too. The lake, the boats, I find them calming," Agnes said.

Bixby looked at her. "Agreed."

Agnes sat down, and they both watched in silence as in the distance one of the newer, longer ore boats inched its way toward Duluth's Aerial Bridge. After about fifteen minutes Bixby asked, "Do you own this estate?"

Agnes laughed. "Oh heavens no. I'm the estate manager."

"Who owns it then?"

"Two gentlemen inherited it from John McKnight."

"Oh, I…"

"I am sure they'd love to meet you. Would you like to come up to the house?"

"Yes," She said without further comment.

They walked together in silence, passing Ed Patupick and his machine still on the quest for dead bodies.

Sutherland, sitting on the terrace, stood as the two women approached. Agnes did the introductions. "Where's Mr. Rathkey?" she asked.

"Reading in the library," Sutherland said. "Why don't you get him, and I'll set us up in the gallery."

"You'll love the gallery," Agnes said to Dr. Bixby, "It's a fun room. Everyone is amazed by it. Keep your eye out for the cat."

"Oh, I like cats!" Dr. Bixby exclaimed. "Let's go."

Sutherland led her into the glass-domed room where Bixby spotted Annie, up in her favorite tree. "What's her name?" Bixby asked.

"Annie," Sutherland said.

Dr. Bixby looked up. "Annie are you going to come down and meet me?"

For the moment, Annie wasn't interested but kept a watchful eye on Professor Bixby who informed Sutherland, "You can't hurry a cat."

They sat down in one of the seating areas. Bixby looked around at the trees, the birds, the glass-domed ceiling and said, "Ms. Larson was right. This room is fun. It has changed so much."

Sutherland was surprised. "Have you been here before?"

"I played in this room as a child. Of course, it didn't look like this."

"Professor Bixby?" Milo asked as he came in from the library. "I'm Milo Rathkey."

As they shook hands Sutherland informed Milo of the professor's previous visits to the house. "Professor Bixby was one of the children who played here."

"Maybe you can help us clear up a mystery," Milo said.

"I love mysteries," Bixby said.

Agnes came in with more of Martha's cookies.

"We're all proud of Breanna," Sutherland said.

Bixby took a cookie. "Whose idea was it to turn this room into a park?"

Sutherland explained that the gallery was his mother's project to brighten up the winters. Her plan was to include real birds but his father balked at that idea and they compromised with hand-painted, papier-mâché birds.

Bixby, in a stare down with the cat, agreed. "I would have preferred live birds too." Without so much as a meow, Annie came down from her perch and walked over to Bixby, rubbing against her leg. "Hello there," Bixby said picking her up. "I'm glad you came down to meet me. I've gotten too old to climb up in your tree, but you knew that didn't you?"

Annie gave her a silent meow and curled up in the professor's lap. Sutherland stared. "That cat likes you even more than it likes Milo. She only follows him for bacon."

Bixby looked at Milo as if seeing him for the first time. "Ms. Larson said you both inherited this house. Who are you?"

Sutherland jumped in. "To steal from Emily Dickinson,"

He's nobody

Bixby added, "It's one of my favorites."

Then there's a pair of us–don't tell.
They'd banish us you know.

"I only know poetry from Agatha Christie," Milo said.

Four and twenty blackbirds baked in a pie.

"That's a children's rhyme not poetry," Sutherland corrected.

"To answer Professor Bixby's original question before Sutherland waxed poetic, I'm the house detective," Milo said.

"Well, you mentioned a mystery," Bixby said, "Are you here to solve it?"

"I am. We are trying to find…"

The door to the terrace opened and Ed stepped into the gallery. "I'm done. There are no bodies in the back lawn."

"Good!" Agnes almost yelled.

Professor Bixby stood up. "Bodies buried in the back lawn…how interesting. But I must go. I have to teach a class soon."

Ed left to pack up his gear. Professor Bixby exited onto the terrace and walked back to Martha's cottage. Sutherland mused as to how they should have Ed check the front lawn.

"Still sure there are dead bodies on the grounds?" Milo teased.

"Of course. We know, or at least I know, they were murdered."

"How do you know that woman who just left isn't Annie? She's looks to be the right age and visited here as a child."

Sutherland hit his head with his hand. "We didn't ask her for a first name?"

"Bella," Agnes said. "Not Annie."

"I guess the only Annie here is the four legged kind," Sutherland said. "Ask Ed to check the front lawn."

"After the wedding," Agnes ordered.

19

Milo parked the Honda alongside Sutherland's bike-laden SUV. He grabbed two Excedrin from the giant Costco container on the floor behind the passenger seat, and put them in the zip pocket of his seldom-worn, quick-dry biking shorts.

Sutherland walked Milo's bike over to the Honda. "Here's the plan. We'll take the picture and then we'll do some serious trail riding. I think it may be too intense and athletic for you."

Milo bristled. "Bring it on," he bragged, patting the two pills in his pocket.

Sutherland laughed. "I'm serious. When the trail gets too intense pedal back up."

"Up the trail?" Milo questioned. "I don't do up the trail."

"Then don't go too far down the trail. In fact, don't go down the trail at all."

Other members of the Zenith City Cyclers began to arrive as did Megan and Reggie. Both looked like models on the cover of Cycle Magazine—trim and fit.

As they began to assemble for a group picture, Milo asked if they were going to wait for Larry and Danielle.

"I told you they couldn't make it," Sutherland explained.

"No you didn't."

"When we first talked about doing this, I said some people could not make the picture. Some people were Larry and Danielle."

"Oh."

Megan began to ask questions about the trails as she tucked her blond wisps into her helmet. "How far are we going today?"

Sutherland pointed to the posted trail map. "We are at the far western edge of the trails. I thought we would pedal east until we decide to turn around. There are a couple of side trails that are a little more extreme if you want to do them."

She glanced at Reggie who nodded his approval as he adjusted his helmet over his dreads. "I think Reggie and I are up for it. We'll need to stop from time to time for Reggie's pictures."

Milo was checking out Reggie's cameras which included GoPro cameras attached to his bike and helmet, along with a DSL camera and a slew of lenses.

"What happens here when it rains?" Megan asked.

"Like most places, when the trails are wet, we can't use them. There's a daily update on trail conditions, and today all trails are dry and open. By the way most of these trails are single track. We have to yield to horses, hikers, and bikes going uphill."

"Horses? There are horses? Horses don't like me," Milo stated.

Megan laughed.

Sutherland mumbled, "Horses have good taste," as he assembled everyone for the photo.

Reggie set up his camera, dealt with a few minor lighting problems, and set the timer, giving himself fifteen seconds to get into place. It all worked and after three takes they headed down the trail called *Calculated Risk*. Sutherland led the way. Milo pulled up the rear.

The track was a little uneven since it was a dirt trail rather than smooth blacktop. Meandering right for fifty yards, the wide track narrowed as it turned to the left. Milo knew he was going downhill, but it was gradual until it wasn't. Without warning, the trail changed from rutted to gnarled and plunged in bobsled fashion.

Milo bounced from rut to rock all the time gaining speed. Thick, solid trees on each side kept him trapped in an ever narrowing, ever steeper chute. His tires bumped and skidded over the rocks as he fought to maintain control.

This is a hospital visit waiting to happen, Milo thought as he panicked and applied all the brakes he could remember. Unfortunately, he forgot to do them in order, squeezing the front breaks first. As the back end of the bike raised up, the front tires skidded sideways causing Milo to lurch off the bike and careen across the rocky trail slamming to a stop between two thick trees.

Crumpled on the ground, he began moving body parts—plenty of aches but no sharp pains. He inched over to one of the trees, sat up, and leaned against it. His knee and shin were bloodied as was his right hand and elbow.

I don't think a couple of small Band-Aids are going to fix this.

He stood up, balancing against the tree, and looked for the bike. It had wedged itself between two large boulders on the other side of the trail. Fighting the urge to leave it there, he freed it from the boulders and used it to lean on, rolling his way up the hill.

Milo leaned the bike on Sutherland's SUV, and, using the water bottle, downed the two pocketed Excedrin. The Bike's front tire was a little wonky but then so was Milo. He was sure he would never touch that bike again. By the end of the summer, with great enthusiasm, Milo let Sutherland donate it to an organization that provided trail bikes for kids.

Steering the Honda into the Lakesong garage, Milo limped into his bathroom to clean up. His knee needed a wide Band-Aid as did his elbow. They had taken the brunt of the fall. The minor raspberries up his arms and legs didn't need any more than cleaning. What he needed now was a sandwich and time in the library with a good mystery.

§

"Where's Milo?" Megan asked as they stopped to let Reggie take pictures.

Sutherland looked at the group. Milo was missing. "I guess he's headed back up the hill. The trail was too steep for him."

"Shouldn't we check?"

Sutherland took his phone from the bike phone mount and called Milo.

"Emergency room," Milo answered.

"Ha ha, funny. Where are you?"

"I'm home, reading a book."

"Good. We'll be a couple more hours. I invited Megan and Reggie to dinner."

"Okay," Milo hung up.

"He's back at Lakesong," Sutherland told Megan.

"He's missing this wonderful ride,"

"Milo's not ready for this yet," Sutherland said with misplaced optimism.

Megan was about to go over to Reggie when her phone rang. It was the Duluth Police department. Lieutenant Gramm asked if she could stop up sometime this afternoon to answer a few questions.

"The police want to talk to me about Saturday morning," She told Sutherland.

"Does that impact dinner?"

"It shouldn't—unless of course they arrest me," she laughed.

§

Liz Brooks packed up her remaining clothes and wheeled her suitcase to the elevator. Agnes Larson's Lakeside house was comfortable, and the company was fun. Being urged by police to stay in Duluth, she was glad to spend time in the warmth of a home rather than a lonely hotel. When Liz called Bob to tell him she would be staying a few more days, he told her about the phone call from the police checking the lawsuit story.

"Did they buy it?" Liz asked.

"Seemed to," he said.

The elevator door opened to the hotel's front desk. Liz clicked off and slipped her phone into her purse. It looked like checking out would be fast—two desk people, one customer.

She was told she missed checkout time and would be charged for a half day. As she waited for her bill, she noticed the woman next to her resembled an LA celebrity evading the paparazzi, complete with sunglasses and wrap around scarf. Intrigued, Liz began to listen to the woman's conversation.

"I'm sorry ma'am but these two credit cards have been denied," the man at the reservation desk said as he handed her back her cards.

"That's impossible! I used them this morning," the woman argued. "Why are they being denied?"

"I don't know ma'am. All we get is a code that says denied. They don't tell us why. Maybe you would like to call your credit card companies."

The woman took out her phone and tried to dial, but the phone did not respond. "My phone won't work. What do I do?"

Liz chimed in, "If you set your phone to Wi-Fi calling, you can use the hotel Wi-Fi to call out."

The woman fumbled with her phone before finally admitting, "I don't know how to do that."

Liz held out her hand. "Here, I'll help you."

As the woman handed over her phone, the scarf began slipping off her head. Liz was shocked. The out-of-place celebrity was Maureen. The scarf wasn't hiding her from the cameras; it was hiding two dark bruises and a cut lip.

"Oh my God! Maureen, what happened?"

Maureen grabbed onto the front desk to steady herself. As she spoke, Liz could smell the gin on her breath. "I would say I ran into a door but screw it. I ran into Cliff's fist. He wasn't careful today."

"Sign here, Ms. Brooks," Liz's desk attended held out a copy of her bill.

"Cancel that," Liz said. "I'm keeping the room."

"Very well," the man said, looking a little put out.

"Let's go up to my room Maureen," Liz said. Turning to the desk person, she added, "Have a pot of coffee and an ice bag sent to 1103 please."

"Yes ma'am."

She handed him a twenty-dollar bill. "Tell them to rush."

The man nodded and in a hushed tone asked if her friend needed a doctor.

"No!" Maureen almost shouted.

"We'll let you know," Liz said. "Thank you."

§

Martha joined Agnes on the back terrace, handing her a large glass of iced tea. Agnes' angst over her disrupted wedding schedule was dissipating.

"Oh, thanks. I was going to get tea but was afraid to leave for fear that this progress was an illusion." Agnes pointed to the activity on the back lawn. "Look, my decking is finished, the tents are going up on schedule, and there's no rain in the forecast."

"It looks real to me," Martha said, watching the work.

"The tent people added more workers to get it done. Milo approved the extra expense and said to send the bill to Sutherland."

Both women laughed.

"What was that guy doing out here this morning?" Martha asked.

Agnes closed her eyes as if trying to erase the memory. "Looking for dead bodies."

"What?"

"I swear Sutherland is trying to be Milo and was sure somebody—who disappeared in the fifties—was buried in the back yard."

"For real?"

"Yeah for real, but don't worry, he didn't find a thing," Agnes sighed. "I thought at first being a house manager was going to be dull. So far this week, we are trying to find dead bodies in the back yard while preparing a wedding for a mobster's granddaughter."

"Happily, I have no cadavers interrupting my plans, and I am cooking a wedding feast in a kitchen I never knew existed until Mr. Rathkey showed up."

"How's that going? The wedding feast I mean," Agnes asked.

"Great," Martha said as she put her feet up on a hassock. "My sous chefs are working away. There are perks to this executive chef gig."

Agnes took a sip of her drink as she watched Peggy directing the crews. "It's only Thursday. I wonder what's going to happen next."

§

Annie was curled up on the rug as Milo woke up in one of two oversized brown leather chairs that flanked the large fireplace in the book-lined library. The last thing he remembered was Poirot extolling the virtues of the little gray cells. Milo's little gray cells had decided to take a snooze. He rubbed his eyes and stretched his legs. Both movements reminded him of his dreadful morning on two wheels. The trip down the trail had loaded his body with adrenaline masking the pain. Now he hurt.

Annie gave him a side-eye and a silent meow.

"Okay, cat, I get you bacon…how about you get me two Excedrin, and a glass of water."

Annie got up, stretched, and strolled out of the room.

"I'll take that as a no," Milo said, inching to the edge of the chair. He put his hands on the overstuffed arms and on a count of three pushed his body to an upright position. Looking down at his bandaged right knee he decided to move the left leg first. That seemed to work. He dragged the right up to the left, keeping it stiff.

Milo checked the time and decided the first order of business was Excedrin. Carrying his sandwich plate with him, he limped through the gallery to his bedroom stopping in the bathroom where he rested by bracing himself on the sink, taking weight off his leg.

Why are these rooms so big?

He opened the medicine cabinet, grabbed his favorite medicine, cupped his hand under the facet to catch a mouthful of water, and downed two more tablets. Milo thought about hiding the plate in a drawer until he didn't hurt as much but his conscience got the better of him. He limped back through the gallery and returned the plate to the kitchen.

Martha told him if he needed anything to just leave a note on the island where she kept a notepad. Limping to the island he wrote the words, *paper plates.*

Milo needed to sit down and thought Martha wouldn't mind if he sat down for a minute at her kitchen desk. This was the first time he noticed the framed picture of Martha, her parents, and her sibs. It was a nice group picture, everyone was smiling. It reminded him of the group picture taken this morning where he was not smiling. Framing that picture in his mind made him uncomfortable. Something wasn't right. *I don't get it. It makes no sense.* Milo limped to his office. *I need more information.* He fired up the computer.

What should have been a standard search kept hitting a dead end. On a lark, Milo checked out a crazy idea he had been harboring for several days.

He began again, this time looking for an old photograph. It took a while, but from an internet copy of a defunct business magazine, he found it. Calling Patupick for Photoshop instruction, he was able to take the small, grainy photo and improve it.

Looking at the corrected picture, Milo whispered, "Crazy, but I was right."

Expanding his search beyond the photo, the dots began to connect. He wrote down notes and called Gramm.

"Hey Milo, find any more tunnels?"

"No smart guy. I've been connecting dots."

Knowing this was a good sign, Gramm was excited.

Milo continued. "Find out if Vogel ever did any business with a Druid Development Company in Atlanta."

"Okay," Gramm said, with hesitation. "And your dots led you to this?"

"Maybe."

"Do I need to know about these dots?"

"Not yet. Just get the information."

Milo heard Gramm yell for White. "We have to get information for our esteemed consultant. He's doing that brain thing again."

Gramm hung up.

§

White listened on the speaker phone as Gramm talked to Jessica Vogel's ex-husband Phil Berg once again. Berg confirmed that Vogel had worked with the people at Druid Development Company selling new condos for them. He added that the Druid Company was the one with the suspicious deaths he had mentioned before, the CEO and the CFO.

"Why are we checking on this?" she asked, after Berg hung up.

"I don't have a clue, something Milo came up with," Gramm said.

White's phone buzzed. She checked the screen. "Megan Davis is in the lobby."

"I'm debating where we should do this interview. I'm thinking here in the office," Gramm said.

"I agree, less formal. After all, the only reason we're talking to her is because Milo wants to know why she wasn't in the drone video."

"Tell me again—does he work for us, or do we work for him?"

White laughed, called the front desk, and brought in another chair. Megan was ushered into the office by one of the desk people. She shook hands with Gramm and White and sat down. "Sorry I look so dusty. I have been biking your magnificent trails. How can I help?"

Gramm turned the computer around and hit play on the drone video. "Your photographer shot this Saturday morning when we think the murder was being committed."

Megan looked at the video. "Yes?" She seemed puzzled.

"Where are you?"

Megan laughed. "That's what this is about? I was in the bathroom."

Gramm paused the video. "The bathroom that's halfway between your photographer and Enger Tower?"

"I guess." Megan said.

"Did you hear a scream?" White asked.

"No. I was in the bathroom."

White flipped through pages of her notes. "That's not what you told us the morning of the murder, Ms. Davis."

"It isn't? I don't remember," Megan answered, feeling uncomfortable.

"Twice you said, *we* heard the scream. Now you're saying you didn't hear the scream."

"Am I in trouble? Reggie told me he heard a scream. I didn't think it was that big a deal if I said I heard it too."

"It's a big deal," Gramm insisted.

"Kinda strange you'd lie about something like that," White said.

Megan's discomfort was growing. "I didn't mean to lie. I guess…I just said it. If I had been with Reggie, I would have heard it."

What began as routine questioning was taking on a more adversarial tone.

"Have you ever lived in Atlanta or Minneapolis?" Gramm asked.

"Atlanta. Why?"

"Because I asked you. This is a murder investigation."

"Okay." Megan began to squirm in her chair.

"What did you do when you lived in Atlanta?" White asked.

"I was a student at Emory." Not wanting to be accused of lying again, she told them about her part-time jobs as a waitress, store clerk, and receptionist at a real estate office.

White flipped her pages to Rathkey's question. "The real estate office…was it the Druid Development Company?"

Megan looked shocked. "Yeah. How did you know?"

"Did you know a woman named Jessica Berg?"

Megan closed her eyes and ran her fingers through her disheveled blond hair. "I…I don't remember that name. It was more than ten years ago. I'm trying. I am. What did she do for the Druid people?"

"She sold condos for them."

"Oh, that would make her an agent…you know…a private contractor. I was office help, answering phones, things like that." Thinking this answer got her off the hook she asked, "Who is Jessica Berg?"

"Why would you ask?" White questioned.

Megan shrugged. "I'm a newspaper reporter. You mentioned a name. I'm curious. Who is she?"

"She's the murder victim whose scream you didn't hear."

20

Maureen threw up twice before Liz thought it safe for her to drink coffee. As she began her second cup, she was still drunk, but chatty. She began telling Liz about Kendrick, the foolish picture, and Jessica's blackmail.

"My life's a mess. I don't know what I'm going to do," Maureen worried.

"I do," Liz said. "Here's what's going to happen. First, we are going to a meeting that I think will help you. Then we're going to the police where you are going to file a criminal complaint against your husband."

"I can't do that," Maureen replied. "It will ruin him, and it'll be all my fault."

"Your fault? Is your bruised face and cut lip your fault? That Kendrick picture is you being victimized in high school and it's happening again. It wasn't your fault then. It's not your fault now."

"But Cliff said…"

"Cliff can tell it to the cops."

Maureen stopped and stared out the window. "It sounds so reasonable when you say it."

Liz inched her chair closer to Maureen's, so she was sitting face to face. "That's because it is reasonable. You're going to stay here tonight. You're going to be safe. Right now, go clean up. We're going to that meeting."

Maureen wasn't stupid. She knew an Alcoholics Anonymous meeting when she saw one. She had even attended one once. Half of the chairs in the basement of the First Lutheran Church on Second Street were filled. She and Liz sat down in the back. The group leader introduced himself and asked if anyone wanted to speak. Maureen's head was pounding.

Liz got up and walked to the front. Maureen closed her eyes and lowered her head. Fearing that she would be recognized and her situation would become a public spectacle, she started to get up to leave.

From the front of the room she heard, "Good evening. My name is Liz. I'm an alcoholic."

A chorus of 'Hi Liz' filled the room. Maureen was the only one not to offer the expected greeting. She sat back down in stunned silence.

§

"Were you planning on going home at a normal hour?" White asked as she strolled into Gramm's office.

"Apparently not," Gramm grimaced. "Whaddaya got?"

"Guess who's filing a criminal complaint."

"I don't know. Milo? Agnes Larson?"

White smirked. "Close, not quite. Maureen Donahue."

"Against us? We didn't do anything to her."

"No. Not us. She's filing a criminal complaint against her husband Councilman Cliff. He beat her up."

"City councilman Cliff Donahue. Oh, this is going to be a long night. Where is Mrs. Donahue now?"

"At my desk along with Liz Brooks."

"Call Councilman Cliff and tell him to surrender. I'll call the chief and let him know what's going on."

Maureen's thinking was clearer. As her eyes flitted around the bullpen area she confessed, "Before this week, I'd never been to a police station. This is my second visit this week," she said to Liz.

"If you keep drinking, you will see a lot of police stations. I did."

"I didn't know."

"Not many do."

"I'm sorry I told the police about your phone call. If you hired a hitman that's okay with me."

Liz laughed. "You got it wrong. Our hitman was a lawyer to sue Jessica, not kill her."

"Oh. So, you didn't kill her?"

"No, I was at that same AA meeting Saturday morning."

Maureen explained her situation of being in the tower but not remembering.

White returned to her desk and finished filling out the criminal complaint. Writing up domestic violence charges was not a normal part of White's job. In this case it made sense because of Maureen's involvement with the murder.

Fifteen minutes later, Cliff Donahue arrived and identified himself to the desk sergeant who mistakenly let him proceed on his own. He charged into the bullpen area, zeroing in on Maureen. She shuddered when she saw how angry he was.

"You goddamn drunk! What are you trying to do to me now?" he shouted.

White jumped up, careful to get herself between husband and wife. "Calm down Mr. Donahue."

Cliff puffed up to his full six-feet-two height. His cold eyes drilled into hers. "Don't tell me what to do, Missy," Cliff yelled, shoving White out of the way, grabbing his wife by the arm. "Come with me, Maureen!"

White whirled around, grabbed Cliff's wrist, twisting his arm behind his back. The pain forced him to release Maureen. He screamed but struggled. White wrenched his arm farther up his back, slamming his face onto the desk.

"You have the right to remain silent…"

"What? I am…who's in charge here?" he yelled into the desk.

Gramm stood in his office door. "That would be me," he challenged. "Officer White continue to arrest this man for assaulting a police officer. Cuff him. I assure you councilman, I saw the whole thing…it's even on video. You make quite an impression."

Maureen and Liz watched in shocked silence as two officers escorted a still yelling Cliff to a cell. White sat down adding Cliff's assault to her paperwork.

Gramm walked over to White and asked, "That TV reporter, the one who helped us out a couple of times. What's his name?"

White looked up. "Are you talking about Max?"

"Yeah, him. We owe him. Call him up and tell him Councilman Cliff has been arrested."

White laughed. "You are evil."

§

Liz took Maureen back to the hotel and called Agnes, filling her in on the situation, saying she would stay in the hotel with Maureen tonight. Agnes suggested bringing Maureen to her house, but Liz declined. "If Cliff gets out of jail tonight, it could be a dangerous situation. The hotel is safer."

Sophie was listening in on speaker. "I'll be right there. If Cliff comes to the hotel with me there, he'll leave in a body bag."

Liz had to admit that Sophie was better equipped to handle Cliff, so the two switched places.

§

"We would have had drinks out on the terrace," Sutherland told his guests, "but we have a wedding out there on Saturday and the construction still going on. It's noisy… not great for conversation."

"I didn't know weddings needed construction," Megan Davis remarked.

"Either did I," Milo said. "But don't tell our house manager."

"Congratulations. Which one of you is getting married?" Reggie Cuff asked.

Sutherland laughed. "Neither of us. It's a wedding for…"

"A friend," Milo jumped in.

Megan looked around the gallery. "I so enjoy this room. Is that a real cat up there in that tree? I didn't see her before."

Annie did her silent meow to let Megan know that she wasn't paper and paint like the birds.

"That's Annie the cat," Milo said. "She's a full-time resident, part-time critic."

Reggie pointed at Milo. "Where did you go this afternoon? You weren't at the first rest break."

"And we noticed you're limping," Megan added.

"That trail attacked me, and I have scars," he said, presenting his bandaged elbow and knee.

"Did you piled up on the rock gardens?" Megan asked.

"Gardens? There were no flowers in the dirt I hit, just rocks."

Sutherland sighed. "He does well on flat blacktop."

"Hello? I'm right here in the room. People keep talking about me as if I'm not here," Milo complained.

Sutherland turned to him, "I'm sorry you washed out, but I told you not to try it."

"Those trails are challenging, Sutherland," Megan broke in. "I was impressed."

"My whole body was impressed," Milo joked. "I was impressed from rock to rock and then a tree in there somewhere."

"Okay, you had a tough day," Sutherland laughed.

"So did I," Megan said, "but not on the trail…in the police station."

"What? Why?" Sutherland blurted.

Megan put her arm on Reggie's shoulder. "My partner's drone video of that tower on Saturday morning didn't show my smiling face. The cops noticed and wanted to know where I was," She laughed. "I was in the bathroom."

Milo stayed silent.

"Well…as the police and I were chatting, I found out the dead woman sold condos for a company that I work for in college. I don't remember her. I answered phones to make my rent. She was at a much higher pay grade."

"The Druid Development Company?" Milo asked.

"Yeah! How do you know about that company? It's been out of business for years," Megan asked.

"Just guessing," Milo said.

Guess? I doubt it. Sutherland thought there was much more to Milo's guess, but this was not the time to inquire.

Megan changed the subject back to biking. "Did the city build those trails?"

"The money is both public and private. I supported them and a number of other business people chipped in. It's good for tourism which helps the whole area," Sutherland explained.

Milo didn't realize Sutherland invested his own money in the trails.

Sutherland continued. "We only did a small portion of the trails today. Milo and I will be busy the next two days, but we can start at Twin Ponds Sunday morning and go farther east."

"I'm going to be taking scenics of Duluth on Sunday," Reggie said. "Can you pick Megan up from the hotel? We only rented one car—cutbacks."

"Sure," Sutherland said. "My friend—the one who hates my bike—may be with us, so you can chide him vigorously."

"Will do," Megan agreed. "Are you coming, Milo?"

"I would love to, but I have some extreme healing to do."

Megan laughed. "Healing is good, but when you're healed what do you like to do Milo?"

"Swim and play tennis," Milo said.

"Is there a court on the grounds?" Megan asked.

"Yup."

"We'll have to play a friendly match before we leave."

"No!" Sutherland almost shouted. Everyone looked at him. "I have learned Milo does not put tennis and friendly in the same sentence."

"He exaggerates," Milo said.

Martha announced dinner, and the group headed to the family room.

§

Joining team Maureen, Agnes called Milo for the name of his lawyer friend, so Maureen could have representation. Saul Feinberg was more than happy to oblige, having never liked Cliff Donahue. With that call to Feinberg, wheels were set in in motion for a restraining order which a judge signed that evening.

When Cliff's lawyer bailed him out around midnight, Saul was waiting to serve him with the order in front of

Channel Ten's cameras. Someone tipped them off. Cliff was fuming, but rather than bothering with his wife, he and his campaign manager spent the night trying to figure out how to spin this mess.

21

ilo was looking forward to a calm and healing Friday. No trails to ride, no tennis to play, not even a kidnapping. He was hoping to stay awake long enough to finish his reread of Christie's *A Murder Is Announced*, but first, breakfast. Milo slipped two Excedrin into his mouth and washed them down with orange juice.

"Still taking those little white pills?" Sutherland chided.

Rathkey gave him a nasty look. "Between you and Mary Alice, I'm lucky I can move."

"I meant it last night when I said I was sorry you got hurt." Sutherland pushed two of his pills over to Milo. "Try these."

"Are these the two strippers—Tammy and Gilda?"

"Yes, Turmeric and Ginger," Sutherland corrected, getting used to Milo's dry humor.

Milo shrugged and downed the pills with more orange juice. "The trail was a plot to get me hooked on these. What are Tammy and Gilda?"

"When pronounced properly, they're spices."

"Like salt and pepper?" Milo cracked.

"Yes, exactly like salt and pepper."

Entering the morning room, Agnes proclaimed, "Gentlemen, so glad I caught you together. I have two clipboards here, one for each of you."

"How wonderful," Milo said. "And it's not even my birthday."

Sutherland took a cue from Milo. "I was about to rush Milo to the hospital for his heart attack."

"He looks fine to me," Agnes said.

"For his…heart attack!" Sutherland over enunciated trying to get Milo on board.

"Oh yeah right." Milo stopped eating his hash browns and grabbed his chest feigning an attack.

Agnes wondered if they were grown men or teenage boys. "Are you two finished?"

"We can do three or four more minutes," Milo said.

"Please don't!" Agnes handed each one a clipboard. "Trucks will be coming and going all morning. I have a guy named Fred stopping them on the side street in front of the back gate. When they come up to unload, you two have lists of what each truck should be carrying. Both of you are to make sure they unload everything they're supposed to. If we are short something, you must radio me at once."

"We have radios?" Sutherland blurted. "This could be fun."

"Does he get a special whistle too?" Milo asked.

Walking out of the morning room Agnes added, "The trucks will begin arriving in fifteen minutes, so eat up."

"I think I'm back in the Navy," Milo complained. "She could be a Chief Petty Officer."

"Cast off sailor; we have work to do," Sutherland said.

"I thought I was having a heart attack."

"Yeah about that. You're a terrible actor."

§

Ilene was sporting shorts and a tank top as she stepped down from the bakery delivery van. "Milo left the luxury apartment above my bakery for this hovel?" she joked as she shook hands with Martha.

"The man has no taste," Martha laughed. "You know most bakers show up in a white uniform."

"Yeah, Martha, but I'm a walking work of art." Ilene laughed, displaying the tattoos on her arm and her current hair color, blue.

"You are creative, Ilene."

"And so is my baking."

Martha knew that was no lie. "Let me show you how to get the cake down to the big refrigerators in the catering kitchen. It's through the garage."

Martha raised one of the garage doors and Ilene started to laugh. "I love Milo's Honda sitting next to these babies." She pointed to the Bentley and the Rolls. "The man has no shame."

Martha nodded. "You know him well." She guided Ilene into the hallway and the door leading to the elevator.

"I love this," Ilene said. "This is going to help. Ever try to bring a cake up and down stairs?"

"The elevator was a Milo revelation," Martha said as she pulled the elevator doors shut.

"You have an elevator, and you didn't know about it?"

"We have a catering kitchen, and I didn't know about it."

Pushing through the kitchen *IN* door, Ilene looked around. "You could feed an army from here!"

"Tomorrow I'll be doing that."

Three sous chefs were busy cutting and chopping vegies, small filets, whitefish, and creating hors d'oeuvres to Martha's specifications. "Do you need help with the cake?" Martha asked.

"I've got my nephew in the van, we'll get it done. Which refrigerator?"

"Take the left one; the middle one has sushi and whitefish, the one on the end has everything else."

"I didn't know the refrigerators were this big, so I left the cake in sections. Tomorrow morning I'll come and put it together. I'll also bring the other bakery items. Lucky bride to get in here. You don't usually do weddings, do you?"

"No, never."

"How did she wrangle this place?"

"The bride's the granddaughter of one of Milo's friends."

"Milo has friends? Go figure."

§

The trucks were set to arrive every thirty minutes. Agnes was not naïve enough to think the process would proceed without a hitch, so she planned for problems. Most important to her plan was Fred, an eager college student stationed at the side gate to keep too many trucks from entering the grounds at one time.

Milo and Sutherland were performing their due diligence, counting tables, chairs, boxes of linens, plates, silverware, glasses, sound equipment, bar stations, coolers, freezers, fans, and ice makers. The list went on and on.

This was one of Duluth's hot days, ninety-two degrees and rising. Milo kept waiting for the wind to shift off the lake. It didn't.

"Ah, Ms. Larson," The radio crackled.

"Yes Fred?"

"There's a large angry man in a truck here who doesn't want to wait his turn. He says if he doesn't get in now, he will break my kneecaps. Ms. Larson, I believe him."

"Mr. Rathkey!" Agnes yelled into the radio.

Milo clicked the talk button. "That would be the booze from the Rasa Bar...not on my clipboard, but I suggest letting him in unless Fred wants to walk with a limp. Sutherland can direct him."

Hearing the chatter of an angry, threatening man heading his way, Sutherland sprinted over to Milo and shoved the liquor list at him. "Yours."

"Coward," Milo charged, waving Milosh and Benny forward to his line.

"Where do you want this stuff, Milo?" Milosh asked as Agnes radioed, "Liquor goes in the middle tent."

Without warning, Milosh took off over the lawn. Milo, still nursing a sore leg, hobbled over, arriving as Benny began unloading cases of liquor.

"I have orders to count the cases," Milo apologized.

Milosh walked up to him smiling. That was a good sign. "Milo, do you think Morrie is going to cheat his granddaughter?"

"No. I'm doing what I'm told."

"Trust me. You got everything and then some. Go take a load off. We got this."

Milo leaned against one of the deck railings meant to kept people from falling off during the reception. His phone did the *Gramm* ring. Milo answered.

"Milo?"

Milo put his finger in his unused ear to drown out the beeping sound of a backing truck then someone started a generator. Adding to the noise, Agnes was giving radio directions to Sutherland.

"What the hell is going on Milo? Are you running a circus?"

Agnes yelled over the radio. "Mr. Rathkey! Where are you? Are you checking the liquor truck?" Milo turned it off.

"Working a loading dock?" Gramm asked again.

"I needed a part-time job. Millions of bucks don't go as far as it used to." As soon as he said it Milo mentally slapped himself. He had never told Ernie, or any of his old friends, how much money he inherited. It embarrassed him.

"Millions! Are you kidding me? I thought you got like a couple hundred grand. Millions?"

"Yeah, like I got millions. I made that up. You needed to feel bad today."

"Nice try asshole. Millions. Wow. I mean I kidded about you being a millionaire…but you are one."

"Why did you call?" Milo asked.

"This Druid Development Company—how did you know our victim did work for them?"

"Lucky guess?"

"I got my boss breathing down my neck. Last night I arrested a city councilman. There's no time for lucky guesses. I need to know how you knew."

"Soon."

"This Druid Company had suspicious deaths weeks before Vogel left Atlanta. The CEO and the CFO died."

"Both?"

"Yeah. CEO killed in a boating accident. The CFO fell from a construction site."

Agnes charged over to Milo and yelled, "Your radio is off!"

"Gotta go," Milo said.

"We've gotta talk about this!" Gramm insisted.

"Later," Milo hung up.

"Your radio..." Agnes repeated.

Milo looked at the yellow and black device. "Oh yeah, how did that happen?"

"Are you counting the liquor?"

"No need to, it's coming from Morrie."

Agnes went over to Morrie's men. "Who's in charge here?"

Milosh lumbered over. "Me. I'm in charge."

Looking up at the tall, muscled man, Agnes fumed. "Sir, I don't appreciate you threatening my gate person."

"Oh, we didn't threaten him Ma'am. We were just speculating on how he could get around should both his legs be broken. You know, it was just a question."

"Fred, that young man at the gate, is doing his job, unlike some people," Agnes said, giving Milo a dirty look. "It seems I have to make sure we have enough liquor."

"Hey Bennie, how much vodka we got?" Milosh asked.

"Two cases."

"I asked for only one case," Agnes said, looking at the cases still coming off the truck.

"Yeah, Morrie wants to make sure you don't run out."

"That's nice of Mr. Wolf, but if you multiplied my entire order by two, I have no room for those boxes."

Milosh looked around. "Big house…gotta be room somewhere. Tell you what, I'll send a couple of the boys here, and they'll put those boxes anywhere you want."

Agnes was about to protest further when Milo jumped in. "Sounds good, thanks."

Agnes whispered to Milo. "Will they pick them up after the wedding?"

"No, I don't think so. Whatever the bride and groom leave behind is a gift to Lakesong."

Agnes shook her head and started walking away, muttering, "More is not always better."

§

Sophie was watching television in the sitting area when Liz arrived at her hotel room. "Where's Maureen?" she asked Sophie.

"She's on the phone in the bedroom."

"She's not talking to that husband, is she?"

"No, I checked. She's talking to her brother."

"Good," Liz said as she sat down on a nearby chair. "How was last night?"

"The usual, some crying, some sleeping."

"And how was Maureen?" Liz kidded.

Moscatelli flipped her middle finger just as Maureen joined the conversation.

"Good news," Maureen said, sitting down.

Liz handed her a bottle of Gatorade. "Drink it. It'll rebalance your electrolytes."

"What's the good news?" Sophie asked.

"I have money," Maureen said responding to the question. "When my esteemed father died, he left all his money to my brother."

"Why?" Sophie asked.

"He didn't believe women should have their own money."

"You're kidding?" Liz asked in disbelief. "Was he born in the sixteen hundreds?"

"Might as well have been. My brother is kinder and more enlightened. Matt told me he invested what should have been my share in a separate account."

"That's great, but why didn't he give it to you before?" Liz asked.

Maureen laughed. "He never liked Cliff or trusted him. Matt didn't want him getting his hands on my money."

"Wise man," Liz added.

Maureen sighed. "I also talked to that lawyer you got me Liz. How did you know him?"

"Agnes knows him," Liz said. "She says he's exceptional."

"I hope so because I will need a good one."

"For a divorce?" Sophie asked.

Maureen looked surprised. "Yeah...I guess. Right now, I need help with a possible murder charge. I don't remember Saturday morning at all."

Sophie looked shocked. "What are you talking about?"

Liz jumped in. "She was drinking Saturday morning, and she must have binged because she had a blackout."

"Liz took me to an AA meeting with her," Maureen said.

Sophie looked surprised. "With her?" she asked.

"I'm an alcoholic," Liz said. "It's how I coped after Molly's murder. It's where I was Saturday morning."

"I...I...don't know what to say. I thought you weren't drinking because you were pregnant," Sophie said.

"Well, that's true, but I haven't had a drink in five years."

"That lets you off the hook," Sophie said.

"Hardly. It's Alcoholics Anonymous, and I'm new in town. Nobody there knows who I am and I don't know them. If the cops check, they'll have trouble verifying my story."

Maureen got up and looked out the hotel window. She was appreciative for Liz's and Sophie's support, but she couldn't help thinking that they all had a reason to want Jessica dead. Which one of them acted on it?

§

The clamor and chaos of the last delivery day dissipated and was replaced by the chatter of guests as they began to arrive for the rehearsal dinner. Agnes stood back and watched the gallery fill with family and friends of the bride and groom. Voices grew in number and volume, a symphony of celebration.

"This is gorgeous!"

"How did you find this place?"

Agnes glowed, catching snippets of conversation.

"Look outside! You can see the lake!"

The squeals and hugs of the bridesmaids came from the left. "Can you believe the day is finally here?"

"I can't believe it!"

"I'm so excited!"

"Joe is so lucky."

From the bro corner on the right, a much different conversation. "Dude! You ready for this?"

"I just stand there right?"

"Is there an open bar?"

The bride and groom broke away and stood side by side looking out at the back lawn. "Joe!" Brittany exclaimed, as she saw the back lawn set up for their wedding, "This is wonderful!"

"You are wonderful." Joe smiled at her.

"I am so excited!" Brittany said, squeezing his arm and leaning against him. "How about you?" she whispered.

He looked at her and kissed her lightly on the forehead. "Let's do this."

Agnes and Peggy visited all the groups, ushering them onto the back lawn.

"Welcome to Lakesong," Agnes said. "Who's taking charge of the rehearsal?"

"I am." A freckled, red haired, friendly looking woman raised her hand. "Reverend Joy Atkin."

Agnes shook her hand. "Good to meet you. Let's begin."

As guests not in the rehearsal took their seats, Stephanie, mother of the bride, said to Agnes, "Everything looks wonderful! Thank you!"

"This is so much more than we could have ever expected," Brittany gushed. "The only thing we're missing are the twinkling lights on the walls, but then we have no walls."

Agnes cued her radio. "Peggy, hit the tree lights."

Brittany gasped as the trees nearest the tents lit up against the darkening sky in a delicate array of twinkling light.

"It's not a wall, but..."

"It's wonderful!" Brittany answered.

Joy called the wedding party down to the archway overlooking the lake. Being a veteran of many weddings, she knew most of the people were anxious to get on with it and begin the rehearsal dinner.

"Okay, ushers escort the grandmothers to the front chairs. Grandfathers walk behind. Good. Next the mothers; fathers walk behind. The groom and best man come in from the side. Excellent. Now let's pair up the bridesmaids and groomsmen."

Sutherland and Milo were sitting on the terrace watching the proceedings. "I never realized groomsmen and bridesmaids were paired by height," Sutherland said.

"I didn't either, and I've been married," Milo added. "I should have paid more attention."

"If no one was murdered at your wedding, chances are you wouldn't have noticed," Sutherland joked. "By the way, do you have a plus one?"

"Who am I bringing? Just Mary Alice."

Sutherland stared at him. "One does not *just* bring Mary Alice."

Milo knew exactly what Sutherland was saying but underplayed it. "She's my tennis partner."

"Yeah right. You tell yourself that," Sutherland laughed. "More shocking than you asking is her accepting?"

Milo had no clue why the mesmerizing Mary Alice would want to spend time with him, but she had accepted. "Why not? It's free food. It's good free food. It's Martha's. Who are you plus oneing, wise guy?"

"I've asked Agnes to sit with me."

"Sit with you? What does that mean?"

"I will be her escort if she needs one."

"Why would she need one?" Milo persisted

Sutherland was flustered. He wasn't quite sure what he meant either. He was attracted to Agnes, but he was her employer. That made it complicated. *Sitting with* and *escorting* seemed safer than *plus oneing*. "Her assistant, Peggy, is handling the day of the wedding. Agnes is going to try to be a guest. I thought she might need an escort.

"I want to thank you gentlemen," Linda Baer, the bride's grandmother, interrupted. "You were true to your word; no Morrie anywhere."

Milo almost didn't recognize Linda without her jeans and steel-toed boots. "He'll be here tomorrow."

"I know. He's got a pass on the wedding and reception." Linda paused and stared at the two men. "I have a question for you two."

"Shoot." Milo said.

"How long have you guys lived here?"

"All my life," Sutherland said.

Not wanting to go into a long history, Milo said, "About six months."

"And Morrie knows you, Mr. Six-Monther, right?" Linda pointed at Milo "Did he know about this place?"

Milo nodded, remembering an uncomfortable conversation at the Rasa Bar six months ago.

"You see where I'm going with this?" Linda asked.

"No, not at all," Sutherland blurted.

Milo caught her drift. "She's thinking Morrie had Bullard Hall torched so the wedding could be held here, and he could attend."

"You're not as dumb as you look, Rathbone."

"Rathkey," Milo corrected. "You couldn't prove it, but it does makes sense."

"It does." Linda smiled.

"It does?" Sutherland asked. "You two are kidding, right? Right?"

22

M ilo was surprised to find Ilene in the Lakesong kitchen as he limped down for Saturday morning breakfast. "Ilene, you miss me so much you needed to deliver cream puffs personally."

"Yeah, right, keep telling yourself that. Does a three-tiered wedding cake, frosting, and pastry bags in front of me give you a clue as to why I'm here?"

Ignoring her sarcasm, Milo said, "I like your new nose sparkle thing."

"You mean my stud?"

"I thought Vern was your stud," Milo joked, referring to Ilene's husband.

Ilene laughed. "Always. In fact, Vern's home from the boats for a few days. I always like to shine for my Vern."

Sutherland poked his head around the corner from the morning room. "Hello, I'm Sutherland McKnight."

"Sutherland, this is Ilene of Ilene's Bakery," Milo said as he poured himself a cup of coffee.

Sutherland stood up, crossed to the kitchen, and shook Ilene's hand. "We meet at last. Are you the gifted creator of my goat-cheese-filled, honey-fig muffin?"

"Guilty." Ilene smiled.

"It's a pleasure to put a face to a muffin." Sutherland laughed at his own joke.

"As a matter of fact, there's a goat-cheese-filled, honey-fig muffin waiting for you," Ilene said pointing to the refrigerator.

"Yes!" Sutherland shouted as he headed for the muffin. "I've been on vacation for a week, and I've missed my Monday morning meeting muffin fix." Sutherland admired his poetic alliteration.

"What about me?" Milo whined.

"Such a child. Okay, there's one cream puff in the refrigerator, for old time sake."

Milo limped to the refrigerator, grabbed the cream puff, and licked the oozing cream from the side. "Heaven as usual Ilene, thank you. I'm gonna need this today. Nice cake by the way."

Ilene sighed. "Thank you...king of the understatement."

Martha popped up from the wedding preparations in the basement kitchen as Ilene was placing piped yellow roses on the first tier of the cake. "Ilene it's beautiful...so delicate."

Ilene looked at Milo. "Take a lesson, Milo, Martha knows how to compliment my cake."

"I said nice cake," Milo mumbled.

"I was checking in," Martha explained, "to let you gentlemen know your breakfasts are ready. Mr. McKnight, your usual is in the refrigerator, and Mr. Rathkey yours is in the warming drawer."

Sutherland hid the muffin behind his back. Milo could not hide the cream puff.

"What are you enjoying, Mr. Rathkey?" Martha asked.

"Queam pah," he garbled, having just taken a healthy bite.

"He's got a thing for cream puffs," Ilene explained. "He came to the shop last week to get his fix. I presented him with a fine work of art."

"It's going up in my office," Milo said. "Agnes is framing it."

"What is it?" Martha wondered.

"My old door," Milo said.

Martha looked at Ilene.

"Not the whole door…a chunk of it."

"Glad that's Agnes' problem and not mine," Martha laughed. "How do you frame a door?"

§

Gramm and White spent Saturday morning in the office going over evidence. The arrest of Maureen Donahue's husband had ratcheted up the pressure. Their boss wanted this case solved, as he put it, before we incarcerate anymore city officials.

"How did Milo know about that Druid Development Company?" White asked.

"He sounded like he was in the middle of a loading dock and couldn't tell me."

White looked at the transcripts of interviews, her notes, and the various forensic pictures. "Let's hope he's getting close. We aren't."

§

Milo, all spiffed up in a N&J medium blue-linen suit and coral paisley tie, pulled the Bentley into Mary Alice's driveway at six-fifteen. He now owned two suits that fit. His somewhat officious, but helpful guy at N&J fine men's clothing did well by him. Of course, the cost of this suit was far beyond his comfort level, but even he knew the suit he bought in December would be too heavy for summer. Now that he had one suit for each season, he was set for years. He resisted his guy's attempt to sell him a new shirt and shoes. He had only used the old ones once.

Milo exited the Bentley, buttoned his new suit jacket, and straightened his tie.

Mary Alice greeted him with a smiled. It was that *you're the only one in the room* smile—Mary Alice's gift—and tonight Milo was the receiver. "You know we're so close, I could have walked to Lakesong, or at the least driven myself," she said.

"View it as car maintenance; our car guy says we have to drive it."

"Why not take the Rolls?"

Milo grimaced. "I can't work myself up to the Rolls yet. Remember, my comfort level is an old Honda."

Mary Alice laughed as Milo helped her into the Bentley. Her chiffon halter-neck, mint-floral dress with a flirty flowing skirt looked at home in the luxury vehicle. Milo only saw what wasn't covered. He thought her soft, tan shoulders and back were stunning. Milo struggled to say something appropriate, but the only things that came to his brain sounded stupid, so he said nothing.

Mary Alice noticed the lack of a compliment. She was used to men remarking on her beauty. Milo didn't. This might be an important moment to discuss with her therapist. She was, after all, working on different.

"You look quite dashing this evening, Mr. Rathkey...and coral paisley...sharp. It's not black-Metallica-t-shirt sharp but still sharp."

Milo smiled. "Thanks. N&J dresses me when it matters." Mary Alice turned the blue eyes on him. "And when has it mattered?"

"Twice. Your New Year's Eve party, and now."
Was that a compliment? Mary Alice wondered.

§

Martha prepped the waiters while Peggy instructed the bartenders, valets, and drink servers in the geography of the venue and the duties to each group. Agnes watched, impressed with her assistant's thoroughness.

As the wedding clock ticked down to thirty minutes and counting, Agnes and her assistant were excited. There was one major malfunction. Fred, yesterday's gate keeper and one of the today's bartenders had disappeared, probably taking a smoke break.

Fred was not smoking. Fred was making money on the side. As instructed, he opened the side gate, let an old Lincoln

Town Car cruise through and locked the gate behind it. Rather than broken legs, Fred received five crisp twenty-dollar bills from Milosh.

"The other half comes when you let us out," Milosh grumbled and drove to the parking lot next to Martha's cottage. Ever since an associate in Chicago died in a car bombing, Morrie did not trust valet parking.

All the other guests were arriving at the front of the estate and were greeted by an army of valets who whisked their cars to the side roads and parking areas around the grounds. Agnes had created a system of color-coded key tags, indicating which area held the car.

Guests were guided around the house to the back lawn and the ceremony area in front of the lake. Service people driving golf carts assisted the people who could not make the long walk.

Milo, Sutherland, Agnes, and Mary Alice were standing near a clump of trees waiting for the invited guests to sit down in the wedding ceremony area before taking their seats.

Mary Alice, looking over the crowd, couldn't remember the last event she attended where she didn't know most of the guests. Again, this was different.

Sutherland was also looking over the crowd, except he was trying to identify the infamous Morrie Wolf.

The answer to Sutherland's quest came from Mary Alice who had turned to look back towards Martha's Cottage. A dapper, gray-haired gentleman was walking toward her with a slow, deliberate pace.

"Mr. Wolf!" she called, holding out her hand.

Morrie stopped and took her hand.

"Mary Alice Higgins, now Bonner," she said not knowing if he would remember her. "You knew my father."

Morrie smiled. "Of course. I remember. It's been a long time. How are you Mary Alice?"

"I'm fine. You look well. Are you here for the bride or groom?"

Without skipping a beat, he replied, "I knew the bride's grandfather. I'm here to pay my respects." Noticing Milo and Sutherland approach, he nodded to Milo and turned to Sutherland.

Milo stepped up and introduced Sutherland, not knowing how he would handle meeting Morrie.

Offering his hand, Sutherland said, "Good to meet you Mr. Wolf." It was said with more courage than he felt.

Morrie shook his hand and walked toward the ceremony area.

"That's Morrie Wolf?" Sutherland asked, after he was out of earshot.

"That's Morrie Wolf, minus the skinny tie," Milo said.

"And striped sport coat," Mary Alice added.

Both Rathkey and Sutherland turned to her in surprise. "Are you a frequent visitor of the Rasa?" Milo asked.

Mary Alice fluttered her eyelashes in a teasing fashion, hooked her arm through Milo's and said, "Let's sit down."

Sutherland stood alone for a moment under the trees. *Does everybody know Morrie Wolf but me? Even Mary Alice knows him.*

Brittany and Joe were married, and the wedding party paraded past the tents to the terrace for pictures. The guests were directed to the nearest tent to chat about the wedding and enjoy the couple's chosen signature cocktails and hors d'oeuvres prepared by Martha and staff.

Milo and Sutherland headed to the bar for their preferred drinks while Mary Alice and Agnes took a signature cocktail from one of the waiters. As Mary Alice sipped her drink, she noticed Milo being intercepted on his way to the bar.

"Morrie wants to see you two by the trees," Milosh said.

As they followed him, Sutherland whispered, "This is going to end well, right?"

Mary Alice, intrigued by Morrie Wolf's attendance at a simple garden wedding, moved to the edge of the tent. Sipping her drink, she watched as Milo and Sutherland walked up to Morrie and shook hands.

"You did well. I'm grateful. I owe you both a favor," Morrie said.

Sutherland, even though he had seen the Godfather movies multiple times, was about to decline the favor when Milo jumped in. "We were glad to do it…for your granddaughter."

Morrie left them and walked along the path to Martha's parking lot. Noticing him, the bride grabbed her husband and ran off the terrace where the pictures were being taken. "Mr. Wolf!" she yelled.

Morrie stopped and turned.

Brittany hugged him and whispered. "I know you're my grandfather. Thank you so much!" They talked for several minutes then Morrie shook Joe's hand and led him away from his bride.

"I wonder what he's saying," Sutherland asked.

"I'm sure it's something grandfatherly," Milo said. "Maybe like welcome to the family."

Sutherland wasn't sure that was true.

When Britany and Joe returned to the terrace, Linda walked up to her ex-husband and talked to him for several minutes. Milo tried to imagine them as nineteen-year-old newlyweds. It was hard.

Not wanting to be seen spying on Morrie's family moment, Milo nudged Sutherland and led the way back to the signature-cocktail tent where he found Mary Alice watching Morrie and Linda talking. As Milo came up beside her, Mary Alice didn't move but continued to gaze at the two figures near the cottage. "Am I correct in assuming I'm not seeing any of this?"

Milo glanced at her with admiration. *Beauty and street smarts.* "You got it. None of this is happening."

"A fun, summer-garden-wedding for friends you said."

"Did I lie?"

"No," She smiled, looked at her empty glass and said, "Let's go get a real drink."

"What do you drink?"

"Vodka martini, extra olives."

"Oh, a health drink. Coming up." Milo left for one of the bars.

Mary Alice drifted over to the other side of the tent, watching Martha's crew ready the buffet stations. Nearest to Mary Alice, servers were delivering trays of filet mignon. In the center of the tent, a sign said sushi, but it had not yet arrived. The chicken station featured lemon caper, honey garlic, and Dijon baked. The far station, labeled vegetarian, provided tofu dumplings bowls with ginger, soy, hoisin, and brown sugar sauce.

Mary Alice wondered about the fish when yet another crew descended with three more trays. She heard hard-soled shoes on the wooden decking and turned to find Milo with her martini and three extra olives. "Lovely," she said, munching an olive. "Martha has done a beautiful job, as usual."

"Looks good, but at these events I just try not to spill," Milo said.

"You say what everyone thinks," Mary Alice laughed. "I scoped out the hors d'oeuvres—no little hot dogs in a bun."

Mary Alice smiled and brushed a piece of lint from Milo's lapel. "Maybe you didn't notice, there's a garden wedding going on here, not a beer bust." She stopped a waiter, picked up smoked salmon on cucumber with horseradish sauce. "Try this."

Milo's inclination was to complain about the green cucumber, but, lost once again in those blue eyes, he let it pass. "This is…okay."

"Little-hot-dog-on-a bun okay?"

"Let's not get carried away. Baby steps."

As the bride and groom arrived from the photo session on the terrace, twinkle lights in the trees came to life to the *oohs!* and *ahhs!* of guests. Brittany's father, Dan, rang a large bell to gain a measure of silence. "Our newlyweds, Brittany and Joe Nowicki invite you to join them in the dining tent."

Mary Alice, Milo, Agnes, and Sutherland laid claim to places at one of the tables and decided to wait until the lines for the food were shorter. Mary Alice reported on all the delicious choices and their sides.

Agnes half stood and scanned the far tent to make sure Peggy was getting the band readied for after-dinner dancing.

Sutherland put his hand on hers.

She sat down and looked at him.

"You did a fantastic job. Sit down so you can enjoy it too," Sutherland said.

Sutherland had been her friend and was now her boss. Did he want to become something more? Did she want him to become something more? *Weddings are so romantic and make people's heads spin*, she thought, but said. "You're right, Peggy is a pro." She used her other hand to hold up her cocktail, and said, "Happy wedding."

"And enjoying the rest of the evening," Sutherland added as he removed his hand, and they clinked glasses.

When the lines began to thin, Mary Alice said she was hungry and stood. Milo joined her as did Sutherland and Agnes.

"Don't stand in front of the sushi station," Mary Alice joked, "Milo will run you down."

"She knows me so well," Milo said.

299

23

Brittany and Joe were honeymooning. Sutherland was finishing his smoothie. Annie was vocalizing her displeasure at missing several days of Milo's bacon. Milo, having slept in, followed the cat into the morning room.

Milo was surprised to see Martha, not expecting her to cook breakfast. "Why are you here? You pulled off the event of the year yesterday. You should be sleeping."

"Well thank you, Mr. Rathkey, but between secret weddings, I work here," she said handing him a plate of her brioche French toast and bacon.

"Oh, the special breakfast! Extra swimming in my future," Milo said as he took his feast and sat down, giving Annie her bacon pieces. "I haven't been to a party in ten years and now I've attended two of them in six months."

"But the important thing is, no one died at this party," Sutherland said, referencing the death of Mary Alice's husband after her New Year's Eve bash. "And given our special guest, that could have happened."

"Your imagination is wild. No one was going to die," Milo protested.

"Either way, what Martha and Agnes pulled off in less than two weeks was incredible. We," Sutherland said pointing to Milo and himself, "will give them bonuses for going above and beyond, but I kinda wish Morrie would have thanked them."

"Are you sure he didn't?" Milo asked.

"I asked Agnes. As of last night, he hadn't."

"Well, he did leave early."

"Martha, did Morrie thank you?" Sutherland asked.

Martha shook her head. "I don't know. The entire family did many times, but I don't remember someone named Morrie."

"Morning Martha, gentlemen," Agnes called as she arrived in the morning room and helped herself to coffee. "Would this be early brunch or late breakfast?"

"This is breakfast. What would you like?" Martha asked.

"Did Ilene leave any goodies?"

"I think there's an unclaimed blueberry muffin."

"I claim it!"

Martha brought the muffin, poured herself a cup of coffee and Sutherland invited her to sit down and join them. They all shared stories about the wedding and their favorite parts. The conversation was interrupted by the front-gate buzzer.

Martha began to stand, but Sutherland waved her back down. "Ed upgraded the intercom," he said. "I can answer it from my phone. Let's see if it works." He fumbled with the app, the intercom rang again. "Yes?" he answered.

"Courier for Ms. Larson and Ms. Gibbson," a voice said.

Sutherland opened the gate from his phone. "You know I could put it on your phone too, Milo."

"And I would accidently open the gate sixteen times a day. No thanks."

"That is genius. I'll take it," Martha said.

"Me too," Agnes chimed in.

"While you two are being upgraded, I'll answer the door," Milo offered.

Agnes and Martha quizzed each other but no special deliveries were expected.

While pushing one large package across the polished marble floor of the gallery, Milo hugged the other package under his arm. He stopped at the family room rug which made pushing difficult and yelled, "Hey guys, I'm needing some help here!"

The trio left the morning room as Milo was placing the smaller package on the family room dining table. Sutherland grabbed the larger package, lifting it onto the table. "What is all this?" he asked.

"Special deliveries for Agnes and Martha," Milo said.

Both Agnes and Martha glanced at each other, shrugged, and checked each package for the name of the sender. There was none.

"I have box cutters," Martha said as she disappeared into the kitchen, returning seconds later.

Agnes eyes darted from Milo to Sutherland.

"What are you waiting for? Open them up," Sutherland urged.

"Did you guys do this…send these to us?" Agnes asked.

"Not me," Milo said. "Sutherland?"

"Nope. Open them up."

Martha handed Agnes one of the box cutters. Inside the box there was a lot of packing material and a rectangle wrapped in brown paper.

Peeling away the paper with care, a painting began to reveal itself. Agnes stopped and held her breath. "Oh my God! It's the Molly Zuckerman Hartung I bid on."

"You bid on art?" Milo asked.

As she inspected the painting, she absently answered Milo's question. "I was in Chicago at a gallery auction. On a whim, I bid on this painting knowing I would quickly be outbid. I was right, but it was exciting."

"Nice copy!" Sutherland said.

Agnes shook her head. "This is not a copy Sutherland, it's the original."

"The one you bid on?" Sutherland was stunned. "Did the art gallery get confused? Did you get a bill?" Sutherland started looking through the box for an invoice. Agnes joined him. There was no bill.

"Well, I'm confused," Sutherland said, scratching his head. Milo, who looked far less confused, turned to Martha. "What did you get?"

Martha had already opened the outside packaging and was holding a black lacquer wooden box with gold leaf decorations on all sides. A note from the seller indicated the box was Japanese from the Meiji period. Martha held it up. "It's lovely, but I don't understand."

"Maybe there's something inside," Milo said.

Martha placed the box on the table and, with great concentration, looked for a clasp.

"I think the top pulls off," Sutherland said.

"Is that from your extensive knowledge of the Magi period?" Milo asked.

"Meiji period," Sutherland corrected.

Taking pains not to damage the box, Martha lifted the top revealing a knife inside. Everyone leaned in to take a look.

"That's it? A knife?" Sutherland asked.

Martha knew what it was in an instant. "It's a Japanese chopping knife, handcrafted with a forged blade and a black Juma handle. Several years ago, I was invited to a culinary cutting techniques class held by a master chef in Japan. Only those who pass the class are allowed to buy this knife. When my parents died, I forgot about the knife. At that point, I couldn't have afforded it, anyway."

"Who sent these?" Sutherland asked.

Milo sat back, put his hands on the table, and looked at both the knife and the painting. "I think Morrie just said thank you."

Agnes looked at her painting in silence for a few minutes, and then whispered, "You're welcome!"

"Indeed," Martha echoed. "Should we send Mr. Wolf a thank you card?" Martha asked Milo.

Sutherland looked to Milo.

"Well, I'm not the expert on all things Morrie, but I wouldn't," Milo said. "He didn't include a card, so, as far as any of us know, these gifts came from the universe."

"How did he know about my knife and Agnes' painting?" Martha asked.

"Yeah, that's a little creepy," Agnes said, "but I do love the painting."

"It's not hard to figure out," Milo said. "Martha, did you ever tell anyone about the knife?"

"Yes, chefs talk about tools."

Milo smiled. "I suspect someone was hired to ask your former associates what would make you happy. Someone remembered you took that class but never bought the knife."

"What about me?" Agnes asked. "No one was with me when I bid on my painting."

"It works the same way. Someone was hired to find out what you want. The answer came back art."

"Oh, my goodness!" Sutherland exclaimed.

All eyes turned to him.

"I got a call from the bride's brother, wondering what Agnes might like as a thank you gift. I said she likes art, thinking they would get you a nice print or a local original."

Agnes looked at Sutherland wide eyed. "The bride doesn't have a brother."

"Now we know that bit of the puzzle," Milo said.

"But we don't know how Mr. Wolf knew about that particular painting and my bidding on it in Chicago. That part is still creepy."

"Who do you discuss art with other than Sutherland?" Milo asked.

"Jules. He's Mary Alice's art buyer and a friend. He lets me know about regional exhibitions I might like."

"Did you tell him about the auction?"

"Of course. I told him how much fun I had bidding on...oh my!"

Milo continued his interrogation. "Did you tell Jules about your auction or did Jules ask?"

Agnes paused. "I honestly don't remember. It came up in conversation at lunch."

"Lunch? Did you invite him or did he invite you?"

"Well, we ran into each other. He said he was checking out a new place for lunch and invited me to join him."

"Ran into each other? How many times have you just run into Jules?"

"Never."

"End of story. Any more questions?" Milo asked, self-satisfied.

"Does he have any more granddaughters?" Martha asked.

"No!" Sutherland pronounced as he stood up to leave. "One and done is good for me, but the gifts are impressive." Checking the time, he said, "I'm sorry to break this up. We're riding this morning, and I have to pick up Megan."

"You're riding with Megan?" Agnes asked with surprise and a discomfort she couldn't define.

"Well...yes...we all are. I thought you'd be sleeping-in this morning or I would have told you about it. Would you like to go?"

"I'd like to, but unless you want this white tent look on the back lawn for the entire summer, I have to prepare for the tear down," Agnes said. "The trucks will begin arriving soon."

"What time are you going to be down off the trail?" Milo asked.

"No double-diamond trails today. We're going east to Hartley Park. We should be back at Twin Ponds about one. Why?"

"No reason—wondering if Agnes needs her two clip-boards manned again."

Sutherland was a bit ashamed he didn't think about the cleanup. "I'll make sure we don't dawdle."

"Dawdle? Who says dawdle?" Milo asked.

"I did. Gotta go. I'll make it short." Sutherland headed for the garage.

Martha left to supervise the final cleanup of the basement kitchen. Before Agnes left she said to Milo, "I wonder how Mr. Wolf knew how to do all those tricks you mentioned."

Milo shrugged. "He could have asked someone."

"Like say a private detective?" Agnes looked at Milo knowingly.

Milo looked down. "I wonder if my shoes are tied."

Agnes laughed and headed outside to wait for the trucks.

Milo, having been abandoned, was deciding what to do when Gramm's *da dunk* ring-tone from *Law and Order*, sounded on his phone.

"I don't hear a loading dock today; tell me what you know that I don't know, now!" Gramm gruffed.

"And good morning to you," Milo said.

"I need to know how you came across that Druid Development Company."

"I followed a hunch," Milo answered.

"I don't even know why I come to work. Have all the dots come together yet? Do you know who killed the Vogel woman?"

"I think I do." Milo added that they might be able to wrap it up if Gramm and White met him a little before one.

"Just us?"

"Yeah, you won't need an army."

As he often did, Gramm hung without saying goodbye. Milo went to the library.

§

Megan was waiting outside the hotel with her bike when Sutherland drove up in the SUV. They secured it to the bike rack and chatted about the weather.

"Nice day for a ride—sunny and dry," Sutherland said.

"Sure is," Megan said as she slid into the front seat.

"What trails have you been riding?" Sutherland asked.

"We've sampled so many. I don't remember their names off hand, but they're in my notes."

"Have you been to Twin Ponds? I thought we'd start there and head over to Hartley Park today."

Megan nodded. "That's Enger Trail...right? I almost wiped out on it last week. It was my fault...going too fast. Let's do it."

"When will your article come out?" Sutherland asked.

"It will take about a month to complete."

Sutherland pulled into the Twin Ponds parking lot noticing that most of the other riders were already there. He introduced Megan to Larry Ashbach. "He's the guy who hates my bike but provided yours."

"Thank you!" Megan said, shaking Larry's hand. "Sorry you are such a purist."

"Don't get him going." Danielle came up to them, strapping on her helmet. "We'll be here all day. Let's ride."

§

At twelve forty-five, Milo parked the Honda next to Gramm's unmarked car. Opening the trunk, he fished around for his digital SLR camera, pausing for a second to remember the settings. The battery meter showed half full which was more than enough to do what he needed to do.

"Are we here for a group picture?" Gramm asked, looking at the camera.

Milo smiled. "Sorta."

Gramm hated not knowing what was going on. They waited almost fifteen minutes in silence, the maximum length of Gramm's patience, before Sutherland appeared in the lead as the Zenith City Cyclers emerged from the trail. Slowing his bike, Sutherland was surprised to see Milo standing there with a camera but smiled and waved in friendly Sutherland style. Milo kept his focus on the emerging string of riders making a production of raising the camera to insure they saw what he was doing. "Smile pretty!" he yelled.

Instantly Megan's bike lurched sideways into Danielle's taking both of them down along with Larry. Several more cyclers rammed into the pile-up, while the rest either braked fast, or veered off into the woods. The air was filled with shouts and swearing.

"Got it!" Milo said.

Gramm looked confused.

White also seemed confused. "What did we just see here, and how does this solve the murder?"

Sutherland, now off his bike, rushed back to help the downed bikers.

As the bikers stood up, Milo walked over. "Camera shy?" he asked.

Megan, wiping dirt off her legs, looked at him surprised. "Not me," she said raising her arms. "Go ahead get a picture, dirt and all."

"Not you," Milo said. "I was talking to Larry."

"What?" Larry seemed shocked.

Milo showed the view panel on his camera to Gramm and White. "I was shooting video. Notice Larry's front wheel knocks Megan's back wheel." Milo looked up to address Larry. "You did that as soon as you saw my camera, didn't you…Steven?"

Larry was silent.

"Steven?" Sutherland questioned. "Who's Steven?"

"Sutherland, I'd like you to meet a hero of yours, Steven Griffith. Steven, this is Sutherland."

"No, Milo. Steven Griffith is dead," Megan said, tending to her scraped knee.

"You are crazy, little man," Danielle said, brushing her way past Milo.

"Sorry Beth, but your secret is out too," Milo said.

"Beth? Who's Beth?" Sutherland shouted, his confusion mounting.

"Beth Griffith, Larry's wife, and the person who murdered Jessica Vogel."

White looked doubtful. "The witness? She was there, but what's her motive?"

Danielle laughed. "This man is delusional. I'm Danielle Ashbach. Sutherland tell him. You've known us for years."

Sutherland agreed. "Milo, I think you're off base here. They are Danielle and Larry Ashbach!"

Gramm, who had too much history with Milo to discount him, stepped up and took charge. "Mr. and Mrs. Ashbach, I think you need to come with me to get this straightened out."

"No!" Danielle shouted. "I'm not going anywhere because this hobby cop is having a moment." She picked up her bike, slammed the wheels on the ground and began heading to her car.

Afraid she was going to bolt, Gramm shouted for her to stop as White sprang in her direction. A booming crack with a trailing echo surrounded them. Stunned and frozen, White saw Danielle's head snap as her body pitched backwards.

"Down! Everybody down!" Gramm yelled, grabbing his gun.

White hit the ground, her shoulder slamming against Danielle's rear tire. The uneven sharp pieces of gravel dug into her side as she scanned the nearby woods for a shooter. "The trees...in the trees," she yelled at Gramm.

"Got it." The way Danielle's head snapped back, he agreed the shot came from the tree and bush-lined hill on the side of the parking lot. Gramm's eyes cordoned off the area and searched for any flash or unnatural movement as he picked up his hand-held radio, "It's Gramm...we've got a shooting in the Twin Ponds parking lot. One person down. Send squads to Twin Ponds and Enger Golf Course; we're looking for a shooter with a high-powered rifle."

Milo, stunned but moving, took cover and began scrambling toward the trail. He shouted to Sutherland to get the others away from the direction of the shot.

Dead air. No sound, not even birds. White glanced at Danielle to see if she needed aid. The burned pit in her forehead and blood seeping from behind her head coating the black gravel told White it was too late. Danielle's eyes were open, wide, and lifeless.

The radio crackled back. "Do you need an ambulance?"

"Ambulance and Doc Smith."

Milo noticed a pale, trembling Larry Ashbach holding onto his bike, staring at the body of his wife. He mumbled something no one heard before collapsing to the ground.

"We've got a problem here," Milo yelled to Gramm.

Gramm looked at Milo's situation but didn't move. "Ambulance coming."

Not hearing another shot, White charged up the hill into the woods.

Gramm's radio began blaring out reports as the sirens and lights of various squads announced their arrival. He ordered Skyline Drive closed off around Twin Ponds and the golf course. "Check every car that comes out of the area for a high-powered rifle."

The K-9 squad pulled up with officer Young and Tricksie. Gramm pointed to the woods. "Take the dog…follow White…between those two tall trees…straight up."

Young nodded. They followed White's path.

Several minutes later, through the chaos and noise, Sutherland crept back down the trail to see if it was safe for the others. Noticing Gramm, White, and Milo all standing, he motioned for the others to follow him.

One by one, they came back into the parking lot, brushing the dirt from their legs and clothes. A few stared at the scene, the medical examiner, the body of Danielle. Others turned their backs not wanting to look. For a few, there were tears and hugs, a reaction to the fear, the thought of dying, and having come close to leaving the people they love.

Sutherland, numb to the scene, watched a small tent being erected over Danielle's body. Shocked at what he was watching, he went back to the group to see if he could be of help.

Megan, ever the reporter, had her phone out and was taking pictures of the police activity.

Two forensic officers were starting to mark off the entire parking lot with police tape and the EMT's were loading Larry into the ambulance.

Gramm asked for more officers at Twin Ponds to interview witnesses and also to check the bikers coming down off the trail. "For all we know, the shooter could be on a bike," he said to Milo.

"He could be anywhere by now."

White reemerged from the woods holding a rifle. "I don't think the vehicle search is going to find anything," she shouted.

"Damn!" Gramm swore. "Give it to forensics."

"My bet…it's clean," Milo said.

Gramm shook his head in disbelief.

"I found the rifle under a tree stand," White said when she reached Gramm. "It was a commercial job—ladder and everything. I climbed up. It gives a perfect shot to the parking lot."

"This was planned?" Milo asked.

"That stand is new. That shot was lethal and perfect, square in the forehead," White declared.

Gramm looked at White. "Could we be talking about Leroy Thompson's hitman?"

"Except the target wasn't Vogel, it was Ashbach?" White asked in disbelief.

"So now we have to figure out who killed Ashbach, and we still don't know who killed Vogel." Gramm turned to Milo.

"Beth Griffith," Milo said. "I already told you that."

Gramm erupted, "Who the hell is Beth Griffith?"

"Danielle. She killed Vogel. Why is this a problem for you?"

"Okay. Stop! Just Stop!" Gramm took a long breath. His frustration evident. "We have yet another crime scene to process. I want you at the hospital before we talk to Larry."

"Steven," Milo corrected.

Gramm sighed. "Of course."

"Stop talking to him," White admonished.

"Good advice. Tell Sutherland once his biking friends give us a statement they can go. Invite him to our hospital… soiree."

"I love a good soiree," Milo said. He was universally ignored.

The ambulance carrying Larry Ashbach turned on its lights and siren roaring out of the parking lot.

§

"You really got into character this time," Erica said to Randy as they merged with south bound traffic on I-35.

"I did, didn't I? I actually sold that RV. Nice couple. What was the name of the town?"

315

"Esko," Erica said looking around at the interior of the pre-owned Volvo. "I like this better than that RV. It was a tank. We cut this one close though. I was barely out of that tree stand when I heard the first siren."

"Yeah, those cops were standing there, and you hadn't even shot her yet. What were they doing there?"

"Beats me. This whole trip has been from the twilight zone."

Randy laughed. "It was one for the books. I mean, we pull into that tower parking lot and the mark runs up to us and introduces herself. You couldn't write that. Nobody'd believe it."

"How did they find her, anyway?" Erica asked. "How did they know she was in Duluth?"

"It had to do with a specialty candy she ordered. People don't change, apparently. They traced the candy."

"You look better without that scratchy beard. I'm glad you finally shave it off." Erica ran her fingers through her red curly hair. "And I'm glad to get rid of that wig. I'm not a blond, and it was so hot."

Randy smiled.

Erica checked her phone. "The money is in our account. Love that Koz—always pays promptly."

They rode in silence until reaching the outskirts of Minneapolis. "Do you ever worry about them coming for us?" Randy asked.

"Us? Why?"

"At some point they may think we know too much."

Erica thought for a minute. "Let's make sure we don't have a special candy."

24

Sgt. White spent the next two hours interviewing witnesses who saw nothing and knew less, but it had to be done. Gramm watched forensics check the deer stand for finger prints, and the general area for anything that would lead to the shooter. There were footprints, shallow and small, possibly a woman.

Gramm met White in the parking lot. "This case gets weirder by the minute."

"What now?" White asked.

"Our hitman might be a hitwoman."

"Oh good, another glass ceiling broken."

"That's where you want to go with this?" Gramm grumbled.

"Crime: an equal opportunity employer," White joked.

"If we stop for coffee, I'd be ready for our hospital soiree," Gramm said.

White agreed. "Oh yum, a stereotypical donut for dinner."

§

Sutherland sat in the hospital waiting room sipping his bottle of PH-balanced, electrolyte water. Larry wasn't Larry. Danielle wasn't Danielle. But the woman who wasn't Danielle was dead.

Several hours had passed since the shooting, and it still didn't make any sense to Sutherland. Fatigue was settling over him. He kept fighting it. He told Milo he was going up to see Larry who had been admitted for observation.

About fifteen minutes later, Sutherland returned, sat down, and continued sipping his drink.

"So, how's your friend?" Milo asked.

"According to the floor nurse, he's not being allowed visitors. There's a cop by his room. Why?"

Before Milo could answer, Gramm marched past them, and identified himself to the volunteer at the information desk. The volunteer smiled and handed him a key to a conference room. Turning to Rathkey and Sutherland he asked, "Coming?"

Both got up and followed.

"How are you doing?" White asked Sutherland as she put a pink box of donuts and four coffees on the table.

"I'm okay, just confused and tired," Sutherland said.

"That's natural. You need sugar and caffeine. It'll perk you right up," White said.

"Does anybody care how I'm feeling?" Milo asked.

"No," White said.

"I haven't eaten since breakfast. I'm not confused—I'm hungry."

Gramm pushed the pink box toward him. "Have a donut." The small, blue-walled conference room held a table, eight chairs, and a painting of a fox hunt.

Sutherland sat at the end of the table, ran his fingers through his hair, and began to massage his neck and shoulder.

Milo grabbed a donut and coffee.

White sat with Sutherland on her left and Gramm on the right, readying her notebook.

Gramm took a sip of coffee and cleared his throat. "I don't even know where the hell to begin."

"Let me start," Milo said, sitting down across from Gramm and White. "The man we know as Larry Ashbach is Steven Griffith, the designer of Sutherland's bike."

Sutherland leaned back and stared at Milo but said nothing.

"Why do I care if he designed Sutherland's bike?" Gramm grumbled.

"Only that it led to my figuring this out. Danielle is—was—Beth Griffith, Steven's wife, and one-time CEO of the Druid Development Company in Atlanta."

"Oh! Now there's a dot we could have connected earlier," Gramm said. "Obviously, Beth Griffith did not die in a boating accident ten years ago."

"That's right," Milo agreed. "Both Beth and Steven faked their deaths, disappeared, and began living in Duluth as Larry and Danielle Ashbach."

Sutherland, folding his arms, shook his head in disbelief.

Gramm's eyebrows furrowed.

"They had a life and friends," Milo said, motioning to Sutherland. "They thought they were safe. It was a fluke that

Vogel was in town for that reunion. It's my guess at some point she ran into Danielle, recognized her, and I'll bet tried to blackmail her. That's what Vogel did— blackmail, only this time she ran into a murderer."

Sutherland gasped. "What are you talking about?"

Gramm put up his hand to stop Sutherland from talking further. "You said murderer, like she's done it before?"

"I'm only guessing here, but you mentioned that financial guy falling from a construction site. What was he doing there? He's a bean counter. I'm thinking he was meeting his boss—Danielle—and she pushed him, like she pushed Vogel."

"If she murdered this financial guy and Vogel, who shot her?" Gramm asked.

Milo sat back, glanced at Sutherland, and then proceeded. "No idea. Did not see that coming," Milo said.

The mood changed as each person tried to come up with their own theory.

Sutherland broke the silence. "Are you saying Larry knew...about Danielle...that she murdered a man in Atlanta and now this Jessica?"

"You know him. He's your friend. What do you think?" Gramm asked.

Sutherland shook his head. "I don't know, but if someone close to me committed murder, I think I would know about it."

Milo checked to make sure his shoe laces were tied.

§

Larry *Steven Griffin* Ashbach had not been resting comfortably. His wife had been murdered in front of him, and for all he knew, he might be next. There was a policeman outside his room. Was he there to protect him, or keep him from leaving? Larry didn't know.

Lieutenant Gramm and Sergeant White came in and read him his rights. After he was interviewed, he was told he would be transported to jail in the morning and charged with obstruction and accessory to murder. If he cooperated, he was told the charges could be reduced. Larry decided not to lawyer up, yet.

Gramm called Milo when the interview was over and was pleased when he and White were invited to dinner. Amy was hosting her mystery book club, so his house was full of wine drinkers and discussions of fictional murders.

White followed Gramm to Lakesong. After a short tour of the gallery for White, Milo offered them a drink. Gramm took a beer and White asked for a virgin Bloody Mary. She explained she didn't drink but loved the mixes. Sutherland did the honors.

They wandered out onto the terrace and made themselves comfortable in the cushioned chairs overlooking the now-clear back lawn and the lake.

"So, what did Larry have to say?" Milo asked.

"We were very direct with Mr. Ashbach or Griffith…"

"Let's call him Ashbach," White said. "I'm getting a headache from all the different names."

"Ashbach it is. He knew his wife was laundering money in Atlanta for drug dealers through the buying and selling of condos. The dealers bought condos from her using dirty money. When she sold their condos, they would get clean money and she would get a chunk of it. It was profitable until the recession hit, and the bottom fell out of the market. The condos wouldn't sell, or sold at a loss, but the dealers didn't care. They still wanted their money."

"That's like the article I just read," Sutherland added.

"For a while, she was using her own personal money to buy the condos, to stay alive," Gramm continued. "As Larry explained it, they were near bankruptcy. They could see no way out, so she and Larry faked their deaths and ran with whatever money they had left."

"Was she killed because of the money?" Sutherland asked.

"I don't think so. I called the Feds…"

"Tonight? After all of this?" Milo asked. "Couldn't it wait until morning?"

Gramm sighed. "This is interstate—their jurisdiction—and I don't want to go through the paperwork of charging Larry if the Feds are only going to walk in and whisk him away."

They were interrupted by Martha saying dinner was ready.

"What are we having?" Gramm asked.

"Wedding leftovers, but they're delicious," Sutherland said.

"Wedding?" Gramm asked.

"A friend of Martha's," Milo explained.

Martha smiled. "I'm afraid the sushi is gone, but we have a whitefish stew, a cold filet salad, and a few vegetable sides."

"As tragic as that sushi thing is, I'll opt for the filet salad," Gramm said.

"Fish stew here," White jumped in.

"I'll bring in the sides, you can pick and choose."

The dinner conversation changed with the location. Everyone needed a break from the day. Somewhere around dessert Sutherland said, "Ernie, you mentioned Danielle's death wasn't about the money."

"It was about the money laundering, like you read in your article. According to the Feds, the money laundering started again when the economy recovered. The agents were looking for Jessica, who was the agent on record, but she was a small player. They were more interested in Danielle. She could tell them how the scheme worked from the inside. That faked death thing was being doubted by both the Feds and the drug dealers."

"But the bad guys got here first," Milo said.

"Yup," Gramm said.

"Is Larry in danger?" Sutherland asked.

"I don't think so," Milo said. "He was standing straight up while the rest of us were belly down in the cinders."

Gramm agreed. "If he was in danger, they would have shot him right there."

Sutherland was relieved by the answer, but he was still concerned. "What about jail?"

White jumped in between bites of butter-cream frosted wedding cake. "Remains to be seen. The Feds may cut him a deal, but at the moment, he's charged with being an accessory to murder, Jessica Vogel's, and pseudocide."

All eyes went to Robin.

"What the heck is that?" Milo asked.

"Gentlemen, I see a bit of education is in order." Robin cleared her throat. "Pseudocide is the act of faking one's own death. When you create a new identity, you could be committing fraud."

Martha announced she was going back to her cottage and asked that the dinner dishes be placed in the sink. She left two pots of coffee, the real stuff, as Milo called it, and decaf. The group grabbed their coffee of choice and sat down in the family room seating area.

Gramm leaned his head back and put his feet up on the ottoman. "I told you our information, now you tell us how all the dots got connected in your brain, Milo."

Milo seemed surprised. "What do I have left to tell?"

White looked at her notes. "In no particular order, we have Maureen Donahue, Sophie Moscatelli, Megan Davis, and Paul Kendrick all up at Enger Tower when Jessica Vogel was murdered. Then there's Liz Brooks, who could have hired someone to do the murder. Why on God's green earth did you suspect the witness, Danielle Ashbach?"

Milo shrugged. "She was there. Everyone who was there is a suspect. I wondered about Megan."

White flipped several pages. "What about Randy and Erica, the RV couple from Iowa? They were there."

"No. Danielle said they came in after the murder," Gramm reminded her.

"So, what moved Danielle up the list?" White asked Milo.

"There were a lot of little things, like the soft drink, which in itself wasn't a big deal."

"What soft drink?" Sutherland asked.

"Larry and Danielle referred to all pop as Coke, something people from Atlanta do. I know that because I had two buddies in the Navy from Atlanta who did it all the time. Like I said no big deal. Then there's the problem of direction after the murder."

"I don't get it," Gramm said.

"Which way did the speeding car go? The one driven by the supposed murderer," Milo asked.

Gramm looked at White who was flipping through her notes. "Erica, the woman in the RV said it was speeding up the hill when they arrive."

Milo nodded. "And what direction did the frightened Danielle go?"

Again, checking her notes White nodded. "Megan said the person on the bike went up the hill. Oh! Why would Danielle go in the same direction as the murderer if she thought he was trying to kill her?"

"That's the direction problem I'm talking about. A car tries to run you over then races up the hill. Then you race up the hill? I found that a bit odd. In her place I would have chosen down the hill," Milo explained.

"She panicked," Sutherland offered.

"Maybe," Milo acknowledged. "That's a reasonable explanation. However, we have a dead woman who worked in Atlanta—Jessica—and a person at the scene who appears to have come from Atlanta—Danielle—with an odd choice of direction."

"Milo, when you realized she went the wrong direction, why didn't you say anything to us?" Gramm asked.

"I didn't realize it right away. Something was bothering me, but it came to me when Heidi Reinakie drove down to the old Fitger's building."

Gramm laughed. "Of course. I solve a lot of murders following someone named Heidi to the Fitger's building. Doesn't everyone?"

Milo enjoyed Gramm's sarcasm. "She went down the hill and up the hill. She never goes down the hill, but that day she did. It was an odd direction. That unclogged my brain."

White shook her head and tried to keep from laughing.

"I can't wait for the next revelation," Gramm said.

"It's about Sutherland's friend, Larry. I didn't know Larry well, but he seemed like a good guy, you know, easy going, even when I made fun of biking. But he got angry over changes on Sutherland's new bike. Why?"

"I thought he was upset because I didn't buy it from him," Sutherland said.

"And I didn't buy that. His anger was over the changes to the bike, not the loss of a sale. Then there was the picture."

"Picture of what?" Gramm asked.

"The Zenith City Cyclers," Milo explained, "of which I am a proud member, through no fault of my own." Milo thought he saw a small glimmer of a smile on Sutherland's face. "Larry and Danielle missed the picture. Larry sells bikes. It's a nationwide publication. I don't know much about advertising, but I think that picture was marketing gold. Why would you miss it? That's why I began to research."

"Research what?" White asked,

"Them, their past. They didn't seem to want their picture taken. I checked. For the last ten years they've lived in Duluth and there was nothing suspicious. However, going beyond ten years there was nothing."

"You mean nothing suspicious?" Sutherland was confused.

"No, I mean nothing at all. No trace of them. They didn't exist, and I used all my PI computer toys. I was stuck—then I took a left turn. Remembering Larry's reaction to Sutherland's bike, I looked for a picture of the dead Steven Griffith." Milo checked his phone and displayed the picture. "I found this old picture and sweetened it on Photoshop…quite proud of that."

Sutherland looked at the photo. "That's a young Larry but no stubble."

"Once I found out Larry was Steven Griffith, I found pictures of his wife Beth and the fact she ran that Druid whatever."

Gramm got up and filled his cup with decaf. "So, in the official police report, I'll put, 'when referring to a liquid beverage in a social setting, the suspect called pop, Coke.' Right?"

White added, "'Went the wrong way up the hill, and didn't have marketing-gold picture taken.'"

"Solid case," Gramm said, sitting down.

"There's more. I haven't even mentioned the car thing," Milo said.

"I was just about to ask about the car thing," White said with false enthusiasm. She turned to Gramm. "Weren't you going to ask about the car thing?"

"Definitely. It was why I got another cup of coffee."

"Oh good, you know about the car thing." Milo added to the sarcasm. "So, I don't have to explain it."

"Don't be an asshole. Tell us about the car thing," Gramm demanded.

"Danielle said the car that came at her in the parking lot was the cheap BMW sports car. Checking with my good friend, Sutherland, about the price of sports cars, I would not consider the cheap BMW sports car cheap, but Sutherland would. It kinda said Danielle had big bucks at some point in time."

"Wait? You're not getting a sports car?" Sutherland complained.

"It started as research, but the idea is growing on me." Milo smiled.

Sutherland still doubted Danielle was a murderer. "None of these odd bits and pieces go together. They're Milo's... mind lint."

"Oh yeah, sorry Sutherland," Gramm interrupted. "I didn't say anything earlier, but Larry confirmed that Danielle pushed Vogel and her CFO. If it makes you feel any better, she told Larry they were accidents."

Sutherland leaned his head back on the sofa.

"Mind lint?" Milo complained. "It was brilliant deductive reasoning."

"I think it's inductive not deductive," Sutherland corrected while looking at the ceiling.

"Still brilliant." Milo smiled.

25

Milo dragged himself to breakfast, forgoing his morning swim for another hour of sack time. Weddings, assassinations, and the late-night debriefings had taken their toll.

In contrast, Annie was chipper, almost frisky, pleased to be back to her old routine of demanding bacon from Milo, followed by playing lioness on the hunt among the trees in the gallery. She even ran halfway up the gallery wall—something she hadn't done since she was a kitten—before climbing to rest on her favorite Guiana Chestnut tree.

Sutherland reestablished his usual morning routine: Wall Street Journal and green protein smoothie.

"Suit and tie today?" Milo asked.

"Yes. I'm looking forward to my Monday morning meet-ing, Ilene's fig-and-goat-cheese muffin, and colleagues who talk about real estate rather than murder. But first I have a question about yesterday. Does any of this ever bother you?"

"Any of what?"

Sutherland folded his paper. "I know you didn't know Danielle and Larry long, but does their double life bother you?"

Milo shrugged. "People sometimes aren't who you think they are. I see it all the time."

"Sure, the little old lady up the block smokes pot, but she doesn't murder two people!"

"It bothers you that someone you know could be a murderer."

"It does. It bothers me to no end. I don't see how Larry could know about Danielle and still go along with it. I don't get it."

"So, you and Larry are no longer friends?" Milo asked, getting up to get coffee.

Sutherland tapped his paper on the table. "I didn't say that. This is so complicated!"

Milo returned with his coffee. "Life's complicated."

Sutherland was quiet, leaving Milo to worry that he may have taken insult. He was about to soften his statement when Sutherland asked if he should ask Saul to be Larry's lawyer.

"Saul's the best," Milo said.

"Can I visit Larry…in jail I mean?"

"Sure. He's going to be transferred from the hospital today."

Martha came in from the kitchen with Milo's breakfast, saying it felt good to be back to the old routine. Milo agreed, digging into his full lumberjack feast of eggs, hash browns, pancakes, and bacon.

Coming up for air, he said to Sutherland. "I hope you weren't insulted by my comment on life being complicated."

"No insult taken." Sutherland sighed. "I enjoy my uneventful life. Complications are chaotic for me. Call me silly, but I prefer not to know that my friends have a double life, or murder people."

Knowing Sutherland had taken a body blow and needed to heal, Milo returned to his breakfast.

"Getting back to my scheduled life," Sutherland said, "I have an item of new business."

Milo asked, "New business? Are you practicing for your morning meeting?"

Sutherland ignored the comment. "This morning it hit me—you must join the country club in order to be Mary Alice's tennis partner. I will sponsor you. There's an interview process; it can take weeks. If we start now, we might get it done before the summer tennis season starts."

Milo showed Sutherland an email on his phone. "I got this notice yesterday. It says, 'Welcome to the club, pay your initiation fee and dues.'"

"What? Did you already fill out the application and everything?"

"I didn't do a thing. This is the first I've heard of having to join anything."

"Let me see that?" Sutherland said as he took Milo's phone, read the email and started to scroll down.

"Whaddaya looking for?"

"Your sponsor. I know it wasn't me."

"I could give it a good guess," Milo said being ignored.

Sutherland got to the sponsor portion of the email. "Mary Alice Bonner."

"Funny, that was my guess," Milo mumbled and went back to his breakfast.

"How did she do that so quickly?" Sutherland asked as he slid Milo's phone back across the table. "I mean...there are procedures."

"For you and me there are procedures. For Mary Alice? Nope."

"So, you're in. Welcome. Pay your dues."

"Did you see how much that initiation fee was?" Milo asked.

"It's expensive, but you do get to play tennis with Mary Alice."

"Kind of a pricey date, but you and Creedence say I can afford it."

"Date?"

"Well, I put it in my calendar—which has a date—so..."

"Nice try. You said date. I'm marking that down on my calendar. On this Monday, Milo referred to his *tennis* match with Mary Alice Bonner as a date." Sutherland smirked as he pretended to put that note in his calendar.

"You need to get back to work. You're creating chaos in my uneventful life," Milo complained.

§

Although Leroy Thompson's hitman scenario detailed the wrong target, it provided valuable information and Gramm wanted to develop Thompson as an informant. To that end, he orchestrated Leroy's early release from jail.

Leroy was into a full on strut as he changed from prison orange into his wrinkled white Miami Vice suit and purple shirt. He was still minus the goatee, but it would grow back. As Leroy slipped on his retro optic-classic-eighties sun glasses, he congratulated himself. *I friggin' gamed the system and won. I'm Leroy Thompson goddamn it! Nobody tells me what to do.*

Leroy swaggered out into the morning sun only to be confronted by Milosh and two burly thugs. His swagger stopped. "Oh…hi guys. Nice morning."

"Morrie wants to see you! Get in the damn car!"

"Oh sure. He was going to be my first stop."

Milosh pushed Leroy into the back seat bumping his head. There was no sorry.

§

Paul Kendrick did a quick scan of the tenure email, failing to find his name. He scanned it again, slower this time. His name was missing. "Damn it!" he yelled.

His gut reaction was to threaten a lawsuit. He should have a year to find another place to teach, but if he sued, the whole Jessica thing would be made public and lead to his immediate termination. He was screwed.

Job hunt or career change? He wasn't sure.

§

After the Monday morning meeting, Sutherland called Saul Feinberg, filled him in on the weekend's events, and asked if he could represent his friend, Steven Griffith AKA Larry Ashbach.

Saul listened before saying, "Quite a weekend for you and your friend. What part did Milo play in all of this?"

"He um…solved the first murder, but he didn't see the second one coming."

"The old man is slipping. Where is Larry now?"

"Being transferred from the hospital to the jail."

Saul made a note on his ever-present legal pad. "I will meet with Steven Griffith this afternoon and see if I can get him released on bail."

"How much trouble is he in?" Sutherland asked.

"I have to talk to him. I have to talk to the prosecutor. I might even have to talk with the Feds. Steven may know something or have something we could trade for leniency. First, your friend has to agree to be my client."

"True," Sutherland answered. Sutherland didn't know Steven Griffith. His friend was Larry Ashbach. Were they different? "On another note, you've known Milo longer than I have. Is he always involved in murders?" Sutherland asked.

Saul thought for a minute. "Interesting question. He's helped me with my cases, and done grunt PI work for years, but as to your question; I would say no; you are the problem."

"Me? I've never been near murder before I met him!"

"Look at it from my point of view. Milo didn't know James Bonner until he met…you. And from what you've told me, his connection to Jessica Vogel was through Agnes, who worked for Bonner, whom Milo would have never met if it weren't for…you. Oh, and by the way, the Ashbachs are friends of yours, whom Milo would have never met…see my point."

Sutherland was slightly dizzy. "Saul, I'm glad I don't have to face you in court. The problem is Milo, and you've turned it around so I'm from Murder Incorporated."

"Well, think about it. Am I wrong?"

§

Lakesong was back to normal allowing Agnes time to rush up to the airport and say goodbye to Liz, Sophie, and Maureen at the airport restaurant.

"That was one hell of a reunion—meet and greet plus a murder," Sophie said, after they ordered nachos.

"Yeah Maureen, how you gonna top that in ten years?" Liz kidded.

"Let's hope someone else organizes it. In ten years, who knows where I will be."

"Pretty exciting isn't it?" Liz smiled. "I will be a mom of a nine year old, and maybe a brother or sister for her too."

"Exciting and scary," Sophie said.

"How are you doing Maureen?" Agnes asked.

"I haven't had a drink in four days. According to Liz, I have a couple of rough weeks ahead. I can tell you that so far, I have a monster headache, I'm fidgety, and not sleeping well. So, that part's hard, but there's a good part too. I'm going to live with my brother and his family for a while. I don't think we've ever known each other."

"I've set her up with support in Chicago," Liz said turning to Maureen, "and you know you can call me anytime."

"Have you heard from your husband?" Sophie asked.

"I have a restraining order. He can't contact me. Our lawyers have talked, but that's all. I've heard he's pulling out of the race for state senate, and that's okay. Nobody needs to be represented by someone like him."

"Let's not let ten years go by before we do another night of ice cream therapy," Agnes said.

"Especially because I missed this year's session, but it sounds like it was fun," Maureen said.

"What's your favorite ice cream?" Sophie asked.

"Marshmallow delight."

"Well, you won't have to share that!" Agnes quipped.

They munched nachos talking and laughing about their futures. As they said their goodbyes, Agnes wondered if they would get together again, or if they would avoid revisiting the memories and emotions of the past few days.

The police had told them the case had been solved and they were free to go. No one spoke about the murder of Jessica Vogel.

§

Sutherland was meeting with his development person, Piper, in Two Harbors about four, so he thought he would stop at Lakesong for lunch. Martha had said there was still chicken in the fridge.

Milo was on the terrace, finishing his sandwich, watching Dr. Bixby and Breanna at a picnic table by the lake. Breanna was writing on a legal pad and from time to time showing it to the older woman.

Sutherland came and sat down next to him.

Looking at the chicken, Milo offered, "Want half my sandwich? It's ham and cheese, better than day three of chicken."

Sutherland declined, saying something about lean protein and Keto that Milo ignored.

"Look at those two down there. Did you ever find math that interesting?" Milo asked.

"Never."

"Me either."

Looking at the wall, Sutherland sighed.

"Still upset about the Ashbachs?" Milo asked.

"Yes, but I'm getting over it. I had a chat with Saul. Larry's in good hands. I'm more upset we haven't found Annie. Look at that empty wall. It says we've failed."

"We'll find her, just not in tunnels or under the ground."

"Ever since we found that picture, when I look at that wall, I see Dad as a boy, running around down there by the lake with his friend Annie."

> *I was a child and she was a child*
> *In this kingdom by the sea,*
> *Something…something,*
> *I and my Annabel Lee.*

Milo looked at Sutherland as if he had lost his mind. "What the hell is that?"

"*Annabel Lee*, a poem by Edgar Allan Poe."

"You're on a poetry kick. Any particular reason you blurted that particular poem?"

"It was one of dad's favorites. I can't remember all of it. He used to recite it now and then, staring out across the back lawn."

"Look it up. Read it to me. The something something part."

"Why?"

"Call it mind lint," Milo chided.

Sutherland Googled the Poem and began reading it.

> *It was many and many a year ago.*
> *In a kingdom by the sea,*
> *That a maiden there lived whom you may know*
> *By the name of Annabel Lee;*
> *And this maiden she lived with no other thought*
> *Than to love and be loved by me.*
>
> *I was a child and she was a child,*
> *In this kingdom by the sea,*
> *But we loved with a love that was more than love—*
> *I and my Annabel Lee—*
> *With a love that the winged…"*

"Stop! That's enough. Stop." Milo closed his eyes. "I can't friggin' believe it. Why didn't you tell me this earlier?"

Sutherland laughed. "Why would I? I just remembered it now."

Breanna and Dr. Bixby walked the back lawn toward the house. Sutherland got up and waved to them.

"We want to see if Martha has cookies," Breanna said. "She said she was going to bake a new batch."

Milo smiled and said to Sutherland, "Margaret is Peggy."

"What?" Sutherland asked.

"Follow me, Poetry Boy. We've been going about this all wrong."

Sutherland shrugged and fell in line behind Breanna, Dr. Bixby, and Milo.

"Breanna, will you go hunt down the cookies?" Milo requested. "Dr. Bixby, please join us in the gallery."

"I like this room," Bixby said as Annie came down and rubbed up against her.

Milo watched her pet the cat. "Dr. Bixby, you said you played here as a child. We found a picture of Sutherland's father as a young boy. Would you mind looking at it?"

"I wouldn't mind at all," she said, following Milo. "Oh my! I remember this picture. June fourth nineteen fifty-four. It was sunny but rained in the afternoon."

"How do you remember the weather that long ago?"

"I have an eidetic memory."

"If you were there, why aren't you in the picture?" Sutherland asked.

Bixby seemed confused. "Are you being sarcastic?"

"No." Now, Sutherland was confused.

"Oh good, I didn't think you were, but I often don't know."

Milo was enjoying the befuddlement but thought it needed to end. "Let me straighten this out. We shouldn't have been looking for a girl named Annie. We should have been looking for a girl named Annabel."

Breanna crossed the gallery carrying a tray of cookies and set them down on a nearby table. "I'm sorry but Martha wants my help in the kitchen. I'll be back."

Bixby moved over to the sitting area, took a cookie and sat down. Sutherland was still confused. "Milo, we're looking for Annabel?"

"Me and my Annabel Lee. Your father's poem says it all."

"I still don't get it?" Sutherland said.

"He wasn't looking at the lake when he recited that poem. I bet he was looking at the wall. Dr. Bixby," Milo called, getting her attention and pointing to the picture, "what did you think of Bennie?"

"He didn't like me," Bixby said.

Milo moved his finger along the picture from Bennie to the next child, "Susan?"

"She was mean."

"John?"

"He was my friend. He told me he was my friend. We played all summer in 1954…the spy game."

Sutherland, remembering his father's list, stood wide eyed.

"And Sutherland, the last child on the wall is Annabel Patterson. Margaret can be Peggy and Bella can be Annabel."

"No, Annabella," Bixby corrected, while taking another cookie. "Good old Scottish name my father used to say."

Sutherland joined Dr. Bixby in the seating area. "You're Annie?"

"I said Annabella. Are you making a joke?" Bixby asked, a bit bewildered.

Milo jumped in. "But John called you Annie?"

"It was an important part of the spy game. John said spies never use their real names, so he was Mac and I was Annie. These are good cookies."

Sutherland shared with her that John never forgot their friendship. "My father never stopped wondering where you went. You know he named all of our cats Annie."

Bixby petted Annie but didn't respond.

"Where did you go?" Sutherland continued.

"Do you have problems? I'm right here." Bixby stated.

"No, when you were young. My dad thought you disappeared. Did your mother take you away?"

"My mother? She died when I was three. I still remember her."

Milo inserted the right question. "Where did you go when you left Lakesong?"

"To a new school in St. Paul with my nanny Patricia. She liked me, and I liked my new school. Nobody thought I was weird there."

"We have a picture of your father and a woman with a baby," Sutherland said.

"That must have been my step mother, Adeline. One day she left with my half-brother and the chauffeur. She didn't like me. She told me I was different and to stay away from the baby. I was glad when she left." Bixby took another cookie.

"Your father knew where you were?" Sutherland asked.

"Of course. He would come and visit when he was in town for business and for Christmas. I lived with Patricia, Patricia Lind. I named the scholarship for her." Dr. Bixby looked at her watch. "I need to go. I have to teach a class."

Breanna, holding a small box of cookies, caught up with her and walked her to her car.

Rathkey and Sutherland returned to the terrace. "So, what's the wall telling you now?" Milo asked.

"My dad could have mentioned her real name was Annabella."

"The list was just bullet points. I'm sure he was planning to. He did mention the spy game."

They both sat in silence for a long time.

"Should I tell Ed to forget about the front lawn, or do you still want to look for bodies?" Milo teased.

Sutherland grinned. "It made sense…at the time." Milo laughed.

The tone became more serious. "I wish Dad had asked you to find Annie sooner. Dad would have enjoyed meeting her again."

"It wouldn't have happened."

"Why do you say that? We found her."

"No. We didn't find Annie. She found us. None of this could have happened before Breanna was old enough to get that scholarship."

"I wonder why my father liked her, Anabella, I mean. It would be my guess she has a form of Asperger's, bright, but doesn't understand social cues. The other children thought she was odd, or weird as she puts it."

"John accepted people for who they were. Anabella was just Anabella. She is who she is."

Sutherland's eyes got a little watery, but he tried to hide it. "Dad was a nice man. I miss him."

Milo agreed. "So, do I."

§

Milo limped out onto the back lawn. The day was sunny, with a cool breeze. The deep blue sky had a few puffy clouds, and several sail boats were crisscrossing the lake in a lazy fashion. It was a perfect summer day, the kind the tourist bureau touted in its brochures.

Milo made his way down to the stone wall mid-lawn and sat down. His feet were firmly planted on the ground. As a boy when he first arrived at Lakesong, he would grab on to the wall and belly up with all of his strength, sit down and let his feet dangle. He thought about those days and smiled.

"Well, John," Milo said out loud, "we found your friend Annie; sorry it didn't happen while you were alive, but she is back at Lakesong…from time to time."

He thought about how John had spent his life wrapped in the childhood mystery of what happened to his friend. Milo had his own mystery which he had successfully avoided. It was time. He picked up his phone and dialed Gramm.

"I'm doing paperwork. Whaddaya want?"

"I need a file on an old murder."

"What? What is with you and old murders?"

"It's a quirk."

"Who are we talking about?"

"Police Detective Karl Rathkey."

FUN REUNION! MEET, GREET, MURDER

If you wish to contact the authors, email us at authors@dbelrogg.com or leave a message at www.dbelrogg.com.

If you enjoyed this book please leave a review on Amazon.

BOOKS BY D.B. ELROGG

GREAT PARTY! SORRY ABOUT THE MURDER

FUN REUNION! MEET, GREET, MURDER

MISSED THE MURDER. WENT TO YOGA

MURDER AGAIN! HAPPY NEW YEAR!

SNAP, ZAP, MURDER

CLUES, CASH, PIECES OF MURDER

OLD MURDER, NEW MURDER, WHERE ARE THE COWS?

Made in the USA
Coppell, TX
25 August 2024

36435037R00204